THE RAT BECOMES LIGHT

THE RAT BECOMES LIGHT

stories

———*Donald Secreast*

1817

HARPER & ROW, PUBLISHERS, New York
Grand Rapids, Philadelphia, St. Louis, San Francisco
London, Singapore, Sydney, Tokyo, Toronto

The following stories have appeared in these periodicals:
   in the *Carolina Quarterly*—"Factory Hand"
                              "The Rat Becomes Light"
                              "When Loads Shift"
   in *Charlotte Writers' Club Journal*—"Private Drive"
   in the *North American Review*—"Lady Luck"

FIRST EDITION

Designed by Cassandra J. Pappas

Library of Congress Cataloging-in-Publication Data

Secreast, Donald, 1949–
      The rat becomes light / Donald Secreast.
         p.   cm.
      ISBN 0-06-016440-9
      1. North Carolina—Fiction.   I. Title.
      PS3569.E287R3   1990   89-46573
      813'.54—dc20

---

90 91 92 93 94 CC/HC 10 9 8 7 6 5 4 3 2 1

Contents

Summer Help

Wanda Dey sat in the culled Louis XVI banquet chair, a gift from the man who had dropped it from the loading platform; she was eating a banana for her breakfast. Beside her, sitting in another banquet chair, Marleen Craig was drinking a cup of canteen coffee, telling Wanda the rumor about Old Man Chalfant's son. As Marleen talked, she kept sliding her eyes toward the door that led to the canteen. It was almost time for the seven o'clock whistle, and Marleen had to time her exit from Wanda's workroom so she could get back to the machine room before Mayhew got back from the boiler room, where he lingered every morning to smoke and talk about trolling. Mayhew insisted that Marleen have at least three headboard patterns traced out and ready to be cut by the time he turned on the band saw. Wanda was glad she didn't have to work with a man like Mayhew.

"But his boy really hates the factory," Marleen said through her upper lip, her lower lip pressed against the Vendomatic coffee cup.

"And I bet he can't stand the money it makes for Old Man Chalfant." Wanda twirled the peel of the banana draping over

1

her wrist and fingers like a deflated bouquet.

"From what I hear, he's not the kind of boy who'd think the two are connected. He's an artist."

"So are a lot of people." Wanda was aware of the striping brushes in her smock pocket and the pleasant odor of enamel paint coming from the center of the room where she was working on a gigantic hutch, painting Chinese ladies on the panels of the lower doors.

Marleen stood up. She was about forty-five but still had a nice figure. She wore the tight pants to prove it. Wanda suspected that her bright auburn hair was not completely honest. Once every two weeks, Marleen's hair had a pungent chemical smell, and it was not a smell that came from the furniture factory. Still, Marleen was a reliable source of information. All the men in the factory talked to her. "I'm just surprised she don't pick up more than gossip," Hutson, Wanda's husband, had remarked after last year's Christmas party.

"Well, he starts to work today." Marleen crumpled her cup as the factory whistle pierced the heavy air of the room. As soon as the whistle cut off, the snarl of the exhaust fans being switched on momentarily obliterated all human voices and the sounds of scuffling chairs in the canteen. Off to the left, one of the finishing room men had turned on the compressed-air pump, and it rattled like a skull inside a bass drum. The floor trembled slightly, indicating that the endlessly long conveyor belt, the chain, was now clacking through the factory, insinuating its rhythm into all the motions of the people who worked around it. Out in the rough end, the sound of a cutoff saw screeching through the first piece of raw lumber of the day reminded Marleen of Mayhew.

"The Old Man and the boy have some kind of deal going is all I know," Marleen said on her way to the door. "Otherwise, he'd never got the boy to step foot in this place."

Wanda was able to relax once Marleen left her workroom. She liked to be alone with her work first thing in the morning. Of course, by nine o'clock break, she was ready to talk to somebody—Marleen, sometimes, but she really felt more comfortable with Rachel from the cabinet room. Wanda had been working at Chalfant Furniture for five years now, and she still found

Hutson's original advice accurate. He had warned her to avoid the men from the lumberyard and the men from the rough end. "Most of them've not been too long out of the woods. And you're liable to get fleas or ticks off of them. Or something worse." He'd also warned her about the men from the finishing room. "Most of them have brain damage," he said, only half jokingly. "I swear. For eight or ten hours a day, they breathe the shellac, the stain, the varnish. Even with the little masks they wear, some of the chemicals gets through and busts brain cells like they was little balloons. Besides," he added, "they're the nastiest people to walk the earth."

Wanda knew that Hutson was protective, but what he'd said about the finishing room workers was true, especially for the men at the end of the spray booth chain who had to rub off all the excess finish. One little man who never seemed to leave the factory was known to everyone only as the Rat because of his color—a dull mahogany from his hair, over his clothes, down to his pointed shoes. His low forehead and large nose added to the resemblance. He never spoke to anyone, but about three minutes before break time, lunchtime, and quitting time, he'd wiggle out from between the large packing boxes and sniff the air as if he could tell time with his nose.

Wanda had just opened her bottles of paint and was in the process of tearing open a package of new striping brushes when the door from the canteen opened. The personnel manager, Huntly Vanderveldt, walked into her workroom, followed by a tall man wearing a seersucker suit. At first, Wanda assumed the tall man was a salesman that Vanderveldt was taking to the shipping room. However, instead of walking across to the door that led to the shipping room where the furniture was crated up and loaded on trucks or boxcars, Vanderveldt stopped just inside the door.

"Wanda, you're not in the middle of something, are you?"

"Just getting ready to be." Wanda turned to face him. Vanderveldt was from the front office, but Wanda liked him. In a way, he was the one most responsible for getting her out of the machine room and settling her in as a furniture striper. But because he was from the front office, he didn't come into the factory unless something was wrong. All Wanda could think of was that she'd used the wrong pattern on one of the custom-made commodes that they rushed through last week. Usually, she could take her time and do the job right, but lately some new hotshot salesman was getting quantity orders on custom pieces. She braced herself for Vanderveldt's quiet criticism, his reminding her about the importance of her work because it was done on their highest quality pieces and not easily corrected—the whole piece had to be taken apart, sanded down, and completely refinished. But she hadn't made such a mistake in three years.

Rather than criticize her, Vanderveldt said, "Well, you're doing wonderful work, Wanda. I certainly like what you're doing with that hutch." During his pause, while he walked closer to the hutch to admire her work, Wanda glimpsed the tall man leaning over to the left and then back to the right as if he too were inspecting her painting. "You're almost as rushed this week as you were last week, aren't you?" Vanderveldt stooped to be on an even level with the Chinese ladies, each of whom held an armful of cherry blossoms or dogwood blossoms, Wanda wasn't sure which; she just made them white.

"It's just starting to crank up," she answered.

"Well, when I found out what kind of orders Gray Westfall was calling in—and for custom stock—I knew you'd be standing on your head over here. No problem getting the pieces made: just speed up the chain. But no chain runs through here."

"Sometimes when they crank it up," Wanda said, "it feels like it's trying to work its way through."

"I know what you mean. I can feel it vibrate all the way up to the front office. Last week, though, I told Fonsielle that what makes that furniture custom furniture is Wanda Dey. Without her pictures and striping, it's just so much expensive wood screwed and glued together."

Wanda looked down into her lap where she had dumped the six striping brushes, whose long sable bristles were the shape of tiny foxtails. Often, she had thought exactly what Vanderveldt was saying, but to have one of the bosses say it out loud in front of a tall man in a seersucker suit was more than she could hear and keep looking him in the eye.

"Well, Mr. Vanderveldt, you know it's more than just a job with me."

"I certainly do." Vanderveldt stood up. "And that's why I think you deserve special consideration." He turned to the tall man and said, "Zavier, come over here and let me introduce you to the best striper we've ever had at Chalfant Furniture Factory."

The tall man approached, and for the first time Wanda noticed that he wasn't wearing a tie. He wasn't even wearing a dress shirt with his suit. He was wearing a turquoise T-shirt with crimson lettering, but Wanda couldn't make out the words because the seersucker jacket covered most of them. He was also wearing sandals of woven leather, Mexican looking. In the buttonhole of his jacket was a dandelion blossom.

"Wanda Dey," Vanderveldt said, a hint of formality creeping into his voice—enough to pull Wanda off her stool and turn her around to face the tall man. "I want you to meet Zavier Chalfant. He's going to be with us for a couple of months, and knowing your interest in art, I thought you might enjoy having his help while he's here because Zavier is already a serious artist."

All the time Vanderveldt was making this introduction, Zavier Chalfant was letting his gaze rest lightly on Wanda. Most boys—and that's what Zavier was, after all, a boy of about twenty-one—were very embarrassed their first day on the job. Zavier, in contrast, seemed more amused than embarrassed by what Vanderveldt was saying. His thick blond hair covered the collar of his jacket but was clean and expertly cut so he looked more like a knight than a hippie. His face was perfectly balanced above and below his cheekbones. The delicacy of his chin, however, prevented his jaw from seeming too long. He had green eyes, which he would occasionally force open wider than they were meant to be. Wanda noticed him do it the first time when Vanderveldt began his introduction, a second time when he mentioned how long Zavier was going to be working, and a third time when he made the remark about being a serious artist. Although Wanda didn't know what he meant by the wide eyes, the rest of Zavier's face was so friendly that she couldn't help but smile at him. She decided that his face looked like a Viking's face; she'd always been partial to Vikings. Of course, Zavier was too thin to be a Viking all the way down, but he had the face of an adventurer. Of an artist.

"So for a couple of months, with Zavier to help you," Vanderveldt was saying, "it'll be kind of like a vacation for you. Then come August, it'll be time for you to take your real vacation. Where are you and Hutson going this year?"

Wanda turned from Zavier. "Oh, we're still fighting about that. I want to go to Florida, you know, so I can paint some sunsets, but he wants to go to the mountains."

"If things work out for Zavier," Vanderveldt said, grasping the boy's elbow, "he'll be spending August in Paris."

This time, when Vanderveldt said Paris, Zavier not only widened his eyes, he also tilted his head back slightly. "Provided I can come to work here every morning for two months and get through the day without needing a transfusion or shock treatments."

Vanderveldt laughed. "Well, Zavier, you're going to be keeping company with one of the best people in the whole plant. Why, I wouldn't be surprised if Wanda got you to liking this place so much you just forgot about going to Paris."

Zavier's eyes got wide once more. "Well, she's certainly lovely enough to do that." He smiled. "But my girlfriend is also counting on this trip, and I'm sure she'd have something to say about my deciding to stay in Boehm to finish out the summer painting furniture."

"Okay, then." Vanderveldt sidestepped toward the canteen door. "I've got some people to interview. If any problems come up, Zavier, drop by the office. But I'm sure Wanda can tell you anything you need to know. Once you get in the routine, you'll find yourself having a good time, I bet. Just keep telling yourself you're earning that ticket to Paris."

"You bet, coach." Zavier's nose flared along with his eyes.

With an ease that bordered on stealth, Vanderveldt slipped out of the room, leaving Wanda with the tall Viking and a blade of panic sliding up her throat. This is Old Man Chalfant's own boy, she thought to herself. She had never been comfortable with the bosses, the big bosses, and now here she was with the owner's son.

"Have you done any striping before?" Wanda brushed her upper lip with one of the new brushes.

"No." Zavier tossed his hands up and hunched his shoulders. "I'm completely ignorant. I *am* a fast learner, though." He squatted in front of the hutch. "You know, this isn't bad work at all." He gave her a sideways nod of approval.

"I've been doing it long enough." Wanda already felt comfortable with the boy.

"But you've had some lessons." He picked up a jar of gold enamel paint and smelled it. "I can tell."

"I've taken all the art courses they offer over at the community college."

"That's a good place to start," Zavier replied. "Can I try finishing this lady? She's supposed to match the one you've got on the other panel, isn't she?"

Wanda handed him a brush. She didn't know what else to do. She wanted to tell him about how to mix the gold with the white in order to get the right flesh tone, but before she could get the correct proportions out of her mouth, he'd already applied the gold, then started daubing on the white, actually mixing the colors on the wood—and getting them to match.

"How can you mix like that right on the wood?" Wanda stooped beside him.

"Color is my specialty." Zavier deftly added the highlights to the woman's face and hands. "It's everything." He finished the flesh parts in a matter of minutes. He took another brush from Wanda and in six or seven strokes had filled in the woman's robe. Without seeming to look closely, he added the colors to the dogwood blossoms.

"I've never seen anybody work so fast." Wanda stepped back to her stool, where she sat down and studied the picture with her chin propped in her palms.

"Well, I was going by what you'd already done," Zavier said, wiping a brush. "My speed is simply a testimony to your ability." His eyes widened beyond their normal size. "We complement each other, I think."

"I bet you've had some lessons yourself."

"Lots and lots." Zavier stood up and studied a far corner of the workroom. "I've been taking lessons since I sent off one of those Draw Me pictures. Before then, I'd watch Jon Gnagy every Wednesday night. I even took a few classes at the community college when I was in high school. Now there's college—"

"I'd like to see your paintings. I've never met anyone who took it so seriously. I mean, I take it seriously, but you're making a career out of it."

"That's very good," Zavier said. "You've picked up in about fifteen minutes what my father has failed to grasp in twenty-one years."

"I'd still like to see your paintings." Wanda wasn't certain if the trouble between Old Man Chalfant and his son was any of her business. She had the feeling that Zavier Chalfant could show her real art. Marleen might be interested in the Chalfant family struggles, but Wanda wanted to be an artist.

As they waited for two men from the shipping room to remove the hutch, Zavier talked to Wanda about color. "You've got to know what direction a particular color will take when it's mixed with, say, white. And you've got to know its velocity, too."

"What do you paint?" Wanda felt herself lost in his color theory.

Before he could answer, two men from the finishing room dragged in another hutch. "Use the same pattern on this one that you did on the last one," the foreman said as they left the room. He gave a long look at Zavier and shook his head as he closed the door. Wanda could understand how the men in the factory might disapprove of Zavier; he didn't really belong there.

"I paint surfaces," Zavier replied.

"You don't paint pictures?" Wanda tried to hide her discomfort.

Zavier paused before answering. He was running his fingers over the lightly varnished surface of the hutch. "I think it's a shame to put pictures on this wood. Don't you?"

"But the pictures are what make it custom crafted." Wanda

began looking for the wax pencil she used to trace the pattern on the wood.

"Oh, yeah. It has to have that distinctive Chalfant Furniture Factory touch."

As Wanda traced the first Chinese lady onto the door panel, without even an offer of help from Zavier, she asked, "If you don't paint pictures, what do you paint?"

Zavier picked up the other pattern and handed it to her. Carefully, she lined it up and began tracing again.

"See, Wanda," he explained, leaning back against a large cardboard box containing a discontinued style of dresser, "I've spent the last few years working with colors. Color is a caption for reality. Shape is haphazard; color is pure, musical." He picked up a striping brush. Before Wanda had finished tracing the second Chinese lady, Zavier had gotten a good start on the first lady's face. "Have you ever noticed it's the edges of things that fade first? Color hates edges. When I realized this, I knew I had to stop painting shapes." He said "shapes" as if it had bristles that punctured his tongue.

For the rest of the morning, Wanda and Zavier fell into a routine: she would trace the patterns, and Zavier would paint the two Chinese ladies. At nine o'clock, when the break whistle blew, Zavier settled down in the Louis XVI chair and pulled a magazine out of his jacket pocket. He didn't seem interested in getting to know the other people in the factory.

"You're not bashful, are you, Zavier?"

"Not a bit," Zavier replied. "But you're all the company I need for the short time I'm going to be here." He gave Wanda one of his wide-eyed looks. "On your way back, would you bring me a Pepsi?" He handed her the money.

As soon as she got into the canteen, Wanda saw Marleen waving her to a seat beside her. Rachel was already sitting across from Marleen, and Wanda felt a little disappointed when she saw that Rachel looked as curious and excited as Marleen.

"As soon as I saw Vanderveldt leading that tall boy through the machine room," Marleen said, "I knew he could fit in just one place—in the striping room with Wanda."

"Is he as good-looking as Marleen says?" Rachel was a pale

woman with blond hair and blond eyelashes. Her husband was a preacher and expected Rachel to be a model for the other women in the factory, but she sometimes forgot herself.

"You'd better get all this straightened out with Hutson just as soon as you can." Marleen stirred her coffee.

Wanda sat next to Rachel. She liked to sit so she could keep both eyes on Marleen. For the next ten minutes, she told them all she had learned about Zavier Chalfant. She wasn't surprised to see both women as confused by Zavier's ideas about color as she was. Neither of the other two women had taken any kind of art course. However, Mrs. Mills, who taught the art classes at the community college, never mentioned color's dislike for shapes. When the whistle blew, Marleen wanted to go introduce herself, but Wanda advised her to give the boy more time to get used to the factory.

"I think he's kind of bashful." Wanda moved to the drink machine.

"Or he might be a snob," Marleen replied. "I can't figure out why he didn't go to work in the design room, or maybe over in advertising, if he's such an artist." Her speculations were cut short when she saw Mayhew draining off the last ounce of his Sun-Drop. "Well, I've got to get back to my own art." She stood up and adjusted the seams of her pants.

Quietly, Rachel followed Wanda back to the striping room. Rachel worked in the cabinet room, which was located an equal distance from the canteen whether she circled through the machine room or through the finishing room. As a rule, she preferred to circle through the machine room because she didn't like the smell of the finishing room. Wanda knew why Rachel was following her, but she didn't mind—better Rachel than Marleen.

Zavier was in the same position that he occupied when Wanda left the room. As soon as he saw Wanda and Rachel enter, he jumped to his feet and made a low bow. The dandelion in his lapel was looking limp and overcome. "Wanda, you've brought company." His eyes were wide. "And my Pepsi too."

"Zavier, this is Rachel Prevette. She works over in the cabinet room."

Rachel smiled, calm in the wake of Wanda's introduction.

After all, she was a preacher's wife and used to meeting strangers. "I just wanted to come by and invite you to services at my husband's church, Zavier."

"Which church is that?" Zavier asked.

"The Gospel Wind Church of Daily Salvation."

"Up past the prison camp, isn't it?"

"About five miles." Rachel was flattered that the son of Old Man Chalfant would know her husband's church.

"It used to be a grocery store, didn't it?" Zavier took a deep drink from his Pepsi. "I bought a Sunbeam Bread sign from them just after the store closed. It was an interesting little building when it was a grocery store." Zavier munched ice from his drink. "I would never have thought about turning it into a church. Tell your husband I admire his imagination."

"I will." Rachel made her way for the door that led to the finishing room. "Don't work too hard." She turned toward Wanda and raised her eyebrows while giving a quick jerk of her head toward Zavier.

Wanda could have guessed that Rachel wouldn't know how to take Zavier. While she had been talking to her and Marleen in the canteen, she had realized just how much of an artist Zavier was. And he was nice. Rachel didn't know how a serious painter related to people. That was all. Surely, part of the problem, Wanda reasoned, was that Zavier was a genius. He had to be—the way he mixed paint, the way he talked about color as if it were something alive and moving. And the way he dressed. This was a side of art that Wanda had only heard about from television, certainly not from Mrs. Mills.

As they started back to work, Zavier took off his jacket. The factory hoards its heat. "Did you notice that your flower's wilting?" Wanda asked.

"I'm interested in that process, the process of wilting. Process is the closest we can get to color in terms of action—as in the process of travel."

"And you're painting it?"

"I'm painting the process," Zavier corrected. "Give color a chance to escape shape, and you have an ocean. Color is the source of all life on this planet."

Wanda noticed that the writing on his turquoise T-shirt said *Klee Is for Mee.* She wanted to ask him what it meant, but she decided she'd wait until later. There was already too much she didn't understand, and she felt she'd reached her limit, at least until after lunch. Besides, Zavier seemed to have gone into a trance, filling in the colors of the Chinese lady's dress.

The two men from the finishing room noticed the increased pace and started bringing in the hutches much faster than usual. This kept Wanda and Zavier busy, too busy to talk. They fell into a rhythm that demanded only the periphery of their attention. Wanda was already trying to figure out how she was going to explain Zavier to her husband. She was also trying to decide if Zavier was the kind of person who might give her lessons. She didn't care about all that color-is-life business. She wanted her pictures to look nicer. All the sketches she did left her dissatisfied. Especially when she tried to do pictures of people she knew, she could feel her limitations as an artist. Every time she did a drawing of Hutson, he came out looking like a caveman—and it wasn't entirely his fault. His head was shaped a little like a block, and his hair did come down too far on his forehead, but his jaw really was solid and wide—stable.

When sitting in the cab of his Mack truck, he did sometimes look ferocious. He drove for Boehm Glass and Mirror Company. At first he'd worked there making frames, back before he and Wanda got married. Then, when he found out that truck drivers made more money than frame makers, he'd learned to drive trucks. Still, he made frames for all the pictures that Wanda painted or drew. He also liked everything that Wanda produced, even the pictures of his square, shaggy head.

At lunch, Zavier disappeared, probably to eat with his father in the Old Man's air-conditioned office, Wanda decided. Apparently, Marleen and Rachel had been discussing the boy at length. Wanda could tell from the way Rachel was dedicating herself to her Vendomatic chili and franks that she had told Marleen everything Zavier said to her during her brief visit.

"Well," Marleen said, raising her voice and letting her eyes sweep around the room, "any man who gets his thrills from dried-up grocery stores certainly ain't going to like me."

Most of the men in the canteen looked at her and smiled, their mouths full of sandwiches or pork and beans. Wanda knew every person in the factory had to have his place, even if the person was the factory's owner. Marleen was in the process of putting Zavier in his place. Wanda thought for a moment about saying something nice about Zavier, but that would give the people in the canteen the wrong idea. Besides, she realized it was possible that Zavier didn't feel a normal need, one she might feel, to be liked by the people who worked for his father. A serious artist probably wouldn't.

"Why's he not eating lunch?" Marleen asked. "Is he afraid Vendomatic might poison him?"

"He had somewhere else to eat." Wanda sprinkled pepper on her egg salad sandwich. "Probably with Old Man Chalfant. They *are* related, you know."

"If that's his idea of fun, I can see where he gets his fondness for creaky old buildings. I bet you didn't ask him why he wound up in the factory instead of design or advertising."

"We've been busy."

"Well, Mayhew thinks the boy might have problems." Marleen dropped her voice and shifted her eyes from Rachel to Wanda, back and forth, as if trying to weave some sort of insinuation between them.

"I can see that." Rachel tore open a package of crackers with her teeth.

"He's just a serious painter." Wanda spoke only to Marleen but knew that Mayhew would hear about it in the next hour.

"You're a serious painter too," Marleen replied. "But you're here eating lunch where you belong, and you don't spend the weekends admiring twisted-up little buildings."

"No," Wanda agreed, "but he's different—"

"He's a fruit." Marleen slanted her hand through the air and shook her head.

After lunch, Zavier came through the canteen just as everyone was leaving. He was taller than the crowd he moved through, and he looked over everyone's head. Wanda noticed that he was looking at her, his eyes wide. He didn't seem to notice how everyone was measuring him from head to foot as if they were about to try jumping over him.

Marleen was standing beside Wanda. Rachel, as soon as Zavier started walking toward them, left through the door that led to the machine room.

"You must be Marleen." Zavier stopped at the table where they were straightening their chairs.

"Must be because I am." Despite her suspicions, Marleen was cautiously pleasant. She liked to be recognized.

"When Huntly led me through this morning, I saw you drawing . . . what was it . . . patterns for tabletops?"

"Headboards." A layer of Marleen's caution dissolved.

"And I said to Huntly, 'Why do we waste such beautiful women by hiding them back here behind all these machines? A woman like that ought to be a model.' "

Marleen looked at Wanda and said, "That Mayhew is the dumbest baboon in this factory."

"Then I asked Huntly what your name was. I hope you don't mind. But you see, I have some friends who paint—"

"I hear you paint too." Marleen stood up as straight as she could.

"Nothing you'd recognize as painting," Zavier said quickly and almost humbly. "But these other friends of mine are always looking for models. In a town like Boehm, it's hard to find someone with the classic proportions."

"You mean I've got classic proportions?" Marleen put her arm through Zavier's arm.

"Up one side and down the other." Zavier patted her hand. He looked at Wanda once more with his eyes wide.

"When I was younger, I thought I'd like to be a model, but then I found out you had to go to Atlanta or New York, and while I like to go to the beach two or three times a year, I don't really care for such long trips."

"Well, most of my friends are out of town for the summer, but when they get back, I'll talk to them. Tell them I have found the model of their dreams. The last I heard, they were paying about twenty dollars an hour—"

"Tell 'em they'd get their money's worth." Marleen patted Zavier on his stomach. "Meanwhile, you can find me at band saw number three being abused by Mayhew." As she was walking toward the door, she turned in such a way that all of her moving parts shifted from right to left in a lush arc. "By the way, Wanda and I were wondering why you didn't go to work in design or advertising."

"I wanted to," Zavier replied, "but I know too many guys over there, and my father was afraid I wouldn't get anything done."

"If you get too bored, you can always find me drawing headboards out there in the machine room. Just tell 'em you're looking for Marleen."

"I'll keep that in mind. But from the looks of things, Wanda is going to make sure my father gets his money's worth out of me."

"She can be a drudge," Marleen agreed.

Back in the striping room, Zavier talked about his lunch with his friends in the design room. But Wanda could only half listen because she was trying to figure out if she really was a drudge. She was thirty-six and had yet to win any of the local community art contests—not the industrial fair contest, not the Women's Club annual art contest, not the Community Arts Council contest. Maybe, she thought, it's not that my drawing is bad so much as it's dull. This thought made her feel more determined about asking Zavier for lessons. Even if she didn't understand what he said about color, she could surely understand suggestions about drawing.

All afternoon, she tried to ask him for drawing lessons, but as soon as she mentioned anything about art, Zavier would begin talking about color and how it must be left alone in order to grow, like a fungus in a dark room. For about thirty minutes, he explained a theory he had that all color started in the mushroom and ended up in the ocean. "That's why most mushrooms have so little color. They've given it all to the world around them."

Finally, just before the three-thirty whistle, Wanda asked, "Have you ever given art lessons? I don't mean fancy lessons, just drawing and maybe some painting."

"I'll tell you what, Wanda," Zavier said, "once we get to be better friends, we'll sneak in some drawing lessons right under my father's factory nose. I have to know a person pretty well, though, because giving lessons is a very personal thing for me."

This all made sense to Wanda. Perhaps, she thought, that was why Mrs. Mills never helped her that much. She didn't take time to be friends with her students. But here was a rich and serious artist who wanted to wait until the friendship was established. This was the way one artist should treat another artist, Wanda concluded, as she drove home.

When Wanda pulled into her driveway, she saw that Hutson was already home, raking the stones in their front yard. One of the courses she had taken at the community college had been a ceramics and cement course in which she had learned to make her own yard ornaments. By the time she finished the course, she had so many cement and ceramic animals in the yard that Hutson couldn't mow the grass. He resolved the problem by hauling several tons of river rock down from the Gorge. All of the stones were round, varying in color from dark brown to pink. It took a while for the neighborhood to get used to Wanda's yard, but the previous spring it had won an honorable mention in the Women's Club Yard of the Year contest.

As they were eating supper, Wanda told Hutson about Zavier. Hutson always listened carefully when she talked to him. They'd been married for ten years, and he still acted as if he considered himself lucky that she accepted his proposal. Hutson, despite his love of television and big trucks, was an unpredictable man. Wanda assumed that on his long trips he must do an awful lot of thinking; he had a CB, but he seldom used it. What Wanda really appreciated about Hutson was how he never lost his excitement about her being an artist. Anything she did was acceptable to him because she was an artist.

"Does he look like Old Man Chalfant?" Hutson asked after Wanda finished talking about her day with Zavier.

"He's taller . . . and he has blond hair."

"The Old Man had blond hair. A long time ago." Hutson poured himself another glass of tea. "Blonds lose their hair quicker. Light hair can't hold roots." He avoided looking at Wanda.

"Then Zavier'll probably be bald as his father by the time he's thirty."

"I guess in two months he can't do too much damage to the factory." Hutson poured honey on top of two biscuits he'd broken open on his plate.

"Then he'll be in Paris." Wanda began to clean the table.

"Personally, I'd rather be in the Great Smoky Mountains."

"Or at the beach?" Wanda turned to face Hutson.

"But don't you want to spend our vacation up there where I proposed to you? That was ten years ago, come September." Now Hutson was gazing intently at Wanda. He had honey in the corners of his mouth. "You remember that, don't you?"

Wanda leaned against the sink and laughed. Each year, Hutson reminded her of his proposal. They had gone up to Linville Gorge to see the Brown Mountain lights. As they stood on the overlook, Hutson had busied himself with his binoculars. Wanda noticed that to her left was a fresh pile of dog manure. She had stepped next to the brown pile and slid a bright red maple leaf over it. "Hut," she challenged, "I bet I can pick up this red leaf before you can." Before she had finished speaking, Hutson had swooped down beside her, grabbing the leaf. While he was still down on one knee, he'd grabbed her hand with both of his and begged her to marry him. She was laughing too hard at first to answer him, but had managed finally to gasp out a yes. Hutson started to kiss her, but she wouldn't let him until they'd found a place to wash their hands.

"We could start up at Asheville," Hutson was saying, his voice lowered in an attempt to be persuasive. "And head toward Virginia, trout fishing all the way, bass fishing all the way. And there are some campgrounds that have trails where you can hike."

"But if we go to the ocean, we can go out on one of them big boats and you could fish from it, fish for something big, so big they'll have to strap you in a chair to keep from getting pulled in by it."

"If they have to strap me in to fish for it, I don't have any business hooking it in the first place."

"And there's the ocean, Hut. All that color running loose

like it was trying to come alive." Still leaning back against the sink, Wanda tilted her head back as if enjoying a salt spray. Her brown hair almost dipped into the dishwater.

"Sounds like a monster movie to me."

Wanda could hear in his voice that he was full of appreciation for her pose.

"By August, I might even be ready to try a painting of you in your bathing suit." Wanda looked at her husband through the frame of her two hands, touching thumb to thumb.

For the next three weeks, Wanda worked every day with Zavier. He continued to talk about color in the same difficult way, but he never mentioned any drawing lessons. Wanda assumed they weren't good enough friends. At break time, Zavier would stay in the striping room, and at lunch he would eat with his friends in the design department. He continued to wear the decaying dandelion in his jacket. On payday, he took his brown envelope out of the foreman's hand just like everybody else. At least twice a week, Wanda mentioned that she would like to see some of Zavier's work.

Finally, in the first week of July, Zavier banged into the striping room, carrying a large, battered portfolio under one arm and a frame covered by a cloth sack under his other arm. "To celebrate my last month in the factory, I've brought a few of my old old old pieces." He settled his burdens down in a corner. "Despite the anachronistic, the obsolete, quality of the work, I think these are works you'll be able to best appreciate."

For the rest of the day, every spare minute that Wanda could get, she spent looking at drawings that Zavier pulled from the portfolio. At the end of the day, all that was left to see was the framed picture. A few minutes before the three-thirty whistle, Zavier removed the cover and turned the picture toward Wanda. All day long she had been marveling at Zavier's talent. Several times she'd told him he was a genius. At lunch, Marleen had come to look at the pictures, and she also declared that he was a genius. She wanted to know when his friends were going to get back to town. Zavier promised her that he himself would use her for a model before he went to Paris and take the picture with him to sell over there to a count.

Wanda let out a small gasp when she saw the picture in the frame. It was done in pen and ink, a picture of a young woman standing on a hill, but she was somehow part of the landscape. Her dress was part of the hill where she was standing. And her hair, thick tresses being styled by the wind, curled over her head to become branches of the tree against which she was leaning. The branches, in turn, reached up to form a moon and clouds. But what really held Wanda's attention was the face of the girl. It resembled her own.

"Is that me?"

"I knew you'd ask that." Zavier's eyes went wide. "Look at the date." Zavier pointed to the right-hand corner below the initials z.c.

"Nineteen seventy-six," Wanda read.

"I was fifteen at the time. I was deep in my romantic period then. I happened to be thumbing through an old high school annual that belonged to my aunt—a *Boehm Beacon, 1964*—"

"I was a senior that year." Wanda took a step closer to the picture of the girl.

"And you had the most romantic wide round forehead, and the most romantic diminutive nose, and the most romantic spheroidical chin—by far the Girl Most Likely to Be Descended from Edgar Allan Poe." Zavier widened his eyes.

"It's beautiful." Wanda touched the face that she had eighteen years before.

"For what it is, it is," Zavier agreed. "It won the Women's Club Art Contest Best of Show in 1977. But now, what's even more interesting to me than the picture is the frame. My mother was afraid somebody at the Women's Club might steal my masterpiece, so she bought this special frame—had it made to order. See, it locks." Zavier pointed to a small round hole. "But the big joke is that about a month after I won the contest, my mother lost the key. I'd have burned the picture years ago if I could have gotten it out of this beautiful frame."

"Would you sell the picture and the frame?"

Zavier's eyes grew very wide. "I don't sell art. Even bad art shouldn't be sold, especially bad art that is likely to embarrass me in the future. No, I couldn't sell this picture because years from now, an unscrupulous person might use it to blackmail me. It will have to sit, as it does now, in the darkest corner of my darkest closet." Biting his lower lip, Zavier began putting the linen cover back over the picture. He tied the strings with sharp irritated flicks of his wrists.

"I'd certainly like to be able to draw like that." Wanda wondered how long it took to become Zavier's friend.

"If you were my friend, you wouldn't talk like that." Zavier didn't look up from the strings.

For the remaining weeks of July, Wanda didn't bother Zavier about art lessons. He didn't seem to notice how much he had hurt her feelings. He continued to talk about color as if it were something he could make stand up on its hind legs—as if it were something *with* hind legs. Wanda continued to feel she was just outside Zavier's conversation, that if he would only lean five inches closer to her ear when he was talking about how this red was a heavy breather or how that blue had a ringing in its ears, she might understand what he meant. But he always kept the same distance between them.

Marleen had felt the distance too. Her reaction was to hold it against the boy. "He's a promiser," she declared one day in the parking lot. "He's more full of shit than a goat with a plug in its ass." She spit out her gum to emphasize her point.

"Well." Wanda turned her head away from Marleen to look up between the lumber hacks into the slack afternoon sky. "I can see his point. Art is kind of like a promise."

"A fart is kind of like a promise too, and I don't like being in a small room with either one."

Since that conversation, Marleen had made a point of eating lunch with Mayhew, and Wanda would eat her lunch sitting in her Louis XVI banquet chair. She had started trying to read the magazine that Zavier would leave lying around after his nine o'clock reading: *Art in America*. She read names like Arnulf Rainer, Cy Twombly, Ruth Snyder, Jan Commandeur, Andy Warhol, Anselm Kiefer, Jerry Concha, but as soon as she put the magazine down, she forgot them. She tried to work her way through articles about Pollock, de Kooning, Kline, Olitski, and Van Buren, but they made no sense at all, less sense than Zavier's talk about color. The fact that she came closer to understanding Zavier than she did to understanding the magazines convinced her even further that Zavier was a genius.

On Zavier's last day of work, he came in dressed as usual, even down to the remnants of the dandelion in his lapel hole. However, he was also wearing a light gray beret. All day long, he paced about the striping room. When he paused to paint in the faces and dresses of the Chinese ladies, he would sing to himself and to Wanda when he caught her staring at him. Wanda was irritated, but she didn't know if it was because he was leaving without giving her the lessons or because she hadn't qualified as his friend.

"I can tell you're upset that today is my last day." He painted a mustache on one of the Chinese ladies. When Wanda gasped, he wiped it off. "I'm having a going-away party tomorrow night. A large blast to launch me properly on Sunday. We're going to have fireworks—"

"Sunday!"

"It was the soonest flight I could get. I've been booked since June. The first day I walked in here and saw you, I knew it was ordained, that I'd be able to get through the whole two months. So, in a way, this party is a tribute to your success as well as mine."

"If it was such a success, if I was such a success, why didn't you ever give me any art lessons?"

"Wanda, Wanda, Wanda." Zavier opened his eyes too wide. "This trip has had me tied in knots. I'm so disorganized. It has taken all my spare time to get myself ready. But I promise you; when I get back, first thing I plan to do is give you some lessons."

"Because I qualify as a friend now?" Wanda thought that being a serious artist's friend was getting pretty close to being a serious artist oneself.

"The best. That's why you have to promise to come to my party tomorrow night—and bring your husband. We're going to have beer and all kinds of other refreshments. You'll get to meet some more serious artists. None of them as serious as me, of course, because if they were more serious than me, they'd have to be living in Russia, in Siberia, in a cave, with only wolf paws to eat."

To Wanda's surprise, Hutson was not as hard to persuade as she thought he would be. She had been taking her irritation out on him lately, and when she did that, he always responded by being stubborn. In one week, she knew they would be headed for the glittering shores of Panama City. Even if Zavier was gone, she hoped she still might be able to track down some loose colors just joining the ocean. So far, the best she could do was to imagine a flock of pelicans slowly dissolving into the water, leaving a gray and white stain that would eventually turn green.

The main reason Hutson wanted to go to the party was to see the picture of the girl that looked like Wanda. She had told him about the drawing, and for the past few weeks, he suggested several times that he talk to Zavier about buying the picture. "I could get it out of that frame," he assured her, twisting his empty beer can in two. When Hutson was in this kind of mood, all Wanda could do was pretend to agree with him. She'd promise to ask Zavier about selling the picture, and Hutson would be soothed. The next morning, he would avoid the subject of the picture and quietly take his split beer cans out to the trash can. Wanda always left the cans on the nightstand by his side of the bed.

Zavier lived on the outskirts of town in a small stone house with a red tile roof. "It was the most French-looking place I could find," he explained as he led them inside. They got to the party around eight o'clock. Hutson had insisted on eating at the Western Sizzler because he hated trying to fill up on potato chips. When Zavier answered the door, the first thing he did was hand Hutson a beer. "Some people don't like to shake hands with a stranger, so I find it safer just to hand out beers," Zavier explained. Wanda could tell that Hutson approved of the practice.

The house was crowded with people, all trying to talk over the music spewing from speakers in every corner of every room. Hutson dealt with the communication problem by keeping his beer to his mouth. Every few minutes, he would disappear to get a fresh can. He refused to stoop to the hypocrisy of carrying around an empty beer can. After thirty minutes, Wanda knew she was going to be driving them home when the party ended. She didn't mind. He had come because she wanted to be here. Her main concern was that he would be able to find a soft place to fall asleep. And she also wanted to know where that place was.

After an hour, he disappeared and didn't come back. Wanda knew this was her cue to find where he was hibernating. It couldn't be a place where he'd be in people's way, like on a kitchen table or in the bathroom. However, she knew she had misjudged his drinking when she saw him huddled in a dark corner with Zavier. Somehow, he had managed to talk the artist into letting him see the picture of the girl. He was leaning over the picture with his hands propped on his knees. He was swaying slightly, but he was completely absorbed in the picture.

"And you're sure you won't sell it?" he was asking Zavier when Wanda walked up.

"I'd be too embarrassed to sell it even if I could." Zavier patted Hutson on the back. "Besides, it's locked up in that frame. And the frame was a present from my mother. So I guess both the frame and the picture will always be with me. Actually, I'm too fond of the frame for its own aesthetic worth to let it go. It's a work of art."

"It sure is." Hutson ran his fingers over the polished surface. He helped Zavier put the cover over the picture.

"Tomorrow, all of it goes in storage," Zavier said. "It'll be a relief to have the excesses of my youth locked up for a few years."

Eventually, Hutson wandered off, looking for a place to get off his feet.

"Beer always works from the bottom up on him," Wanda said to a girl standing beside her. The girl glanced in Hutson's direction. Her stare made Wanda painfully aware of how out of place her husband was. As he wobbled among the casual but elegant artists, he looked like a coconut rolling through a room of crystal vases. Wanda drifted from one group to the next, never quite understanding what they were talking about. Once she tried to wedge herself in closer to a woman who was talking about stereotypic responses to pastels, but a very thin boy turned and said, "Behave yourself."

She would have left then, but she saw Zavier sitting with his girlfriend and five other people. He motioned for her to come over. They were circled around a large water pipe. Wanda didn't know what to do once she got to the smokers.

"Sit here." Zavier moved to his right and patted the space beside him. "You don't know any of these people," he said ceremoniously. "And actually, you're better off not knowing them—except for my traveling companion, Tobynne Neustadt." He pointed the mouthpiece of the pipe toward the girl sitting on his left.

What Wanda first noticed was that she had the same Viking features as Zavier. Her eyes were the blue of the fifty-point circle on an archery target, and even though she was sitting, the girl was obviously tall, perhaps not quite as slim as Zavier but just as satisfied with her body. Wanda glanced back in the direction where Hutson had disappeared. By now, he was asleep, waiting to go home where she would have to undress him. She felt a need to go check on him, but Zavier handed her the mouthpiece. "Get wild," he advised. "Have visions; escape shapes." His eyes were narrow, as if he wanted Wanda to scrutinize the truth he was sharing with her.

Wanda had smoked before. Hutson would sometimes pick up hitchhikers, and they would occasionally express their gratitude by giving him a joint. She hadn't felt much when she tried the twisted little cigarettes. Mostly, she had been bored because Hutson had started talking about his tractor-trailer. He told her how it felt driving through snow, rain, wind, and sand. He went into prolonged detail about how the weather sounded. Then he talked about what tire pressure did to handling, what suspension systems did to handling. From there, he described how a truck should be loaded, because that affected handling too.

Wanda took a deep draw. She realized if smoking could get Hutson to talk so much about what he deeply loved, maybe these artists would start talking about art. Or if they talked about color instead, maybe with the right buzz she would be able to move closer to them, to understand them, to be like them enough to follow what they meant. The mouthpiece went around leisurely four or five times. Mostly, Tobynne talked about how much trouble she had packing, but Wanda didn't mind. She had begun to feel like one of her ceramic animals, one of the frogs. She felt green, the green of Zavier's eyes. Maybe, she thought to herself, this is where he gets all his talk about color.

Sometime later, Zavier propped himself up on his knees and announced, "Before I leave Boehm, I want to make one contribution to the culture of my hometown. But this must be a group effort. There might be danger. So all of those who would join me in this adventure into vengeful art must gird up his or her loins—those of you who still have them—and assemble out in Tobynne's van." All the circle followed Zavier outside. Wanda went along because, as they were getting to their feet, Zavier had whispered in her ear, "You should come, because after I'm gone you'll be the only one to carry on. I've spent this whole summer training you. Don't let me down."

On their way out, Wanda asked Zavier to check on Hutson. She pointed out the general direction he had taken. When he came back, Zavier told her that her husband was stretched out on the couch.

"He won't be in the way, will he?" she asked.

"Naaaah." Zavier checked his watch. "Pretty soon, everybody's going outside to look at the fireworks. And we're going to be out making Boehm a little bit safer for whatever sensitive children might be walking the streets."

Wanda was sitting in the back of the van on the floor. She couldn't see where they were going, and she could hear only part of what Zavier was saying. She kept hearing words like atrocious, insipid, and vulgar. Once, she caught a glimpse of Zavier laughing, his teeth shining in the glare of an oncoming car. Then all of them started singing a song in French. Wanda tried to hum the melody. Soon, Zavier hushed them, turned off the van's lights and engine, and coasted for a hundred or so yards.

She recognized the rocks in her yard as soon as she climbed out of the van.

"I don't know who lives here," Zavier was saying, "but it looks like all of Walt Disney's abortions are buried here."

Everyone laughed. Wanda leaned against the side of the van and kept her head down. The voices around her, soft and shimmering as they were, floated in the air like jellyfish, stinging Wanda whenever one bumped against her. She was glad she and Hutson had a post office box instead of a regular mailbox with their name on it.

"What we must do is load up as many of these ghastly effigies as possible; we must stop this cement cancer before it spreads through the entire town. There are pregnant women to consider." Zavier crept with exaggerated care to a cement donkey and tried to lift it. He straightened up and motioned for Tobynne to come and help him.

For the next twenty minutes, they loaded the animals into the van. Wanda worked harder than anyone, never looking up from the cement figures she dragged from her yard. She wanted to get away and back to Hutson as soon as possible. She tried not to think of what the yard would look like in the morning. All she wanted was the evening to be finished.

"Keep working like this," Zavier said as helped her slide a fawn into the van, "and you'll be ready to go to Paris in a year or two yourself. Enthusiasm is the heart of color."

When the yard was empty, Zavier and his friends squeezed into the sagging van. "Wanda, since you're the smallest, you sit up front on the floorboards. You can lean back against Tobynne's legs." Zavier cranked up the van and rumbled toward the part of Boehm that dramatically surrendered to fields and forest. "We must dispose of these heathen artifacts in such a way that they will not torment my people again—nor be a temptation unto them."

He backed the van so close to the edge of the granite quarry that even Tobynne yelled for him to stop. Fifty feet below, moonlight streaked the dark water, so still it seemed solid. Wanda was glad, in a way, that Zavier had picked the granite quarry. If there were any official tragic places in Boehm, the quarry had to be one of them. People came here to dispose of their guilt. Stolen cars, after they were stripped, were pushed off this cliff; two people had jumped from it; and now they were tossing in her ceramic and cement animals with a strange dignity. Each time a statue was thrown—or rolled off the cliff—everyone in the group watched its slow gyrations until it hit the water and disappeared with a hungry *plunk*, like a fist hitting a canvas bag.

On the drive back, Wanda ignored the conversation. Her arms ached from the lifting. Her fingers were raw. Back at Zavier's house, the fireworks were tormenting the sky. Wanda could see the party crowd silhouetted on the hill.

"Listen to that color!" Zavier collected several beers from the refrigerator. "Now make sure he takes you to the ocean, Wanda. Let the tide of tints carry you to true art."

"Will you help me carry Hutson to the car?" she asked.

Hutson was partially conscious, but he moved too stiffly to cover the tricky ground between the couch and their car.

"Are you going to tell him about your adventure tonight?" Zavier propped Hutson in the passenger's seat and leaned him toward Wanda.

"If he asks me"—Wanda cranked the engine—"I'll tell him."

She had such a hard time getting Hutson out of the car that she managed to avoid looking at her empty yard. Because she couldn't get him to sit on the bed, Wanda let him slide to the floor with his back against the foot of the bed.

As she was removing his shirt, he woke up. "Are you mad?" he asked.

Before answering, Wanda pulled his sleeveless T-shirt over his head, ruffling his thick hair as if it were feathers.

"You know I don't get mad about you getting like this." She took off his watch.

"I'm not talking about this." Hutson placed his hands flat on his chest.

Wanda had pulled his pants down to his knees when she noticed the long white cylinder tied to his right leg. "What have you got in your pants?"

"That's what you'll be mad about." Hutson's eyelids drooped. "That tall bastard had no right to it. Put in storage . . . shit. It's your picture—it's you, know what I mean? It's yours. His going-away present to you. Only he don't know it."

Wanda unrolled the cylinder. It was the picture that had been locked in the frame. "How did you get it out?"

"I just waited till everybody went outside. I heard people talking about the fireworks." Hutson pulled himself up to the foot of the bed, then squirmed to his regular sleeping position. "Then I took the frame apart, got the picture out, and put the frame back together. It was like old times. Then I put the cover back over the frame and stuck it back in the closet. After I got the picture in my pants, I had a few more beers."

"You took the frame apart?" Wanda sat down beside Hutson and turned his face toward hers.

"Yep. Where do you think them things are made? Boehm Glass and Mirror Company. When I think about how many of them fucking frames I riveted together, them little toy rivets that you can pull out with your teeth, it makes me sick." Hutson closed his eyes. "Or maybe it's the beer."

"Well, try to get better before we head for the mountains. We can't have you throwing up on the bears."

Wanda pulled the sheet over him. She switched off the light. Once her eyes adjusted, she could make out the shape of her husband. As she watched the soft rising and falling of his chest, she slowly became aware of her own shape, how it was composed without edges and how her heart was beating—a wise sound that had nothing to do with color.

Workmen's Compensation

tanding on top of the lumber hack, Galax Tuttle could see the Blue Ridge Mountains in such clear outline that they made his teeth ache. Off to the west of the range, opalescent clouds were mounting the blue peaks. When the snow was that far away, Galax liked to think about it, just as long as the sky was clear above his house and where he worked. Stacking lumber in snow was not the kind of work a sixty-three-year-old man should be doing. He couldn't afford a broken leg or a cracked hip—not with the bank and the hospital counting on him. And pretty soon, if Esther and their grandson Cecil won the custody suit tomorrow, Galax Tuttle would have a year-old baby depending on him too.

A gust of February wind swept across the lumberyard. Fifteen feet off the ground, Galax was very exposed. Even through his plaid wool jacket and his insulated Air Force flight overalls, he felt chilled. "It's the wind of retirement," he shouted down to Dempsey Walsh and Waters Blair.

The two men looked up from the foundation they were laying for another lumber hack. Dempsey, whose fat protected him from extremes of hot and cold, was wearing his Red Camel overalls and his denim coat with the fuzz collar—the outfit he wore both summer and winter. He paused in his squaring of the railroad ties that were used for the foundation and raised a hand to shade his eyes.

"The cold make you feel old, Galax?" Dempsey's mouth was juicy from the tobacco he chewed constantly, except when he was eating.

"It's more than the cold." Galax scratched his chest thoughtfully. March, almost a year ago, they'd taken the tumor off his chest. It'd had roots like a small bush. The scar was in the shape of a large star. Whenever he happened to think about it, he could feel the tightness of the scar.

"I'll tell you what's wearing Galax out." Waters shoved another railroad tie into place. "No man should try to live in two houses the way he does."

"I'm not living in two houses—" Galax interrupted himself in order to search for a chip off one of the planks he was stacking. Then he slapped his thigh crookedly. Waters was too quick for him to hit with a wood chip.

"Three houses if you count his chicken house." Waters nodded and launched a slack smile in Galax's direction.

Galax shook his head and walked to the far side of his lumber hack so he wouldn't have to look at Dempsey and Waters. They were in their prime, and it didn't matter if they were fools. Their wives worked, and they hadn't picked out a hospital to start supporting yet. He looked at the mountains again. They were supposed to be the oldest mountains in the world. Galax wished he could get old like that, blue and shimmering, clear and powerful.

Of course, Esther wasn't holding up any better than he was. She kept getting those clots in her legs. Her blood pressure bounced up and down. Her plumbing didn't seem to be any better than what those crooks had put in their new house. They'd had that house for twelve years now, but he and Esther still called it the new house.

When the government had started to build the dam across the Yadkin River, a lawyer had come to visit Galax and Esther in their shack. Even then, the wood was weathered black; their toilet was the furthest away from the back door that it'd ever been, and Esther was still cooking on her wood stove. Very carefully, the lawyer explained to them that the government had to buy one hundred acres of their land because that was how much would eventually be under water. Esther wouldn't hear of selling their land. Selling anything that belonged to her or Galax was completely against her nature. Still, very carefully, the lawyer explained to her that if she didn't cooperate, the land would—could easily—be placed in the public domain and taken from them. As a matter of fact, Galax recalled, the lawyer was the one who suggested that they could afford to get their house fixed up with the money they'd get from the land.

Galax stepped on the forks of the lift after he'd finished taking all the wood off of it. He motioned for the driver to lower him to the ground. There was a time when he could have climbed from the hack on his own power, but the cold made his shoulders stiff, and his balance had been off for the last couple of years. He knew that a part of his problem was his having to go to court in the morning. As far as he was concerned, going to court was just as bad as going to the hospital. When you couldn't untangle your own problems, you wound up in court or in the hospital.

"Sometimes, you just feel helpless. You know what I mean?" Galax asked Dempsey when he got to the ground.

"I've not felt that way since I was five." Waters kicked one of the railroad ties to even it up.

"Well, maybe it does have something to do with age after all." Galax counted the number of cross braces in the hack he'd just completed. He liked to have twenty for a fifteen-foot hack. That kept it as straight and stable as it needed to be.

"I don't know." Dempsey had been in deep thought since Galax had asked him the question. This was apparent from the meditative way he had been cutting off a mouth-size cube from his tobacco plug. "A while back, I was out tracking deer in Sawmills Bog with Woodrow Redwine. We weren't hunting, just looking for signs. After a couple of hours, he went wandering off on his own—you know how that Cherokee can drift off—and I got turned around. Before I knew where I was, I sunk up to my crotch in a sinkhole. There for about twenty minutes, I felt more helpless than a baby in a jar. All I could do was yell. I guess I scared every buck out of the bog and back up to Pisgah Forest."

"Anybody as fat as you are," Waters observed, "shouldn't be out where the ground is soft in the first place."

"You'll know how fat I am when I ram one of these railroad ties up your ass." Dempsey picked up one of the ties and moved toward Waters.

"Your wife might like that kind of treatment, but I don't care for it." Waters scrambled up the nearest lumber hack.

"You boys are a real pair of roosters." Galax stepped in front of Dempsey. "If I had a couple like you in my henhouse, I wouldn't have to collect the eggs. The hens would bring them to me out of sheer gratitude. Maybe I could stop raising chicks for Holly Farms and just get egg rich. If you two are going to fight like guinea cocks, you might as well try to make my hens happy."

Dempsey tossed the tie onto the frozen ground, where it bounced three times, making deep, almost fleshy sounds but leaving no marks. Waters climbed down the stack of lumber, keeping his eyes on Dempsey. By keeping his eyes on the big man, Waters was acknowledging that he knew what Dempsey could do to him if he got his hands on him. Both Galax and Dempsey knew this was Waters's way of apologizing. By the next day, though, Waters would manage to say something else that would bring Dempsey charging after him.

Still, as far as Galax could tell, these two boys weren't much different from any of the other younger men he knew. All of them were roosters. He'd been a rooster once himself. Not too long ago, either. Even when he and Esther were moving back and forth, living in the new house in the summer and in the shack in the winter because it was easier and cheaper to heat. When they'd started building the new house, the contractor had convinced them that electric heat was the thing to have. Didn't have to worry about running out, didn't have to worry about delivery, didn't have to worry about furnace repair. Just hook up the juice and enjoy the heat. They'd used that electric heat two months—the first two months of winter. After that, they started living in the shack during cold weather.

This year, it had been different. All summer long, he and his grandson had worked to wall up the double garage doors of the carport. When that was done, they put in a chimney. Then Cecil brought over a fifty-gallon oil drum and by welding some legs on it and torching out a hole in the back for a stovepipe and a hole in the front for a door, he'd fixed up a passable wood stove. It really put out the heat, too. There was enough dead timber lying around the farm that Galax didn't think he'd ever have to cut down a tree.

He and Esther lived in the carport. They'd turn up the heat in the bathroom a couple hours each day. But in the rest of the house, it was either turned completely off or on just enough to keep the pipes from freezing. Just keeping the pipes from freezing was costing Galax much more than he was comfortable with. If they got custody of the baby, Esther might get it into her head to move into one of the bedrooms. He'd lost count of how many times he'd asked himself why they built all the rooms so large. The carport was built for two cars with lots of room in between, and it was still the smallest room in the whole house.

As he was punching out that evening, Galax saw Vanderveldt, the personnel manager, standing beside the time clock, making sure nobody was punching someone else out. Galax didn't have anything against the man personally—only that he always kept too clean, the kind of clean Galax didn't trust. As far as he could recall, all the people who talked him into doing foolish things kept themselves too clean, the way a rooster always looked cleaner than it was. Hens weren't like that.

As Galax passed by Vanderveldt, the personnel manager said, "Tomorrow's court day for you, isn't it?"

"Has been for nearly three months now." Galax wondered how the man kept those creases in his pants so sharp.

"Well, I know it'll turn out right for you, Galax. I don't know of two better people to raise a child than you and your wife." Vanderveldt smiled as if he had done his duty.

The smile reminded Galax of a glove advertisement he'd heard on the radio, something about one size fits all hands. That smile was like one of those gloves—it'd fit anything. So he couldn't exactly resent Vanderveldt, but he couldn't get any real encouragement from the man either. "Well, if being old and worn out makes you fit to raise a baby, me and Esther will raise a president for sure."

Vanderveldt smiled again, the corners of his mouth penetrating higher into his cheeks this time. "I don't think you're quite ready to be put to pasture yet."

"I guess not—not as long as the quality fertilizer holds out anyway." By this time, Galax was out of Vanderveldt's conversational range, and except for the tightness across his chest he felt relieved. The longer you talked to those smooth fellows, the more likely you were to get in trouble.

The drive home took Galax and his Chevrolet about thirty minutes once they got out of the congested city limits. The Chevrolet had suspension problems and steering problems, so the drive home was not a time when Galax could relax—not physically. Through the years, his mind had gotten to where it could detach itself from the shimmy of the car's steering wheel and the wobble of the rear end. But that custody suit tomorrow had his brain acting as if its own shock absorbers were ruptured.

Galax kept assuring himself that he didn't have all that much to do. Esther and Cecil were going to do all the talking, the testifying. Esther would certainly be good at that. Nobody spoke her mind more readily than Esther. And she certainly had a load to drop on Cecil's sorry wife, LaPonda. The lawyer that Esther had hired laid out his strategy for them just a few days ago. He planned to show first that LaPonda wasn't a fit mother. She was only seventeen, and just three months after being married, she had started seeing other men. He could verify this. He also had a doctor's report describing the signs of neglect that he'd found when the baby had finally been brought in because of its diaper rash—which had become infected because LaPonda wouldn't even change its diapers.

Once this point was made, the lawyer said he planned to show how Cecil, living with Galax and Esther, could provide a much healthier home because the grandparents could be responsible for the child while Cecil worked at the garage. It all sounded right to Galax, but he just hoped the judge wouldn't look too closely at him and Esther. Both of them had hands gnarled with arthritis. Galax knew he stooped some since his operation because it made the scar feel less tight. He could stand up straight if he had to. When he got home, he wanted to remind Esther to wear her heavy support hose so her blood clots wouldn't show. If she could get to the stand and start talking, then everything would be fine. She was mighty persuasive when her heart was in it, and she wanted the baby with a determination you could use to pull up tree trunks.

The last three miles of the drive were over a road whose surface had probably done the most to make the car's palsied suspension system what it was. It was narrow and rough, making everything inside the car—except the upholstery—rattle. Despite the jolting, Galax valued the road because it did keep traffic from being so heavy; half the people who drove along the road usually flagged him over to find out where they were. On the right-hand side of the road, the dammed-up waters of the Yadkin River waited, stalled into a reservoir, slow as Jell-O, a mixture of lime and blackberry Jell-O. On the left side of the road, kudzu had enveloped the trees and lapped into the ditch at the very edge of the road. In February, this stretch of gravel and mud didn't look as if it led anywhere.

Galax's driveway cut sharply off to the right of the dirt road and climbed steeply past a row of Norwegian poplars that he and Esther had planted twelve years ago when they started the new house. They'd planned for the trees to line the driveway all the way to the new house, but after they'd planted twenty and still had over a mile to go, they knew they couldn't afford that touch of elegance. From the dirt road, just before turning into his driveway, Galax could see the new house. From a mile away, it looked exactly like the architect said it would. All those windows facing out over the river below. The cinder-block retaining wall, painted white, swooping away from the house like a cloud being released from the downstairs windows.

This far away, nobody could see how all the rooms were empty except for the furniture they'd lugged up from the shack. This far away, the corroded gutters didn't show up either. Neither did the cement porch, which was crumbling along the edges. To get those repairs made today would cost almost as much as the whole house cost to build.

The car swayed and slid up the washed-out driveway. Passing the shack, Galax rubbed his hand through his thinning hair; seemed like each day it took him less and less time to run his hand through his hair. Each day also seemed to make the shack more and more dilapidated. He loved the old place, but there was nothing he could do for it. It was like an old heart that simply gets worn out. Everything about it had gotten so fragile you couldn't live in it without destroying it. Now, all it was used for was storage—storage for all the odds and ends that Esther had collected in her sixty-three years of never throwing anything away. Of course, the shack could hold only a part of what she had collected.

Just below the chicken house, the road got better because Galax had bought three loads of gravel and spread them along this section up to the chicken house. The truck driver who came to pick up the chickens every three months had told Galax if that part of the road wasn't fixed, he wouldn't be able to get his truck in. This thought reminded Galax that it was about time to refill the automatic feeders. Within the next week, the chickens would hit their period of fast growing, and he dreaded having to go through each evening, picking up the dead ones. The ones with weak constitutions simply couldn't take that sudden increase in size and weight. But that was what the feed did to them: blowed them up twice as fast and twice as big as an ordinary chicken. He didn't like to raise chickens like that, but now he had to raise three more batches just to pay for the gravel he'd bought.

When he pulled in behind his house, Esther's five dogs came out to greet him. He waded through their squirming attention. At the back porch, seven cats, disdaining the dogs' enthusiasm, uncoiled, stretched, and began to circulate around the piece of rug where Galax was trying to wipe his feet. Galax mumbled to himself that he was glad there were no stray elephants or alligators in the neighborhood or he'd have to climb over them to get to his supper. The back door was his favorite part of the house. It was oak. He'd ordered it special all the way from Vermont.

The contractor had tried to pass off one of those hollow veneer jobs on him, but the door was the one and only thing that Galax had caught the crooks cheating him on.

During supper, Galax kept studying the two faces that sat on either side of him. Esther had her share of wrinkles, but her chin and cheeks had stayed strong and square. Her eyes were the color of smoky quartz, as clear and fresh as a length of shaved pine. Although her hair was mostly gray, it was still thick and hadn't been cut since Galax could remember. Although she wore it rolled up on top of her head most of the time, when she did let it down, it reached below her hips. Years ago, when Galax saw Esther with her hair down, he would tell himself he had married a Hawaiian princess.

Cecil was a fair-skinned boy, nineteen years old. He was good with his hands: cars, toilets, fireplaces, he could fix them. But he was a rooster too, Galax admitted. Married LaPonda when she was sixteen, her trashy mama only too happy to sign the papers. Cecil was going to let the two of them keep the trailer he'd gone into debt for. The boy didn't eat as if he was worried about the trip to court tomorrow. His thick fingers were dark-tipped with car grease that wouldn't come off his pale skin. As he chewed, he gazed out the window into the back yard where three goats were bounding around pretending to fight.

When they finished eating, Cecil went outside to work on his car. Galax helped Esther carry the plastic milk jugs she'd been scalding down to the lower part of the house. The store-room downstairs was filled with plastic jugs. In the fall, she filled them with her apple cider and sent Cecil up the mountain to sell it to the tourists.

"Don't let me forget to take a few of these jugs to Aunt Pansy. She offered to keep some of them for me." Esther descended the steps one at a time.

"Don't you think we're going to have enough to do without making milk jug deliveries?"

"It's on the way," Esther replied. "You won't even have to turn the car off. Cecil and me can take them in to her so you won't need to get out."

"Don't get so sharp with me, Esther." Galax wondered if

Esther would have to climb up any stairs to give her testimony. Neither he nor Esther looked too good even on short stairways. "Remember, you've got to convince them you're a sweet great-granny. Just try and act that way for the few minutes they talk to you." Galax could tell that Esther was worried about the suit. In a way, that was good, like shaking up a bottle of Pepsi with your thumb over the top. He could feel her dignity fizzing up.

"I don't have to put on an act to tell them the truth. I may be old and ugly, but I'm not sorry as a sow in a ship's saloon. That LaPonda needs somebody to take care of her. I don't say that to be quarrelsome. She's just like her mama because her mama is the way she is, but the baby don't have to be that way."

As far as Galax could tell, Esther was in fine form. She was nervous, but she was keeping herself under control. Just to be on the safe side, he reminded himself to take her blood pressure pills with them to the courthouse.

In the morning, everyone felt clinched up inside. At least that's the way Galax felt. When they walked out to the car, each carrying an armload of milk jugs, Galax thought that from a distance they must look like they were carrying a load of bubbles. He did feel as if he were struggling with an armload of something light and slippery. Esther dropped one of the jugs and started to pick it up. Galax shouted for her to keep on going; they had enough jugs to keep Aunt Pansy busy.

In the Wilkes County Courthouse, Galax stood very close to Esther. Over the years, he'd grown accustomed to the powerful ammonia odor of ten thousand chickens cooped up in a warm chicken house—an odor that could kill trees growing too close to the ventilation ducts. The courthouse odors, though, settled over his stomach like a snail track. Everybody's face looked stiff, as if the lights were filled with glue.

Esther looked shorter and stockier than usual in her plaid jacket and her navy blue dress. She was gaping up at the marble arches that formed the roof of the courthouse lobby.

"Don't let your mouth hang open like that, Esther." Galax tugged her elbow.

"People don't care about my mouth hanging open." Esther shook her head. "I don't know what's gotten into you. My manners are fine when they need to be—they're at least as good as they've always been."

Galax patted her back. "I just don't want you looking lost or bewildered."

"But it's easier to look at a roof when you let your mouth hang open. Go ahead and try it yourself."

"I'll look at the roof when we get out of court." Galax thought how nice it would be on Monday to be back out in the lumberyard with all this behind him. "Or better yet, when we get home, we can look at the roof while we eat lunch." Galax pressed his palm against his chest to ease the tightness of his scar.

Esther noticed his gesture and pulled him over to a bench where Cecil was slumped with his hands in his pockets. Galax noticed that one of the boy's socks had a hole just over the ankle. "Pull that pants leg down."

"What you should have done, Galax," Esther said, more softly than was her custom when she gave advice to her husband, "was dressed both of us yourself."

Galax leaned back in the bench. He wished he could be outside looking at the mountains, which knew how to be old. The lobby was crowded, full of echoes—too much like his own head when his arthritis reminded him that he was sixty-three. He looked up at the roof and let his mouth slowly drop open. "You're right. It is easier with your mouth open."

When the lawyer arrived, Galax, Esther, and Cecil filed in behind him and followed him to a small hearing room in the bottom of the courthouse. They were the first people to arrive. While they waited, Galax felt as if his stomach and jaw muscles were turning to stone. Esther sat with her patent leather pocket-book in her lap. She clutched it as if it were loaded.

After fifteen minutes, LaPonda's lawyer came into the room, looked around with a worried face, then disappeared out the door. Galax knew the man was looking for LaPonda and her mother. He felt himself relax slightly. It would be just like LaPonda to forget about the custody suit for her own baby. LaPonda's lawyer came back after a few minutes and stood beside the Tuttles' lawyer. They whispered to each other, but

Galax couldn't catch what they were saying. LaPonda's lawyer kept looking back at the door.

When the judge came in, the lawyer tried to explain that the girl was probably lost somewhere in the courthouse and that he'd go check in the other hearing rooms. The judge let out a loud sigh and told him to go ahead. Galax liked the way the judge leaned back in the chair and studied the ceiling with his hands behind his head. He was a hefty man, an older version of Dempsey Walsh. His large ears were scarlet—looked like frostbite from where Galax was sitting—and his nose looked like a swollen thumb. He had no hair on top of his head except for a narrow white band that seemed to connect one ear with the other.

"Where you all live?" The judge swiveled his chair in Galax's direction.

"Over toward Goshen," Galax replied. "Up on the hill where the old Stony Fork bridge used to cross the Yadkin River."

"In that brick house with the white retaining walls?" The judge leaned forward.

"That's it." Galax pulled his back a little straighter.

"I've been fishing over there, right there below your place. You raise goats, don't you?"

"It's hard to say who raises goats." Galax wondered what the goats had been doing when the judge saw them. "They eat what they want to. And when they get a mind to tour, they'll tour. But my wife keeps a few around for milk."

"People laugh at me," the judge said in a confessional tone, "but I have always thought goats were pretty."

"They're just like deer," Esther said. "Every bit as graceful."

"You're right." The judge nodded. "I watched them goats of yours once, and that's how they moved. Just like deer."

"There's nothing sweeter than goat's milk. It's a whole lot easier to digest than cow's milk." Esther leaned forward and rested her elbow on top of the bench in front of her. "It keeps better than cow's milk too."

"When I was a boy, we used to crumble cornbread in a glass of goat's milk." The judge smiled to himself. "I've not had anything like that in years and years. It was sweet."

Eventually, the lawyer returned with LaPonda and her mother. Both of the women looked as if they'd just gotten out of bed—which was the way they usually looked—but in the somber light of the small hearing room, Galax noticed how much LaPonda resembled her mother. Neither one of them looked her age; it was hard to tell what age they did look. When each woman gave her testimony, she was constantly adjusting a bra strap or twiddling a stray lock of hair. Their lawyer seemed more interested in getting his part over and getting out.

Esther's lawyer began with showing pictures taken by the doctor who had treated the baby's rash. Then he gave a long description of Galax and Esther. As the lawyer talked, Galax couldn't look the judge in the face. The lawyer made both of them sound too good to be true. He even had letters from the Holly Farms supervisor and Mr. Vanderveldt telling the judge what a hard-working man Galax was.

Then Esther took her turn. Even when she talked about debts and bad health, she sounded proud of herself and Galax. She looked the judge in the eye when she told him she didn't want to lay blame on anybody. She just wanted to raise the baby. She'd been raising babies of one kind or another all her life. Cecil also managed to sound reliable. Although he answered in short sentences and the lawyer had to lead him along most of the time, Galax thought the boy looked like a hardworking father.

Only LaPonda and her mother seemed surprised when the judge awarded Cecil custody of the baby—with the understanding that it be cared for by Galax and Esther. All the way home, Galax thought about the reasons the judge had given for his decision. He and Esther were, according to the judge, fine examples of maturity and responsibility. The stoniness was gone from Galax's stomach and jaw.

As they pulled into the back yard of the new house, Esther pointed to where five goats were standing in a semicircle. "Would you look at that foolish rooster!" Esther's voice cracked with delight.

What she was pointing to and what the goats were observing was a rooster that was struggling with all its feathered strength to mount the plastic milk jug Esther had dropped. It would flap its wings and try to find a place to grip the jug, but just as it would begin to hump, the jug would tilt, dumping the bird on the ground.

"Ain't you glad you're not that foolish." Esther laughed, struggling out of the car.

"Yep," Galax replied. "Satisfaction's not how high you climb but how steady you ride." He could say that, he thought, without contradicting those mountains he had grown up with.

Bentley in Her Basement

The gas mask was hanging where it always hung—on a wooden peg three feet above the air compressor. As Lela approached it, taking care not to brush against the '58 Bentley, she noticed that the pink haze building up on the khaki-colored rubber of the mask made it look like a piece of meat that had thawed too long.

As a matter of fact, as she stopped to consider the mask, it looked very much like an unhealthy organ. The ridges of the tube protruding from the front of the mask resembled an old man's throat, and the mask itself could have been part of a lung.

Fumes still hung in the basement garage, and Lela could feel the hairs in her nose getting sticky from them. When her husband, Olin, had first started painting cars down there, she had laughed when he brought the gas mask home. However, after the first coat of paint, the fumes became so thick that eyelashes would stick together.

Lela liked cleaning the gas mask for Olin. They were partners in this business. She took the mask off the peg. The fumes didn't help the taste that had stayed in her mouth since she had come home from the hospital. But it wasn't just the taste, which was a moldy flavor; her mouth had begun to feel like it was lined with cellophane. Sometimes she felt as if she had drunk a mixture of Wesson Oil and stale water, the water that collected in the storage tray when she defrosted her refrigerator.

She put the gas mask on. She had to loosen the head strap because her hair was thicker than Olin's. Her thick hair was one of the reasons why she hated summer in Boehm. Often, her hair would get so hot on her head she felt like she was wearing a wool cap. If she were in Bandana, there would be a nice breeze, and some nights got cool enough for a fire in the fireplace—especially during a rainy spell.

When she wore the gas mask, she could hear herself breathing. The canister dangling at the end of the ridged tube amplified her breath. She felt mechanical, hearing herself breathe this way. A foam-rubber flap opened when she inhaled and snapped shut when she exhaled. Her face began to sweat.

Very carefully, she walked around the Bentley. Olin had given it nineteen coats of glaze, over the metal-flake. Even through the hazed lenses of the mask, Lela could see the glitter of the metal-flake. She didn't want to turn on the fluorescent lamps that Olin had installed. She preferred to study the car in the light coming through the fume-clotted windows of the garage door. But neither the sluggish light nor the film spread over the goggles of the mask could entirely dim Olin's paint job. Lela fairly ached to touch it.

She checked the feather brushes that Olin used to texture the glaze. Tonight, he would spray on the last coat; he would expect his brushes to be in perfect condition. The feathers were looking somewhat tattered—not too bad, really. Ordinarily, Lela would have waited one or two more days before replacing the feathers, but the final coat—especially for the Bentley—was a special occasion.

She wanted to gaze at the car, but if she were going to replace the feathers, she would have to kill another chicken. The muscles along her spine tightened with the thought. She was not in the mood to kill a chicken today.

Before going upstairs, she made a methodical check of the taped windows, headlights, and taillights. As she had expected, the tape was still holding tightly. She had just re-covered all the glass two days earlier, but Olin was very anxious that everything go smoothly with this job. He wanted a chance to paint more vintage cars because the money was so good.

When Lela looked at the Bentley, she knew what a vintage car was. Even before Olin had sanded it down and started spraying it with the metal-flake and red glaze, the car had filled up the small basement garage with more than its large round fenders. The only experience Lela could compare the feeling to was the day when she had actually realized she was pregnant. She had not realized it until about three months after the doctor told her. Having the car was like that—especially before she started getting sick so much.

But she had to admit that being a mother was confusing to her—even after three weeks. It all seemed much easier for Olin. The day she came home from the hospital, Mr. Edge had brought the Bentley over for Olin to paint, and he had painted every night for these past three weeks. He looked at the baby when he came in from work; then, after eating supper, he went downstairs, put on his gas mask, and began painting the car.

Lela stood listening to herself breathe. Each night, Olin would put on one coat of glaze, then spend hours brushing the elusive texture into the tinted acrylic. The car was large, and Olin would go over it three times with his feather brushes. Most other painters would simply have used chamois to rub the car, but when Olin wanted some effect out of the ordinary, Lela had suggested that he try using the kind of feather brush she once played with when she was growing up in the mountains.

The effect had been exactly what Olin was looking for. The stiffness of the feathers worked to smooth the transparent finish, but it also created a certain wavy effect. The car, Olin observed, looked as if it were being seen through very clear but slightly rippled water. He had been so pleased with the feather-brush effect that he made Lela his partner. She cleaned his gas mask, did the tape work, and prepared the feather brushes for him.

As Lela climbed the stairs from the basement, she realized how uncomfortable the narrow passageway made her. Somehow, it reminded her of her worst days of pregnancy when almost every passageway was too narrow for her.

She was constantly surprised by how much room the baby took up. Since she had come home with it, she had been trying to understand what made it seem bigger than it really was. She thought that once it was outside of her, she would start feeling her normal size again. However, that had not happened. In fact, some places that did not seem too small when she was nine months pregnant now seemed stuffy and confining. All the rooms in her garage apartment felt smaller. Even the porch, which formed a deck over the garage door, did not provide the relief that it once did.

Lela checked in the bedroom to see if the baby was still sleeping. Actually, it did not cause many problems. Lela assumed that the hot weather made the baby stay sleepy. The heat certainly had that effect on her. The late-night feedings also had their effects on her. When she got up to feed the baby, she had to peel the sheets away from her skin. Her pajamas felt like moist tissue paper. Olin did not seem to suffer from the weather. His job made him immune to a lot of things, Lela suspected. When he was trying out new sprays, he would work for hours in the heat box, testing how the finishes dried under different temperatures.

Lela inspected the roof of her mouth with the middle of her tongue. She wondered what she was going to do if the taste continued to get worse. Her doctor told her that her body might do unusual things for a while because it had to readjust to being normal once again, but he hadn't said anything about this taste in her mouth. For the past few days, she had been using as much seasoning on her food as Olin used.

Before she started cleaning the gas mask, she went out on the porch to catch what breeze might be coming by. The breezes in Boehm were disappointing. When Olin first told her that they were going to live in Boehm, she thought the place sounded pleasant enough. The name made her think of how the wind sounded when it blew through a hollow tree. But when they had come from Bandana, out of the mountains, the land just lost any ambition it might have had for cool weather.

Lela had been too preoccupied with being pregnant to pay

much attention to the flatness of the land, but now, barely three weeks into June, Boehm was already hotter than she could ever remember Bandana being. And the breezes in Boehm were mongrels compared to the wind in the mountains. The breeze she now felt had something oily in it. It enclosed rather than relieved. Sometimes, when Olin came home from work after having a few beers, his breath had the same odor as the wind.

Twelve feet below where Lela stood, the chickens were inspecting the ground for insects. Lela tried to decide which one would be her next victim. Since she had started killing them regularly for the brushes, she didn't like to think about them except when she had to. And maybe being a mother had something to do with her change of feelings.

A mag wheel was balanced on the rail of the porch. The brushed chrome squeezed the sunlight into a painful dazzle. Lela placed her hand on top of the glare, half expecting it to burst into flames. The chrome was hot, but Lela left her hand on the metal until it cooled to her skin. Olin had given her the wheel. At first, she had planned to make a lamp out of it, but she had stayed so nervous while she was pregnant that she soon lost her ambition to make the lamp. Now the baby and the Bentley kept her too busy for any kind of hobby. The wheel was too heavy for a lamp anyway.

With jerky movements, the chickens continued to look for food. Nothing about a chicken was graceful, Lela thought. When Olin painted a car, his movements were smooth—almost like he was conducting an orchestra. He used the same flowing motion when he smoothed out the metal-flake and the glaze with the feather brush. The car itself was more graceful than the chickens. When she killed a chicken, Lela was more graceful than her victim.

Lately, the feathers had started making her sad. When she first pulled them off, they were damp and limp from the scalding water she had poured over the chicken to make the plucking easier. They looked like a panful of dreary thoughts. Then she had to sort them into three piles according to size. Even after each feather was split and fitted into the grooves of the brushes, they still retained a foolishness about them. Olin claimed he did not know what she was talking about when she tried to explain to him why the brushes depressed her, but she suspected that he had not killed enough chickens to notice how awkward they really were. For the year and a half they had been married, she had killed all the chickens.

If the feathers were going to be dry enough to put in the brushes for tonight's painting, Lela knew she would have to get one of the chickens plucked pretty soon. However, as she looked at her hand blurred in the gleam of the chrome wheel, she decided to wait until after she had cleaned the gas mask.

It was lying on the table, the flexible rubber flopped at an angle, looking like the husk of a bowl. With her longest fingernail, Lela scratched the glaze on the mask and wondered what kind of shape it would be in if she had not been keeping it clean. Olin often brought home the small muzzle masks that he wore at the shop. They had a tissue-paper insert that could be replaced when it got too clogged, but eventually the mask itself became so caked with lacquer that it had to be thrown away. Olin also said that the muzzle masks kept the men from biting the foreman.

To get into the bathroom, Lela had to go through the bedroom where the baby was sleeping. She was very careful not to look at the baby as she passed by the crib. Until she finished with the mask, she did not want to be distracted. As she was standing over the sink, which hadn't been cleaned in nearly two weeks, rubbing linseed oil over the mask, she wondered if it was wrong to want time to herself. After all, she was a mother now, but so much had been changed. She thought back to the week before when she and Olin had tried to make love but had not been able to because the stubble where she had been shaved irritated Olin too much. Before they came together, though, she wasn't sure if she wanted to, wasn't sure if Olin wanted to.

After she rubbed the linseed oil well into the rubber, she applied a film of Noxema. She enjoyed sticking her fingers into the blue jar of cream. The combined odors made her think of dust on glass bricks, and the glass bricks made her think about the texture of the glaze that Olin was putting on the Bentley.

As she wiped the cream and oil off the mask with one of the

rags Olin carried from the factory, Lela rubbed her eyes with her forearm. Everything about Boehm irritated her. While in the hospital, her ward had seemed too clear, too sharply visible, and, coupled with the air conditioning, she had kept a headache the week she had been in. The doctor and the nurses told her it was just tension, but she felt her eyes were letting too much of that clean, harsh world into her brain. Compared to the hospital world, the rest of Boehm, including her bathroom, was vague and poorly lit. She did not remember noticing this when she first moved to the factory town.

Once the mask was clean, Lela slipped it on again. All she could recognize of herself when she looked in the mirror were her eyes, but the pull of the mask on her chin drew her lower lids down, exposing more of her eyeball than was usually visible. This slight distortion gave her a melting and mournful expression. With satisfaction, she decided that, when wearing the mask, she looked closer to the way she felt.

The baby coughed. That was how it had been waking up. At first, she had expected the cough to turn into something, but it hadn't. Her first impulse was to take it to the doctor, but because it hadn't gotten worse and because she didn't feel up to sitting in a waiting room, she had satisfied herself with the conclusion that the cough was just the baby's habit.

When she leaned over the crib, the baby let out a howl—its first since coming home from the hospital. Lela turned quickly away, removing the mask. For a few minutes, the baby cried more intensely than it ever had, and Lela's stomach tightened with guilt. Automatically, she began changing its diaper; the routine soothed the child. Gratefully, Lela went into the kitchen and warmed its formula, while rocking the baby in one arm.

The feeding made both of them feel better. Before the baby had finished its meal, Lela began to feel the heat of its body mixing with hers. Over the last couple of weeks, she had become more and more aware of how their two temperatures mingled, so she was very careful to switch the baby from arm to arm to keep both it and her from getting too warm. That was something Olin did not have to worry about because he never held the baby long enough to feel its warmth. Of course, he was seldom clean enough to hold it. When he came home from work, he had filler or finish all over him, and when he came up from the basement, he had glaze all over him.

As Lela put the baby back in its crib, she realized that Olin did not have a smell of his own. Since she had known him, he had always smelled of lacquer or paint. It had not been so bad in the small shop up in Bandana, but since beginning work in Boehm, he smelled so strong that he could probably go naked and no one would notice for his odor.

On the baby's left leg, the prickly heat was coming back. Lela brought the Noxema from the bathroom and rubbed a two-finger daub on the pink bumps. She still wondered at the smallness of her son's limbs, and she circled her fingers around his leg. She smiled because the smooth skin reminded her of the soft feathers of a chicken's neck. This thought brought her back to her need to get those feathers for the brushes. Guiltily, she let go of the baby's leg.

She walked out of the bedroom, holding her hands under her armpits. She was trying to squeeze out the memory that tingled in her palms and fingers. As a child learning to kill chickens, the wrench of the neck and the almost polite grinding of the cartilage always shocked her. That was how you knew you killed the chicken. And she had become more practiced at the method as she grew older. The moments when the necks snapped had tattooed the sensation into the nerves of her hand, until now her brain could call up the feeling just by anticipating its cause. Maybe, she thought, she had finally reached her limit, like on *Sea Hunt* when the famous diver who was Lloyd Bridges's old friend got to where he could no longer stand to go down in deep water.

Maybe if she faced the chickens, she could get her resolve back. Lela took a pan of feed, went down the steps of the porch, and scattered the cracked corn for the chickens. Watching them scramble for the food, she noticed that although they moved quickly, they never lost their awkwardness. They moved as if they were pregnant. Again, she felt the sensation in her hand, and she squeezed a handful of the corn until the pain was all she could feel.

To escape the insistent clucks, Lela went back up the steps to the porch, where she threw the corn on top of the chickens. Not bothering to notice the corn dropping on their backs, they scurried for what bounced to the ground.

Tentatively, Lela rocked the wheel. The rail was narrow, and the wheel tilted easily. Two chickens were directly below her, and the wheel was pretty wide. As she made these vague calculations, Lela continued to rock the wheel. One of the chickens began to wander off, and before her pulse had a chance to respond to her intention, Lela pushed her palm determinedly against the far side of the wheel. It slid off the rail, turned one stout flip, and landed like a pot lid on top of the chicken that had not walked away. All of the noise was made by the other chickens.

A few white feathers protruded from the spaces in the wheel. Lela anticipated some involuntary response, some final awkwardness resisting that gleaming weight, which had, no doubt, shattered bones as if they had been potato chips.

Broken bones meant chicken and dumplings. That would make Olin happy, and if she waited until tomorrow to fix them, she could tell Olin that she had prepared his favorite dish to celebrate his finishing the job. However, she still had to get the feathers ready for tonight.

Although the chicken showed no sign of expiring spasms, Lela dreaded lifting the wheel. Perhaps all the body was doing was waiting for the weight to be removed. She paused with her toe resting on the rim. Her head ached in several places, but each pain was similar, like a warm grape with the skin removed. The sun made her scalp itch.

Twisting slightly in the sandy ground as she lifted the wheel with her foot, Lela first noticed that none of the large feathers was damaged. The chicken's neck was folded sharply under its breast, and the only blood was coming from the chicken's beak. Its body was flattened, but some of the feathers were already beginning to fluff back out.

Again using her toe, Lela rolled the chicken over to see what kind of damage was done underneath. Here, she found a little more blood where one of the leg bones had broken and cut through the skin. What blood had come out of the wound was smeared in the feathers so that it looked more like dirt than blood.

When he first got home, Olin did not like to talk. Before they were married he had explained to Lela that, when working in a factory, a man is so happy when the day is over that he does not like to think about how it went. Mutely, a definite pace had evolved for the events that began when Olin came from work. As soon as he came in, Lela would give him a glass of iced tea. He took his tea into the small living room where the television was, and he would watch the last half of *Bonanza*. The end of that program signaled the beginning of supper.

Supper had to be on the table, ready to eat, when Olin walked into the kitchen, his glass tilted up to drain the last of the by-now-watery tea. He expected Lela to provide him with a fresh glass—already on the table, beading with condensation—but he also counted on her leaving enough room in the glass so he could empty his broken-in ice cubes into the glass. Lela always suspected that the time they took to eat supper was determined by how quickly the twice-used ice cubes melted. Olin always finished in time to tilt his glass one final time and collect those pebble-sized pieces of ice in his mouth.

Lela would then pour him a half glass of tea, which he would take back to the living room to drink while he watched *The Funny Man*. While Olin watched this show, Lela would feed the baby, then take it into the living room. By this time, Olin felt a safe distance between him and his workday. Now he did not mind being talked to. When the show was over, he was ready to begin painting.

Tonight, Olin's routine was going to be changed slightly. Before beginning to paint, he had to set up the heat lamps around the car. Although he did not usually care for heat lamps, he wanted to make sure that the final glaze was completely hard when Mr. Edge came to pick up the car. Lela could hear Olin downstairs, checking all the patched places in the basement to make sure no bugs would get in.

He had spent the whole evening, when she came home from the hospital, patching little cracks and holes—anywhere that might admit bugs. About the end of that first week, a moth managed somehow to squeeze into the basement. Before it could fly two feet, its wings had become so gummed with the glaze that it plopped to the floor, unable to flutter.

When Olin recognized how powerful his fumes were, he felt more secure about the Bentley. Olin told Lela two days ago that he planned to stay up all night tonight just to make sure nothing happened. With the heat lamps burning most of the night, the bugs would have more reason to try and sneak in.

As Lela dried the dishes, she noticed they still had a sticky feeling to them. Part of the stickiness seemed to be on her fingers. She went to the bathroom and washed her hands with Olin's Boraxo powder. That helped, but when she picked up the metal can to twist the top closed, she could still feel a trace of stickiness when she took her fingers from the can. She could hear the damp click like the sound of moist lips parting.

Since he was going to be up all night, Lela filled Olin's thermos with coffee, wrapped up three ham sandwiches and five chocolate doughnuts, and took them downstairs to him. On top of the bag containing the sandwiches and doughnuts, Lela balanced the feather brushes.

She sat down on the steps to watch him as he set up the heat lamps. He was arranging them along the driver's side of the car, so his back was to Lela. After less than an hour in the basement, his T-shirt was already damp with sweat, and Lela wondered how he was going to stand the heat once he turned the large lamps on. Just the thought of the glare and the warmth cooped up beneath where she would be trying to sleep made Lela uncomfortable.

Despite his thick waist, Olin bent easily, as if he enjoyed it. He was only slightly taller than Lela, but his arms were large, and his hands were a deep mahogany color with fingernails the color of acorns; they matched the color of his eyes. He got his light hair and his sharp cheekbones from his grandmother, who had been Swedish. His eyebrows came and went with his mood.

Slowly, the dense air of the basement gathered in Lela's nose and mouth, reminding her of the film coating her mouth. She felt that if she stayed any longer in the basement the taste in her mouth might take some ugly shape, so she went back upstairs to wash the baby. Its skin also had a sticky feeling. She tried to persuade herself that the baby had always felt sticky. Babies were more oily than adults, and the weather had made both her and the baby more damp than usual.

Tonight's bath took longer than usual because she wanted to make certain that the baby was completely clean. She powdered it until a small cloud hovered over the table. The talc caked along the sides of her damp fingers, cool at first, then becoming annoying because it made her conscious of every movement her fingers made. The child lay on its stomach, its head turned to the side, watching its fingers. Lela ran her hands along its back and down its legs, but the stickiness had been beaten by the powder. When she had put the baby in the crib and turned on the fan, Lela decided to take a bath too. She tried to remember how long it had been since she'd cleaned the bathtub—not since she got back from the hospital. Downstairs, the compressor began its monotonous chuckle, and for a couple of seconds the lights in the house dimmed. Olin was applying the final coat.

On top of the refrigerator, Olin had left half a roll of Lifesavers. Lela put three into her mouth and went back to the bathroom. As she passed through the bedroom, she angled the fan so it would blow on her when she was drying off. She also shifted the candy in her mouth so she had the lime on her tongue; the cherry and the orange were beside her left and right molars. The candy merely decorated the taste in her mouth—like three bulbs of delicate glass hanging from a dead persimmon tree.

As she dried off in front of the fan, she could hear the persistent flutter of the compressor and the hiss of the spray gun. The hiss was a pleasant sound, very crisp and precise like a wasp's wing. The air in the house seemed dense and stale compared to the sound of the spray gun. Realizing how much she felt like the sluggish and dreary air, Lela chose to go to bed early.

Except for the baby's four o'clock feeding, Lela was not disturbed by anything for the entire night. Sleep smothered her. It was heavy as the fumes rising from the basement. When the compressor and the spray gun became silent, Lela did not notice. She was not disturbed when Olin turned off the fan. Nor did she notice the other two times when he came upstairs to use the bathroom.

When she woke up the next morning, she lay on her back with the same headache she had had every morning for the past two weeks. Normally, she would lie in the bed, letting her eyes rove around the room until the baby woke up to be fed. However, as her eyes roved around the room this morning, she threw herself from the bed because she saw a huddled form lying beside the baby's crib. Even as she stooped over to touch the pinkish heap, she was feeling a vague anger. The form on the floor was Olin's gas mask. For some reason, she was deeply insulted by Olin's sloppiness. This meant he was completely finished with the car. He had never brought the mask upstairs before. Overnight, he had somehow changed. With a flash of unpleasant warmth, like the exhaust from a car, Lela took Olin's untidiness as a criticism of her. Maybe he had left it there because she had not gotten up to fix his breakfast. But she could not remember if he had even tried to get her up.

She knew he might have just been so tired that he brought the gas mask upstairs and dropped it without thinking about it, but she knew even more certainly that Olin was too methodical to make such a mistake. There was no reason for him to be carrying the gas mask around. She felt that something between her and Olin had been violated.

The morning was muggy, and just the exertion of changing the baby and washing it made her feel sticky with perspiration. She noticed that the baby was sticky again. Then she observed that both its skin and hers looked flushed. Of course, babies were supposed to have pink skin, but her skin was just as pink as her child's. Perhaps, she decided, it was one of the traits of motherhood. Pink skin could be a compensation for the headaches and the bad taste in her mouth.

Sitting in her damp pajamas in the small kitchen, she knew she would not feel comfortable if she went to look at the car. Because it was finished, it was removed from her. It was no longer something she was helping paint. It was now a rich man's car—a car that, if it were a person, would not even notice her. When the baby finished eating, she took it back into the bedroom. She looked around the room and admitted that she had let her chores slip. Too many naps, too much attention given to a car that did not belong to anyone she knew, had resulted in a messy house and a husband who did not have enough respect to keep his agreement with her.

As she was washing the bathroom sink, she noticed that the mirror had a dull luster to it. Her reflection seemed fuzzy. The glass, when she touched it, was not smooth but textured—almost like nylon stockings; it had a sticky feeling too.

When she tried to wipe the glass with a rag, she found she could not get the rag to slide. It kept sticking and stalling. The mirror's stubbornness sapped her strength. Still in her moist pajamas, she went into the bedroom, turned on the fan, and stretched out on the bed, trying to think about the mountains.

After her nap, which lasted nearly an hour, she woke up to find her pajamas dry and stale-smelling—except where she had been lying on her back. Her hearing had shaped itself around the noise of the fan. If she turned it off, she knew she would still be able to hear it. To ensure that she would not take another nap, she made up the bed, took off her pajamas, and got into the shower to start her day officially. As she stood under the water, she tilted her head to smell of her shoulder. She wanted to remind herself of how her skin smelled. There was no odor. She had expected a faint muskiness that she knew to be her own smell, but she could not detect it. Quickly, she picked up the soap and began to lather.

By the time she got into her clothes and brushed her wet hair straight back over her head, she knew it was time to prepare the chicken for the chicken and dumplings. Her sympathy went out to the carcass boiling on her stove.

Olin came home early, while she was boning the boiled chicken. With him was Mr. Edge. When Olin introduced him, Mr. Edge did not smile but continued to stare at Lela. This made her feel very awkward. For a few seconds, all she was aware of was the crispness of his suit and the embarrassing odor of the half-boned chicken gaping limply behind her. Mr. Edge made her feel sweaty. She swallowed, and she could feel her throat moving clumsily, like an arm muscle caught in a spasm. Still, Mr.

Edge stared at her as Olin went to the basement to bring the car around. As soon as Olin was gone, Mr. Edge walked to the refrigerator and ran his finger down its side. He moved to the table and did the same thing. With distracted fluidity, he moved all around the kitchen, feeling cabinet doors, plates, and glasses in the rack. When he finished feeling of the sink, he was standing beside Lela. He was scowling, looking directly into her eyes, studying her whole face at the same time—as if they were standing far apart.

"How can you let him do this to you?" he asked, his voice making Lela think of sweet pickles.

She cocked her head and tightened the corners of her mouth in question.

"This whole house smells like a paint factory," he continued. "And I've driven cars with less finish on them than you've got on your kitchen table or on your dishes." He leaned toward her until his nose was almost touching her cheek. "God, it's even on you."

Below the kitchen window, Olin was blowing the Bentley's horn. Lela turned to see the car, but the sun bounced from it so brilliantly that she had to shut her eyes, and in that darkness was a glow lined with a spangled red. Mr. Edge let the screen door slam as he left, waking the baby.

Lela picked up the baby and carried it out to the porch. In the sunlight, she could see that both she and it were unnaturally pink. All along, she'd just felt too bad to look closely enough. Olin had coated them with his glaze. More than anything, Lela wanted to be back in the mountains. She wanted to peel off Olin's pink paint and be cool again. But Olin couldn't see anything except how rich he could get painting vintage cars. He was walking back toward the porch, counting the money Mr. Edge had given him.

Anger buzzed in Lela's brain, stung her eyes with bright points of light. Shifting the baby to her left arm, Lela stepped to the porch railing where the mag wheel rested. The metal was already hot, resisting Lela's fingertips. Olin paused beneath her, recounting his money, always afraid of making a mistake in such matters.

Private Drive

Marna had to stop arguing with her father, Bart, because the road they had turned onto was steep and deeply rutted. Attached to a ragged stump at the entrance to the road, a sign—through rust, dents, and faded paint—feebly declared PRIVATE DRIVE.

Although she was driving her husband's truck with the big tires, she and her father bounced around in their seats as if the truck were trying to shake some sense into both of them. Marna knew her father was the one who needed the shaking. Red dust swirled up around them. The knee-deep gullies on both sides of the road were filled with cans and broken bottles. The only vegetation was briars, morning glory, and ragweed. Marna wondered how her father managed to find these isolated houses with their misshapen inhabitants who always had some odd machine or rusty tool her father felt compelled to buy.

This time, he had come to look at a camping trailer. He was so certain this was the trailer he was looking for that he had asked Marna to bring her husband's truck so they could pull his purchase home. Her father's car was at the garage being fitted with a trailer hitch. In Marna's eyes, the trailer represented her father's obstinate nature, his selfish determination to retire.

Everyone who knew him had tried to talk him out of retiring. The factory where he worked wanted him to continue designing the plywood fronts for their furniture. His buddies at the pancake house wanted him to keep working. Marna wanted him to keep working. He didn't need the money, but he did need the activity, the distraction. Marna's mother had died a little over a month ago, and now her father wanted to give up the job he'd been working for thirty-two years.

Marna had tried to explain to her father that he was changing his life too much too soon. She was convinced that his being out of work, alone in the house, couldn't be good for him. He needed his life to be as normal as possible until her mother's absence had lost some of its pain for him. As Marna saw her father's situation, he was hurt by his wife's death, and he wanted to hurt everybody back by doing something wasteful and foolish.

"I don't believe anybody could live at the end of a road as bumpy as this one." But as soon as Marna had let the sentence shake out of her mouth, she saw, in the field on the left side of the road, signs of human settlement: a rusty tractor, one rear wheel missing, the axle propped up on a fifty-gallon oil drum; a small mountain of wooden crates; three aluminum kitchen chairs with either a seat or a back missing; a small cement mixer with a bale of hay stuffed in the mixing barrel; four electric stoves with various parts missing; two refrigerators surrounded by plastic milk cartons; several car engines; bicycles . . . and at the top of the hill stood an old farmhouse, gray, the front porch tilted into luxuriant weeds although the front yard contained no less than eight lawn mowers. Most of the windows lacked glass, and out of them oozed sheets of plastic or sinks or various lengths of pipe or coils of rope or different parts of gardening tools.

Slightly to the right of the house but attached to it by a short walkway made out of uneven two-by-fours and roofed with six or seven different styles of shingles sat a house trailer, clearly the home of the packrat that Marna's father had come to see.

"That trailer wasn't here the last time I came for a deal." Bart was leaning toward the windshield.

"You mean somebody lived in that house?" To Marna, it

looked like a warehouse for useless odds and ends.

"Lonnie Dula is a trader from way back. He just lets his inventory get too close to nature sometimes."

As she pulled up in front of the house, Marna glimpsed a small travel trailer perched in a narrow ravine two or three hundred yards below them. At that distance, all she could make out was its aquamarine paint job and its door hanging open, slanting from a broken hinge or two.

"You know that travel trailer is going to be a piece of junk." Marna turned off the ignition with irritation. Since she had been a child, she and her mother had always had this one problem with Bart. He enjoyed shopping at flea markets and yard sales. Newness had no appeal to him. Perhaps this was why Marna worried so much about her father's determination to retire.

"I can fix it up." Bart searched for the door handle. He could never remember that the lever was inside the elbow rest.

Marna leaned across her father's lap and opened the door for him. "I bet the inside of that trailer down there is filthy."

"I can clean it. Working on something makes it more mine." Her father climbed out of the truck.

"You could buy a new one and work on it." Marna didn't want to get out of the truck. She and her mother had never gotten used to the men with whom Bart did business. To varying degrees, they always struck Marna as nasty. Her mother had worked for years in a bakery, decorating cakes. When she'd come home from work, she'd spend an hour scraping the powdered sugar off the bottoms of her shoes. Marna had inherited her mother's compulsion for tidiness. Marna had never understood how a man could be married to someone like her mother for forty-one years without learning how to be neat. She suspected that her father's stubbornness made him immune to her mother's tidy influence.

"The work has to be needed or I'd just be play-acting." Bart walked up to the house trailer and knocked on the door.

The man who emerged from the trailer was exactly what Marna expected. He was about the same age as her father. He wore a greasy T-shirt under his soiled overalls. His hair was much too long for a man nearing sixty-five and too oily for a man of any age. Marna didn't have to get out of the truck to know that Lonnie Dula smelled of stale sweat and chewing tobacco. All these men did.

On the occasions when such men visited Bart at his own home, Marna's mother wouldn't allow them in the house. If Bart wanted to deal, he had to take his company downstairs. When Marna was young, she worried about her father going into the small basement with these strange men. Now, as Bart and Lonnie Dula stood in front of Lonnie's trailer, Marna realized that she still worried about her father. He always got cheated on these deals. His problem was that he was an honest man who wasn't out to cheat anyone. Whether he traded CB radios or boats, Bart always got rooked. He needed to be watched. He needed to stay with people who appreciated him. He needed to stay in his factory.

Lonnie Dula leaned against his house trailer, occasionally turning his head to spit. Bart stood in front of Lonnie, talking intently. As he talked, he bent slightly forward at the waist. He moved his hands as if he were sketching out his plans for the trailer. That was her father—forever intent with his plans.

Usually, he was so intense that he didn't see what was going on in the eyes of the people around him. Maybe the factory had made him that way, but as far as Marna could tell, the factory was really all he had left. She didn't want him trying to retire, especially if he planned to travel around the country in a trailer bought from the likes of Lonnie Dula.

Instead of waiting for her father to call her over to meet Lonnie Dula, Marna slid out of the truck, determined to let Lonnie know that her father had someone keeping an eye on him. She was relieved to see that all the dogs on the property were mongrels Lonnie had probably collected from other junk dealers. Consequently, they had no definite urges to protect their territory. In fact, only one or two of the animals even took the trouble to raise their heads high enough to study who this second stranger was.

"I was thinking about using it myself," Lonnie was saying as Marna walked up beside her father. She was about five inches taller than either man, and she knew this would make Lonnie take her father more seriously.

Marna looked around the yard before speaking to Lonnie. "What would you use to pull it?"

Lonnie flashed her a brown smile and pulled himself up as straight as he could. "Oh, I'll come by something when the need arrives."

"Then I guess we can get back home." Marna grabbed her father's elbow, hoping that Lonnie really meant that he wanted to keep the trailer.

"Well, don't hurry." Lonnie took a step forward, holding back his need to spit. "Bart knows I can be persuaded to change my mind. And he is closer to retiring than I am."

Marna followed the two men down the slope to the trailer. The closer they got, the more certain she became that her father was about to be cheated again. The travel trailer had an unhealthy tilt to it. At first, she thought maybe one of the tires was flat, but she saw that they seemed to be the sturdiest part of the whole structure.

The trailer was roughly circular in shape. It reminded Marna of a pumpkin. To walk from one end of the trailer to the opposite end took her ten fairly short steps. When the two men climbed inside, the whole thing swayed as if it were resting on a trampoline. Marna stayed outside. From what she heard of Lonnie apologizing for the dirt, she didn't have to see the inside. If it was enough to make Lonnie Dula apologize, she didn't want to go in.

Money must have changed hands while Lonnie and Bart were inside because, when they tumbled out of the trailer, Lonnie said to Marna, "If you'll back your truck down here, I'll help you hitch it up."

Even before they started down the steepest and roughest part of Lonnie Dula's driveway, Marna knew she was going to have problems pulling her father's trailer. She could see it shimmying and wiggling in the rearview mirror. At first, she thought she could ignore the spaces that were appearing between the joints of the trailer's walls. She could feel sharp vibrations through the steering wheel. When she hit the most rutted part of the road, she glanced at her father. He was turned around in his seat, watching the trailer's behavior through the back window. He chewed on both lips and drummed his fingers on the dashboard. Marna tried to ease over the bumps and dips, but the trailer continued to heave and shudder as if it were being battered by hurricanes. Halfway down the road, the cracks between the joints had clearly widened, causing the roof to slide to one side. When Marna tapped the brakes, the change in speed pulled the trailer toward the back of the truck. Fearing damage to her husband's favorite vehicle, Marna slipped her toe back to the gas and watched as the trailer swayed backward, like an old man on a roller coaster, then toppled into a heap behind the warped chassis from which it had worked loose.

"See, that's what happens when you stick something off in a hole and don't keep it active." Marna stopped the truck in the middle of the road.

Her father turned to her from contemplating the ruins of the trailer. "That's what happens when you keep your dreams parked for too long." He climbed out of the truck, fumbling only for a second with the door handle.

For two or three minutes, Marna watched her father pick up the smaller pieces of the trailer. Then she climbed out of the truck, walked to where he was working, and began helping him. "We're going to haul this mess back up to Lonnie Dula. And after we get your money back, I'm going to make you go look at new travel trailers. You can put a used refrigerator in it if you want something to work on."

"You've made your point." Her father patted her shoulder.

"So have you." Marna was glad that the driveway had a place wide enough for them to turn around.

The Last of the Octopus

The fan at the foot of the bed blew upon Fay, who lay entirely naked except for eight slender ribbons tied to the four largest toes on each foot. She had never done anything like this before in her life.

She did not think Cletus would approve. Last night had changed nothing for him. This morning at six o'clock, he had gotten out of bed and quietly used the bathroom; then, when he was half dressed—in his socks and pants—he had sat down in the chair in the corner of the room as if waiting for the inspiration to put on his shirt and shoes.

Even when they were not on vacation, Cletus had to go through his morning pause, always in socks and pants. After two years of marriage, Fay still could not decide if something was physically wrong with her husband. If she asked him what he was thinking about as he sat there at the edge of his shoes, he simply stared at her and smiled.

"I was just about to think of something," he would answer.

Finally Fay had decided, after reading a story to the children at the day-care center about how the human eye worked, that Cletus's brain was like the pupil of an eye. In the morning, he had to pause like he did so his brain could adjust to the light of being awake once again.

This morning, after he finished dressing, Cletus had picked up his Zebco Deep Water Rod and rattled out the door with his tackle box. Watching him leave through her half-closed eyes, Fay felt a familiar disappointment—like being all ready to skate and finding out you could lace your boots up only halfway.

That was how she had met Cletus. She had brought the wrong laces to the roller rink with her, and she was sitting at the edge where everyone else was skating. Then this very polite boy had approached her. He had noticed the trouble she was having, and he happened to have an extra pair of laces. Four years ago.

The ribbons licked at her calves, lightly rubbing in wavy strokes. The fan purred and flowed over her like a stream of cat fur. She kept her eyes shut and tried to concentrate on last night. She had never seen Cletus so lively. Mrs. Garnes thought they were killing each other, but when she understood what had happened, she had even come in—at three o'clock in the morning—and changed the bedclothes for them.

She had been afraid when she woke up, but even at the time she knew she was more afraid of what she did not know was happening than of what actually *was* happening. The memory made her tremble inside the way she used to when she skated over coarse cement. She remembered skating with Cletus that first night, thinking how calm and graceful he was. Everything he did was calm and graceful, soothing as an almost empty rink when the lights are dimmed for the Couples Only. Cletus had been a welcome change from the lunatics she usually met there.

Part of his charm, as Fay's mother pointed out, was that Cletus was an older man—twenty-two—when he first asked Fay out. She had been seventeen. Then he was learning to be a payroll clerk at Chalfant Furniture Company. Nothing ever irritated him, so he made a good clerk. Fay did not really have to work, but she got along well with children, and all the mothers knew that she was every child's favorite in the day care.

And she would certainly have a good story to tell her children when she got back to work. She could get some photographs of octopuses and make a regular show-and-tell out of it.

She could worry about finding the photographs later; they still had another week. Cletus always came to Myrtle Beach for his vacation. He liked to fish from the piers that stuck out into the ocean every mile or so like interrupted daydreams.

From talking to the women she met at work, Fay found out that Cletus was the ideal husband. He was always calm, enjoyed helping around the house, and stayed at home when he was not at work or fishing. And he never failed to invite Fay along with him on his fishing trips. The first three weeks of their marriage, she went every time he asked her. If Cletus had used a boat when he fished, Fay thought that it might not be so dull. Instead, he preferred to squat on various banks along the Catawba—from seven in the morning to seven or eight at night.

Since their honeymoon two years ago, Fay had come to Myrtle Beach with Cletus four times. At first, she thought pier fishing might have some redeeming romantic qualities. After all, it was the Atlantic Ocean you were standing over, but the heat was suffocating, and the bathrooms were always far away.

Cletus would come in at the end of the day with the peeling skin fluffing his forehead and cheeks and nose like down, but Fay did appreciate the way he tanned. Well, she liked the color of it. He insisted on wearing a shirt out in public—and public was anyplace outside the bathroom—so he had always been two-toned since Fay had first seen him naked.

Even with the fan right there at the foot of the bed, blowing on medium, Fay could tell that the day was turning hot. By now, it must be ten o'clock, and she had not exactly decided what to do. She did not want to play bingo with last night still fresh in her mind.

She was not sure if she should try to explain her feelings to her husband. She knew she should not be excited. Before it had happened, she would have sworn that such an experience would have made her sick. She had never been able to handle the bass and catfish that Cletus brought back from his trips to the river. And when he brought that thing in last night, she knew it would give her nightmares.

The empty fish tank in the room they were renting from Mrs. Garnes was what had given Cletus the idea.

She bent her knees slightly to let the ribbons creep up to her knees, then just a little higher. She could feel herself moving inside, the way she did when she skated backward or took a curve just a bit too fast and she could feel the wooden wheels barely beginning to slide.

Mrs. Garnes knocked at the door. Fay could tell Mrs. Garnes's knock because it had a muffled sound, as if she left her knuckles on the door until she was ready to hit it again.

"Fay. I'm going to the Palace now. Do you want to come?"

"No, Mrs. Garnes. I'm not even up yet."

"I could wait, but I know from experience that they give the best cards out before eleven o'clock. After that, you might as well bring one from home."

"Then you go ahead. Last night still has me upset."

"For good reason. That husband of yours is crazy. The quiet ones are always crazy. Do you want me to save you a place?"

"No. I think I'll go see my crazy husband."

"He needs watching. Make sure he doesn't bring any more pets home this evening."

"He won't."

"Okay. I'm going now. . . . I can still get those sheets from the honeymoon cottage."

Fay smiled at her surprise when three days ago, while the caller was checking a woman's card who had just called bingo for the third time in a row, Mrs. Garnes had asked Fay if she had ever slept on satin sheets.

Mrs. Garnes had taken an immediate liking to Fay because, when they were checking into the Garnes Barn Inn, Fay mentioned to her that she could not sunbathe because she was allergic to direct sunlight. Mrs. Garnes suffered from the same sensitivity. While Cletus fished, Fay and Mrs. Garnes played bingo.

Fay liked her, but the woman was just exactly like her knock—she stayed on a subject when you expected her to touch it, then move to something else. But she would hit a topic with her mind and leave it there. Like everyone else, Mrs. Garnes had first thought that Cletus was perfect. Serene, she called him, putting a kernel of corn on N-38. Before thinking, Fay had replied, "Yes, but serene seems to leave a lot out."

Mrs. Garnes raised her eyes from her card long enough to let Fay realize that she understood. Since then, the subject of those satin sheets had come up twice or three times a day. Fay was worried that Mrs. Garnes was going to try to put them on their bed last night, but she had brought in the standard white ones. The mattress had to be turned over because the stain had soaked all the way through the sheets.

Now the ribbons were moving on her thighs. She tried to imagine them as currents, and herself as moving through the ocean. Then, slowly, she tried to make the currents feel heavier, the way they felt last night, heavy as kisses—Cletus had never kissed her legs, although he often used to say how pretty they were. That was when they still skated, and she would deliberately let her toe drag so Cletus's leg would accidentally come between hers.

When he did not take advantage of her playfulness, Fay knew he had to be the gentleman that her mother had always advised her to watch for. But he had never kissed her legs.

She admitted to herself that he had frightened her for the first time since she had known him when he brought that octopus home. It had been the only thing he caught all day. A man on the pier told him that if you bought an octopus from a store, it would cost ten or fifteen dollars. If it was fresh, better bait could not be found. So he had brought the thing home, filled the aquarium with salt water, and dropped it into the tank.

When they came back from the movie, the octopus was still lying in the tangled nest of its legs, looking pretty dead. Fay knew she was supposed to find it ugly—and she did—but while Cletus was taking his bath before going to bed, she had pulled a chair up to the side of the aquarium to stare at the bristly sack she took to be its head. The way the sack leaned back from the eyes reminded her of that statue of the Egyptian queen. Of course, this thing looked nothing like a woman.

A few hours later, she felt something on her legs. At first, she thought Cletus must have gotten one of his legs across hers, but she came fully awake when she realized that whatever it was was making a slow progress up from her calves. That was when she screamed, but she knew even as she heard Cletus fumbling to turn on the light that she was not trying to get the weight off of her; she was not surprised when she saw the octopus sprawled across her knees; its very human eyes—deep green—looked as startled as she felt.

Cletus knocked it off her knees. He had to hit it twice to get it off the bed, and between the first time it was hit and the second time it had spit out a thick blob of ink. Then Cletus pulled a hammer from his tackle box. By the time he got it untangled from a package of Eagle Claw Hooks, the octopus was already changing its color to match the paisley greens and blues of the carpet. Fay did not watch Cletus kill the octopus. She had run into the bathroom to wash the ink off her legs. But Cletus seemed to have a hard time killing it with his hammer. She refused to come out of the bathroom until Cletus had taken the body outside. Mrs. Garnes gave him a plastic bag to put it in; then she helped him fit it into a drink cooler filled with ice. More than ever, Cletus was determined to use it for bait.

Fay got out of bed and took the ribbons off her toes. She was going to see Cletus at the pier. He always let her know which pier he was going to be fishing from because, Fay imagined, he was too polite to be mysterious.

The doctor had advised her when she had come back from her honeymoon, blistered and feverish, that if she planned to spend any amount of time in summer sunlight she should protect herself: wear long sleeves, keep her face shaded, and try to wear white as much as possible. Fay always brought with her about four of what she referred to as her prescription outfits. Today, she put on white slacks and a white jersey top with long sleeves and a very deep neckline.

She also put on a necklace that Cletus had bought for her the first time they had come to Myrtle Beach. It was a large macramé loop with an anchor pendant, which hung over the shadow between her breasts like a smile. Before putting on her shoes, she sat down and tried to decide what she was going to say to Cletus. Something had to change between them after last night. But trying to put it into words was, Fay realized, like skating backward and trying to figure out how close you were to where you had to start curving around to make the corner. She knew the corner was close, but she could not see far enough over her shoulder to know exactly how close.

She put on her sunglasses and her floppy-brimmed hat—the size of a small parasol—her prescription hat. Actually, Fay enjoyed wearing her protective clothes. All you saw on the streets in Myrtle Beach were bathing suits, peeling skin, wet hair, and men in plaid Bermuda shorts. People looked at Fay when she walked.

The Rainbow Pier was almost deserted. Only Cletus and five other men were fishing from it. Even though Fay did not come to the piers very often, she knew that more people should have been there. Cletus stood almost at the very end. He had put on a long-sleeved shirt when he left that morning because the wind made the piers cool early in the day. Now the sleeves were rolled up, and Cletus was staring down into the water.

"Where is everybody?" Fay asked.

"Awww, a windigo is down there."

"Is that some kind of fish?"

"Yeah," Cletus answered, reeling in his line. "It's the kind of fish nobody can catch." He looked at Fay. "Are you okay?"

"I think so. I've felt kind of funny all morning."

"You're not sick, are you?"

"Oh, no. Not sick. Something else."

"What do you mean?"

"Your bait's gone," Fay said, not ready to explain how she felt.

"That's what a windigo does. This morning, there must have been fifty people out here fishing. Then everybody started losing his bait. Sometimes, when the windigo gets your bait, it feels like you've hooked an ocean liner. But after a couple of minutes—nothing. It's just gone. And you reel in, and fifty cents' worth of bait is gone too."

"Why don't you change piers?"

"I don't know, Fay. I kind of like fishing for something that I'm not sure is really there." Cletus inspected his exposed hooks. "I'm going to buy some more bait. The octopus is gone. You want to come with me?"

Fay was listening to the ocean. It sounded different underneath the pier. And although the planks of the pier were very rough, with wide gaps through which the ocean below was clearly visible, Fay could not help but think of the skating rink. Standing above the swaying water with the wind tight against her, she leaned against the rail and smelled the deep water, which came to her like the smell of the old varnish of the rink's floor.

"I think I'll stay here and guard your rod," she replied.

"I won't be gone but a couple of minutes. Do you want something to drink?"

"Yes. Bring me a Pepsi."

"They've got Seven-Up."

"I want something dark today."

Fay watched Cletus walk down the length of the pier. He was still graceful. He was still thoughtful. She glanced in the ice chest. In one corner, beneath the ice she was picking through, looking for a piece clean enough to suck on, she found part of the octopus's arm—a section with a suction cup. She rubbed the smooth cup, which was now a deep blue.

Several times, she had watched Cletus bait the triple hooks on his Zebco Deep Water Rod. The trick was to weave the bait onto the hooks so the current would not pull it off. Fay inserted the dull tinted hooks into the bristly top of the meat and worked them through the smooth underside where the suction cup was. She had never noticed that the sinker was shaped like a small pyramid.

She was not exactly sure about casting. She knew that she was supposed to bring the rod over her shoulder and keep her thumb on the line inside the reel. But the large reel felt too heavy to be moved quickly enough. She thought that if she let the lead weight dangle down about a foot, she could just kind of sling it out into the water. Her cast was awkward.

The backlash sent out a loop from the reel that lassooed the crescent of the anchor on her necklace. Fay did not notice until the spinning reel tightened the loop and jerked her neck. The weight and the heavily baited hooks hung momentarily in the air as if disoriented between the sea and the sky; then they fell clumsily into the water.

Fay stooped over the rod, trying to loosen the tangle of the reel so she could free herself. At first, the line that disappeared into the water allowed itself to be pulled in. When Fay saw she was only making the tangle harder to get to, she started letting the line play itself out.

Just as she had found the place where she was attached to the reel, the line tightened suddenly with a sound that jerked Fay's breath. She found herself pulled against the rail, the rod suspended in the air between her necklace and the black fishing line.

She heard Cletus yelling somewhere from the other end of the pier, but then her hat fell off. She could not grab for it because she was bracing herself with both hands against the rail, and still she was pulled forward. She was leaning over the rail, looking into the water stirring like crumpled satin in the shadow of the pier. She could hear the ocean very distinctly, like thousands of skates rolling over a darkly varnished floor.

Then two things happened: Cletus grabbed her from behind, taking hold of her waist with one arm and grasping the cork handle of the rod with his other hand; and the line abruptly slackened.

Cletus was trembling. Both of them had to sit down to get Fay untangled from the reel. Fay suggested that she could take the necklace off, but Cletus acted as if he had not heard her. For several minutes, he did not look at her face.

"Fay, I'm sorry," he kept saying.

"Cletus," Fay said, taking hold of the small roll of fat just above his hip, "I liked it."

Cletus brushed the hair from her eyes that the wind was blowing there. Then he took off his shirt and, draping the arms around her neck and over her breasts, he shaped a cowl to keep her from getting sunburned.

Visitation

tewart Prevette paused to tap a lidful of Tube Rose snuff into his lower lip. His helper, Zerle, needed the few seconds' pause to straighten the stack of drawer siding that Stewart was running through the belt sander. As the musky sweetness of the tobacco burned into the membranes of his lip and gum, Stewart twisted the lid back onto the squat snuff container and dropped it in his shirt pocket. Now he was ready to concentrate, and if he was going to reach the men at the prison camp tonight, he surely needed to concentrate.

"Crank it back up," Zerle shouted from her end of the sander. "I'm ready."

Stewart allowed the straight line of his mouth to bow up, his version of a smile. Even under the most extreme circumstances, Stewart's face had trouble moving. His was a wide, flat face, apparently made up exclusively of thick slow muscles that served mainly to work his jaw. His skin was too coarse to admit wrinkles, but just underneath it, a bland network of vague ruts and grooves connected his mouth to his cheeks, his cheeks to his eyes.

Stewart picked up a drawer side from the hand truck beside

him, briefly inspecting the edge by rubbing the palm of his hand against the narrow length of wood. This was the second time through for these sides, and Stewart wanted to make sure he was sanding the side that needed it. Zerle was a good helper, but she sometimes stacked the drawer sides with the sanded edge pointed away from him. That meant he had to flip the drawer side over before he pushed it through the sander instead of simply sliding it right from the truck to the sander. Sometimes Zerle didn't pay attention to the job, but today Stewart was the one unable to pay attention. He tried to focus on the snuff in his mouth, a dissolving bull's-eye of flavor.

At seven o'clock tonight, he and Preacher Boyd Keller were supposed to visit Pleasant Hill Prison Camp and hold a prayer meeting. Although Stewart had his own small church—the building was formerly a small grocery store—and he was used to standing up in front of as many as thirty-five people, he felt nervous about standing in front of these prisoners. After all, he wasn't really a full-fledged preacher. He had spent a June month at Fruitland Bible College five years ago when he first got the call to preach, but he'd never been ordained.

Soon after Stewart got back from Fruitland, he found he didn't want to stay with the Baptists. He realized they had a whitewashed view of what sin was all about. Despite what they publicized about their beliefs, they still acted as if a person could avoid being stained by sin—just the way some people actually believed they could dodge raindrops if the storm wasn't too heavy. The Baptists might say that sin came from the inside, but they still allowed members of the congregation to decide when they needed to recommit themselves to God.

The secret of sin that Stewart had discovered was it really did come from inside a man or a woman. A person didn't have any choice about sin. To sin was to be a human being. You did it without having to think about it. Sin grew out of a person, like hair or sweat or fingernails. A person shouldn't go for months or years without grooming his soul. This was the simple truth on which Stewart had built his own church: the Gospel Wind Church of Daily Salvation. He required his congregation to be saved on a day-to-day basis. He wanted them to feel the power of God the way they would feel the wind of a hurricane. They needed to be pushed back and forth by the power of their guilt. They needed to feel themselves being knocked to the edge of immortality every single day. And that was what the Gospel Wind would do for them.

"If you're going to doze off, Stewart, why don't you go run the drum sander and let me operate this belt sander." Zerle, after getting her stack of drawer sidings evened up on the hand truck beside her, had eased down to Stewart's end of the machine. She grabbed his elbow and pretended to push him toward the drum sander. Unlike the belt sander, which was a delicate structure with a narrow bed, just slightly wider than an ironing board, the drum sander with its squat cast-iron legs reminded Stewart of a hippopotamus sliced off through its chest. Rubber treads carried the wood under three humps—the drums, which were wrapped in sandpaper of descending coarseness. It was seldom used once the new lathe sanders were installed.

He pulled his arm out of Zerle's grip. For a moment, he stared into her green eyes. He tried to decide if she had ever been slim, but the flesh of her cheeks and neck wouldn't be penetrated. Gluttony was a sin she needed to talk about, but Stewart had never been comfortable bringing up the Gospel Wind in the factory. The factory was its own place. Stewart had often wondered if something about the factory's bricks and steel beams didn't somehow insulate it from the influence of God. For all the years he'd worked there, Stewart had never been called upon to testify in the sanding room. Lord knew that some of the men in the machine room and the cabinet room needed witnessing to, but the Gospel Wind didn't blow in Chalfant Furniture Factory.

When Stewart was discouraged and felt out of touch with the Gospel Wind, all he could think about was how gray the factory was. The cement floor was a powdery gray that sucked at his soul through his feet. The steel bed of his sander, constantly polished by the passage of drawer sidings across it, punched at Stewart's soul with its glare from the fluorescent lights. Those lights, along with the gray steel of the roof, rained on Stewart's soul no matter what the weather on the outside was like. Today, the weather outside was as gray as the weather on the inside. "Heard any more about the snow that's supposed to be coming?"

Zerle wiped her hands on the army fatigues she wore to work when she didn't wear her faded jeans. "A few flakes slapped my windshield when I drove to work."

As he began running the drawer sidings through the sander, Stewart stirred up the snuff lump in his lip and asked himself why he had to deal with bad weather and slick roads on the same evening he had to deal with prison camp inmates. He didn't like to drive in the snow. He had on his snow tires, but his Galaxy just didn't have much traction. What really made him nervous, though, was having to dodge other people. If they'd let him be careful, he could get along fine, but somebody always wanted to stop at the wrong place or pass at the wrong time or couldn't get slowed down soon enough.

If he could catch Preacher Keller at home, maybe the two of them could go in Preacher Keller's station wagon. It was always loaded up with bronzed baby shoes. Preacher Keller worked for a company that immortalized children's shoes and bolted them to plaques and pedestals. He was always talking about how he had to buy new shocks for the back end of his station wagon at least three times a year. Already feeling a wave of relief warming his insides, Stewart checked his watch. In twenty minutes, he would knock off for lunch. He could call Preacher Keller from the canteen. It was always better to have two people in the car if you had to drive in snow.

Stewart knew that Preacher Keller would take care of most of the prayer meeting. All Stewart really had to do was stand up and give his testimony and maybe comment on a few lines from scripture. But Preacher Keller had warned him that you could never predict how the congregation in a prison camp was going to react. He'd had believers, doubters, blasphemers, shouters, criers, and debaters. Sometimes, their indifference was worse than their hostility. They'd just sit there like bottomless pits of contempt. That bottomless pit in a captive audience was what scared Stewart.

When the whistle blew for lunch, Zerle galloped off to the canteen. Before Stewart was halfway across the sanding room, feeling in his pocket for the right change, Mayhew Blevins—from the machine room—yelled at Stewart that somebody was at the gate, wanting to talk to him: Boyd Keller. Stewart wasn't used to being visited at work. The factory separated itself from the outside world by more than the cyclone fence strung up around it. Stewart had visited churches that could cut off the rest of the world the way the factory could, but they were very old. Stewart knew that size had nothing to do with the feeling of quietness that sometimes enclosed him when he got to the factory very early in the morning before the machines and exhaust fans were switched on. He didn't trust that stillness. Man had to keep moving if he hoped to cleanse his soul. He had to raise the sail of his conscience and catch it full of the Gospel Wind.

As soon as Stewart stepped out into the gray light filtering through the heavy clouds overhead, he knew he had made a mistake in not bringing his coat with him. According to the direction in which Mayhew had pointed, Preacher Keller was parked at the upper lot. Stewart wrapped his arms around his chest and began running. This air was coming straight from the mountains. So were the clouds.

Preacher Keller wasn't the kind of man who would cancel a prayer meeting, especially with those prisoners. Stewart admired Preacher Keller. The white-haired minister was raising his attendance rate every Sunday. Since he and his family had begun appearing on television every Saturday afternoon, he couldn't keep up with the way his congregation was growing. Preacher Keller's church, the Evangelical Tabernacle, had already bought a piece of land down by the river and was getting ready to put up a larger building. Stewart hoped Preacher Keller might give the Gospel Wind congregation a good price on the building he was leaving behind.

The station wagon was parked in the middle of the first row of cars. Stewart saw the fumes raging from Preacher Keller's exhaust pipe. He thought of Elijah being carried to heaven in a whirlwind. Wedged behind his steering wheel, Preacher Keller wore an expression of detoured expectation. For a moment, Stewart was distracted by a frigid tap on his cheek. Fat flakes of snow began to blow across the parking lot, disappearing into the gravel. Just outside the factory fence, the Gospel Wind was shaking the world. Stewart dashed for the station wagon. He knew the wind was purifying, but he had only thirty minutes for lunch.

"Sorry to take you away from lunch." Preacher Keller extended a chubby hand toward Stewart's chest. "I'm having to skip lunch altogether."

The odor of the station wagon was a blend of Stewart's cologne, musky and close, and the more resonant smell of bronze, an odor that made Stewart think of iodine and dizzy spells. Stewart shook Preacher Keller's hand. "It's more satisfying to talk to a minister of God's word than to cultivate a case of heartburn in the canteen."

"How ready are you for tonight's visitation?" Preacher Keller rested his arm along the back of the seat.

Glancing at the back seat, Stewart saw at least two hundred pairs of bronzed baby shoes, and in the compartment behind the back seat were several dozen pairs of shoes waiting to be bronzed. Once or twice, Stewart found himself thinking that bronzed baby shoes might be considered a form of idolatry, but he couldn't bring himself to question Preacher Keller.

"I'm trusting the Lord." Stewart wondered where Preacher Keller got his confidence.

"I knew you'd be prepared." Preacher Keller leaned toward Stewart. "See, I got a call an hour ago from Reverend Williamson in Spartanburg. He's pastor of the Evangelical Tabernacle down there. This week they're having a revival, but Reverend Williamson has come down with the flu, and he's asked me to run the revival for him."

Briefly, Stewart felt a guilty ripple of relief fan across his stomach. But something in Preacher Keller's voice forced Stewart to tighten his abdomen. Preacher Keller wasn't talking as if anything was being called off. His voice was a springy board about to hurl Stewart into the thin air of performing for those prisoners by himself. "You want me to go by myself, don't you?"

Preacher Keller rubbed his hand through his white hair without ruffling a single wave. "Those convicts need to hear the Word."

"I've never done anything like this before."

"Convicts are just like any other congregation." Preacher Keller patted the air between himself and Stewart. "Only they don't have as far to go home as other people who get out of church. Just talk to them the way you'd talk to people in your own church."

"Looks like I might get snowed out anyway." Stewart studied the flakes outside the car. They were falling lightly but more and more steadily. All along, Preacher Keller had been telling him how unpredictable the prison congregation was. Now, all of a sudden, he was telling him they were just like other people.

"Don't let the weather prevent you from spreading the Word. Nobody needs it more than them in prison."

By the time the three-thirty whistle freed the factory workers for the day, two inches of snow had accumulated and Stewart could tell that the storm was just getting cranked up. The flakes weren't really coming from the belly of the clouds yet. The first snow was always like a man coughing, starting with his throat, then down into his lungs, and finally deep down from his stomach. While his Galaxy was warming up, Stewart considered putting on his chains before leaving the parking lot. The snow would make the job messy but Stewart thought about all those other workers fishtailing their way home, people sliding off the side of the road, everybody in a hurry to get home before the roads got worse.

Very deliberately, Stewart climbed out of the chugging warmth of his car, opened his trunk, and pulled out his chains. He never wore gloves, so in straightening out his chains his hands soon turned russet with the rust. As he stretched the chains behind his rear wheels, Stewart detected a new, unsettling sound mixed with the drone of the cars around him. Pebbling the quiet rustle of the snow was the dry click of sleet. Stewart stood up and studied the highway. The traffic had kept the road fairly clear. That meant if the sleet kept falling the road would be icy in a few hours.

When Stewart slid back into his car, the metal roof amplified the clicking of the sleet. He rubbed his hands on his pants before grasping the steering wheel. The feel of rust always reminded him of regret. The sleet fell so thickly it was now visible through the falling snow. There would be ice.

All through supper, Stewart's wife, Rachel, tried to talk him out of going to the prison camp. Her flu was better, but her voice still came out in patches, sometimes smooth and soft—her normal way of speaking—others filmy and shredded, which made Stewart think of those small Mexican dogs that always had runny eyes and tremors. To every objection Rachel raised, Stewart simply reminded her that a preacher's job was to witness and open the heart's windows so the Gospel Wind could circulate. Even as he assured her of his determination, he could hear the sleet tinkling against the kitchen window. That had been a steady sound since he'd come home. Every few minutes, a gust of wind would throw the sleet against the window so hard it sounded as if a handful of sand had struck the glass.

"There's going to be drifts with the wind blowing like that." Rachel scraped three pads of butter into her plate and poured Karo syrup over them. She blended the butter and syrup with her fork, then began wiping the mixture up with a biscuit. Ordinarily, Stewart would have had his own plate of syrup and butter, but his stomach was too knotted. It was six o'clock already. He had to get ready.

After Stewart put on his suit, he tried to pick a tie that the prisoners would respect. He thought about calling the superintendent of the prison. Rachel had suggested that the prison might not be expecting him on a snowy night. School had already been called off for tomorrow. To Rachel's way of thinking, if the kids didn't have to go to school, the preachers didn't have to go witnessing. But Stewart didn't believe in phone calls. Arrangements weren't solid unless they were made face to face. And what was arranged face to face couldn't be called off over the phone. Phones tempted people to be morally irresponsible.

Half a mile from his house, Stewart came to the railroad tracks. This was a dangerous intersection during the day because the train came from the north around a sharp curve. During the night, the train coming from the south blocked the intersection for an hour while it picked up boxcars that had been loaded with furniture. Stewart had been so worried about the snow he had forgotten to worry about the train. There it was, five diesel engines smoking against the storm, throbbing with electricity and power. Stewart eased to a stop. The train was running late. Usually, by this time, the engines would be way down past the intersection, past where the tracks curved out of sight.

For reasons that Stewart never understood, the train, in collecting its boxcars, had to pull up, then back, over and over. He knew they were attaching the boxcars in some specific way, but this forward and backward way of collecting them seemed like a waste of motion. At least when the engines were this close to the intersection, their backing up put them far enough from the crossing to let Stewart get by. As he crossed, the lead engine's headlight seared the corner of his eye and the engineer let loose a blast on his diesel's horn. Hunching farther over the wheel, Stewart nudged his accelerator and slipped across the tracks, forcing himself to look straight ahead. Since he had been a boy, Stewart had always believed that looking directly into the headlight of a freight train was courting disaster. Behind him, his superstition was affirmed as he heard the rumble of those five engines pulling forward.

A gust of wind reminded Stewart that he had men waiting on him. No doubt, most of them would be there because they had nothing better to do. Maybe one would be there because he needed to hear about the Gospel Wind. Stewart thought he could begin with Nahum: "The Lord is slow to anger, and great in power, and will not at all acquit the wicked: the Lord hath his way in the whirlwind and in the storm, and the clouds are the dust of his feet." On the other hand, talking about anger to a group of imprisoned men might not sit right with them. Maybe what they needed was an explanation of God's power like in Zechariah. "But I scattered them with a whirlwind among all the nations whom they knew not. . . . And the Lord shall be seen over them, and his arrow shall go forth as the lightning: and the Lord God shall blow the trumpet, and shall go with whirlwinds of the south."

Coming to a steep hill, Stewart saw another car struggling

in his direction. It didn't have chains and was fishtailing every two or three feet. Stewart shifted to a lower gear and thought of Hosea: "Though he be fruitful among his brethren, an east wind shall come, the wind of the Lord shall come up from the wilderness, and his spring shall become dry, and his fountain shall be dried up: he shall spoil the treasure of all pleasant vessels." Stewart felt the tendons in his neck rising to the surface. The driver in the other car was too busy keeping control of his rear end to dim his lights. Stewart squinted and eased to the side of the road, thinking of Jeremiah: "When he uttereth his voice, there is a multitude of waters in the heavens, and he causeth the vapours to ascend from the ends of the earth: he maketh lightnings with rain, and bringeth forth the wind out of his treasures."

The other car slid toward Stewart. He edged closer to where he feared the ditch dropped off and felt himself thumping onto the shoulder. The other driver overreacted and jerked his wheel. As the car's headlights swept toward him, what drifted into Stewart's mind was John: "The wind bloweth where it listeth, and thou hearest the sound thereof, but canst not tell whence it cometh, and whither it goeth: so is every one that is born of the Spirit." Scripture always helped Stewart through difficult times, but he also felt a sense of relief as he anticipated being sideswiped into the ditch. He'd have to walk back home and call a tow truck. He wouldn't be able to get to the prison camp after all. Immediately, he knew he was off on the wrong thought, but he also knew that he couldn't stop the rear end of that car coming toward him. At that moment, the other car slid in the opposite direction.

Shifting his attention between negotiating the slick road and piecing together what he could say to the prisoners after he'd read to them about the Gospel Wind, Stewart arrived at the cyclone fences that guarded both sides of the road and assured him he had reached his destination. Coming down in damp clumps, the snow had sealed up all the spaces in the fence wires, forming a thin solid wall of white through which Stewart could just barely see the several low wooden buildings where the prisoners lived. Through the membrane of falling snow, the fluorescent light fixtures in the dormitories gave off a blue glow and made the night feel even colder.

Stewart parked close to the visitors' gate located in one corner of the fence. Instead of being reinforced by a short tower like the other three corners of the prison yard, this corner was edged by a small white house that served as the superintendent's office and guard post. On the other side of the road, behind the other fence, sounds of diesel engines and heavy chains rose up to insult the snow, but the noise lacked the conviction it usually carried on clear days. To Stewart, the machines and the wobbling lights that he could barely see through the snow-clogged fence seemed as helpless as the people he had seen sliding off the road. In the few seconds Stewart took to reach the prison office, two road scrapers and a dump truck full of sand had lumbered out of the lot across the road and disappeared into the dark.

The snow softened all the hard edges of the small house, blurred the bars across the windows, and blanked out the plaque over the door that announced NORTH CAROLINA DEPARTMENT OF CORRECTIONS. Vaguely, a smell of disinfectant wavered from behind one of the long white buildings. Stewart, who could put up with the scent of wood being sawed and sanded, of machines running too hot, and furniture being varnished, found the smell of disinfectant making him think of skim milk and indigestion.

The outside door of the cottage opened into a vestibule. Wooden benches flanked both sides of the small room, and the floor, covered with green outdoor carpet, was spotted with darkened chewing gum and spilled soft drinks. At the other end of the vestibule, a metal door, resembling a heavy-duty refrigerator, supported a small television camera. Stewart stood in front of the door, adjusted himself, glanced up at the camera, and pushed the button next to the RING FOR ADMITTANCE sign.

A flow of static dropped from the speaker under the camera, and Stewart heard a snort, as if someone had started to speak, then caught himself.

"What's your business?" The question came after a long pause rubbed raw by the static.

Stewart raised his Bible toward the camera. "I've come to conduct the prayer meeting. Preacher Wheeler had to go out of town."

The pause this time was without static, but Stewart heard mechanisms in the metal door beginning to twist and disengage. When the door pulled open, Stewart felt air being sucked out of the vestibule.

"We didn't expect Preacher Wheeler or you tonight." The man was dressed in a guard's uniform with a large red-flannel shirt over his blue uniform shirt. He wasn't quite as tall as Stewart, but he was nearly three times as thick. Stewart had seen barrel chests before, but this man was so broad he could have used an extra set of elbows for his arms to hang comfortably from his relatively narrow shoulders.

"I guess I am coming like a thief in the night." Stewart wondered if he should have said that.

However, the guard had the grim tact of a man who ignores what people have to say. "Well, them boys who usually come to the meeting are all out scraping the road or spreading salt. This is one of the few times they're allowed to drive around all night." The guard leaned past Stewart to look out the front door of the house. "Looks like they'll be at it on past sunrise."

"It's important work." Stewart turned sideways to look outside. "I'm grateful for what they do."

"We always give them a choice when it's this kind of weather and they have a meeting to go to. All of them wanted to go scrape. When they work for the DOT, they get extra time off."

"Anybody else available for a prayer meeting?"

The guard stretched his mouth the way most people shrug their shoulders. "It don't work that way. The super would have to approve anybody who might want to come. The boys he approved are all out on the road. The ones who are over in the bunkhouses ain't been approved."

"And the superintendent—"

"Went home before dark. He's getting cataracts." The guard rocked the metal door with his shoulder. "Still drives his Cadillac, though."

Not five minutes had passed while Stewart had talked to the guard, but the snow was still coming down so hard that it had already begun covering the tracks left by the road scraper.

Where the road was exposed, Stewart could see the glaze of ice. Traffic had already thinned; although many cars were stranded in ditches and along the shoulder of the road, their owners had apparently given up on getting them out until morning.

Despite how treacherous the road was, Stewart felt much more relaxed as he crept toward home. He had done his duty. He had overcome his own reluctance to spread God's Word. It didn't matter if he didn't preach. He had been obedient. He had proven himself. Caught up in his relief, Stewart let the car churn too far to the right. The snow made the road look wider than it really was. The right rear wheel slid off the pavement, found a firmer grip in the snow-covered red dirt, and pulled the rear of the car sideways. The front tires lost their traction and slid to the right. The skid felt like one that would correct itself, so Stewart let up off the gas and thought slowing down would be enough to straighten his car. Instead, it continued to glide—as if sliding sideways was less tedious than struggling forward. Then he thumped to a halt, his headlights staring at a crazy angle up into the storm.

For a few seconds, Stewart sat in his car. Both tires on the passenger side were in the ditch. Stewart could tell from the tilt of the car that he couldn't get it out by himself. And he didn't want to stand beside the road, looking helpless, trying to flag down somebody to give him a ride home. If he walked to his house following the road, he had maybe a three- or four-mile hike. On the other hand, just above where he was ditched the railroad tracks curved toward where he lived. If he could follow them, he'd cut off at least two and a half miles from his walk.

After getting his door open, Stewart had to push it with his foot, then pull himself out of the seat by holding to the doorpost. He kept a grip on his car, feeling the ice beneath the snow teasing his shoe soles. His car was stuck but not damaged, as far as Stewart could tell. Stewart patted the hood and through the blowing snow tried to locate the railroad track on the hill above him. He could barely see it. The wind plastered snow in his ear, but Stewart was too preoccupied with finding secure footholds. In order to maintain his balance as he climbed, he had to pull his hands out of his pockets. In the darkness he could feel them, the skin tightening against the wind. During the stronger gusts, Stewart couldn't breathe.

At the top of the hill and dizzy from the darkness and the wind, Stewart stumbled onto one rail of the tracks and stumbled again when his foot slid off the crosstie and into a crack between the wood and the gravel. What might have twisted his ankle on a sunny day merely shook Stewart to alertness in the snow. The tracks were hidden, but at least the snow had not been packed down to ice. That meant the factory freight train hadn't come down yet. Stewart started to check his watch but then stared into the darkness ahead of him and began walking.

Through the wind and muffling snow, Stewart was able to make out the scalding chuff of the diesels as they crawled up and back on the side rails between the factories. Punctuating the puffs was the crash of cars colliding and coupling. Less than a quarter of a mile away, Stewart could see a faded patch in the darkness—the train's headlight softened and scattered by the snow. The light would have been brighter except Stewart at this point wasn't looking at the train head on. In addition to the snow, the sharp curve in the tracks was also keeping the light from shining directly in his face.

As Stewart walked, he tried to calculate how close on the other side of the curve the train waited. Considering how long it had taken him to get to and from the prison camp, the train should probably be almost done with its coupling. It should already be done, Stewart repeated to himself whenever the wind pushed against him as if it too were being puffed from some huge eternal diesel engine. But the snow had slowed down the train crew as it had slowed down everything else.

If the train was between the curve and the intersection where Stewart could get on the road, he was going to be in trouble, because, between the curve and the intersection, the tracks passed through a small bog that was twenty feet below either side of the track. The hill that dropped down to the bog was overgrown with briars and thornbushes: nowhere to get off the tracks along that stretch. Then Stewart remembered that on the far side of the bog, just before the hill dropped off so steeply, the man who owned that lot had cut a narrow path through the scraggly pine trees. That path led up to the man's back yard, and right across the road was Stewart's house. If he could get to that path, he could cut off a couple hundred yards of his walk and maybe not have to face that train, if the train hadn't already cut him off.

When Stewart turned the curve, he was holding his breath. The train's headlight struck him in the face, as if he'd walked into a thick pane of cold glass. For a moment, Stewart thought he needed to jump headlong off the tracks. He was still ten or fifteen feet from the bog and the briars, but he squinted, shielding his eyes with both his numb hands. The train was past the intersection, but Stewart was able to see a break in the darkness of the pines that indicated the path. The train was less than thirty feet from cutting Stewart off from that way home, out of the storm. If he turned back, he'd have to walk all the way back to his car. Or he could get off the tracks here and wait for the train to finish its hooking up. That could be two minutes from now or it could be another hour. Even another ten minutes seemed like a long time to Stewart, his feet lost in the darkness and his hands like two squares of unsanded lumber.

The engine chuffed and pulled up ten feet. When it pulled back a few feet, Stewart lurched forward, hoping the crossties were spaced evenly. He took long strides, hoping to make up in length what he couldn't accomplish in speed. The cold squeezed his legs, the wind giving it fingers. The bog dropped on either side of him. Again, the train chuffed and moved back with a crash that stiffened the skin along the sides of Stewart's spine. The ground shivered as the train chuffed forward, its headlight dazzling Stewart's eyes and throat as if he had swallowed too much light and snow. All his muscles squeezed closer to his vital organs. He moved faster, feeling the crossties thud through his legs, wood against wood.

Stewart felt solid, as if all the hollow places had been squeezed out of his body. The train wasn't moving back anymore. Stewart was close enough to the train to hear its metal wheels pressing against the rails, grinding, close enough to hear the engine breathing through the phlegm of its oil and diesel fuel—the kind of sound he might hear from thunderclouds if he could get close enough to them. The breath of thunder was not moving backward an inch now, but not seeming to move forward either, more like it was pulling the tracks into itself. The path creeping closer and closer to the grinding and growling engine of light and wind, Stewart stooped in his rush forward, feeling pulled toward the huge face of steel and thunder, the tracks shaking, full of a pounding, a pulse that Stewart knew belonged to the train and other immense forces.

He reached the path a fraction of a second before the train got there. All the way through the small stand of pines, Stewart stretched out his legs as if he were still on the tracks. He didn't pause to consider how close he had cut it. He was too preoccupied with feeling his skin assume its normal tension. His stomach opened back up, as did his lungs and his throat. He couldn't tell his wife about what he had done. This couldn't be the subject for a sermon. He had always been uneasy trying to preach about Revelation. But the train wasn't the beast. Not the darkness either. Slowing down, Stewart realized that the wind had dropped. The snow fell—a benediction at its own speed, not part of heaven or hell.

The Crooked Couple

E ven in January, the furniture factory has warm currents flowing up and down its concrete floors, weaving around the saws, eddying beside the drills, puffing by the tenon machines. The moist warmth comes from the three large boilers in the back of the factory and dominates the whole sprawling plant, smelling faintly sour like green wood, pressing against the skin with the pressure of nausea. The machines themselves give off another kind of warmth, dry and electric. The men who run these machines, by the end of the day, find themselves drawn to this heat because it seems to counteract the sultry air blown out from the boilers. Most of the workers carry the heat of their machines home with them the way motorcycle riders take the feel of the wind inside with them, nerves tingling as if they were on the verge of oxidation.

As Virgil Rummelhart walked past the band saws, the triple drum sander, and the jigsaws toward his boring machine, he tightened his belt and tried to forget about the humid air. Morning was the worst part of the day as far as Virgil was concerned. Although he was missing three fingers on his right hand and two fingers on his left hand, he had no trouble getting the brass buckle loose enough to pull his worn leather belt tighter. Those fingers had been gone for forty-six years. He'd learned how to get along with a thumb and a fourth finger on his right hand and a thumb, an index finger, and a ring finger on his left hand.

Virgil had a clear view of his belt buckle. His spine was so curved that his eyes were on the same level as his navel. He had to compensate for this curve by adding a very sharp curve to his neck. This posture gave him the appearance of a man whose body has been dropped on top of him, forcing him to peer from underneath the debris. His face was narrow, as if life's more difficult moments had not been quite wide enough for Virgil to slip through without altering his chin and cheeks. Through a flaw in his bathroom mirror and his method of shaving, he never managed to level all of his whiskers—or perhaps they grew too close to the bone in some places.

The last time he stood straight, he was five feet five inches tall, but because of his stoop, he had to wear extra large work shirts so the tail wouldn't pull out in the back. He wore his cuffs rolled back twice and pinned them in place with two of his wife's large black bobby pins. For twenty years, his only hat had been a series of dark blue baseball caps that he started wearing when his son was a first-string pitcher on the high school baseball team. He and his son had gotten into many arguments since those warm afternoons when Virgil used to sneak off from work early to catch the games on that dusty high school diamond, but he'd always liked his dark blue caps. Caps didn't turn on you the way sons, wives, and shoes could turn on you. Virgil looked at his Dickey work shoes and spit.

A week earlier, Virgil had come to work, and his feet had hurt him all morning long. They hurt when he walked. Then they started hurting when he just stood in front of his boring machine. By lunch, all he could think about was how his feet were hurting. Mick Blybone was the one who pointed out—with his big mouth turned on full blast—that Virgil was wearing his shoes on the wrong feet. While the whole canteen yelped and howled at Virgil, he tried to explain that it was his wife's fault. He didn't like to deal with her in the morning so he put his clothes on without turning on the lights. Somehow, after thirty years of dressing in the dark, he had gotten his shoes crossed up.

About two days after the laughter had died down, Virgil returned from the toilet to find, drawn in chalk in front of his machine, the outline of two feet, with the toes pointing in the wrong direction. His new assistant, Kelton Mims, smiled in that stupid way he did, like somebody else had put it on his face for him, and shrugged his shoulders when Virgil demanded to know who had done the drawing. He knew Kelton had seen the person who did it, but being a new man in the plant, he was afraid to mess up the mechanics of a joke. Still, Virgil couldn't forgive the boy for choosing to go along with the plant jokers. An assistant should be loyal to the man who was teaching him the machine. But Kelton was a college boy—just out. Virgil knew he couldn't depend on college boys. His own son proved that. Everybody who went to college turned into a sneak, which was as bad as turning into a joker.

When Virgil told his wife about the joke, she had laughed too. For years, she never missed a chance to let him know he deserved everything that happened to him. He could always count on her to reduce his suffering to his constantly swelling collection of faults. His son had the same habit. So, every day when he would go to the toilet or to the canteen, he'd come back to find the two crossed feet drawn on the floor where he stood. Except for the basic instructions that he barked at Kelton, he'd stopped talking to everyone in the factory.

He planned to fix them all. His wife had given him the idea. She had been telling him, as he tried to eat supper, about all the warts that had started popping up on her skin. Her sister, who'd had the same problem a few months earlier, had gone to a woman on the north edge of town. This woman bought warts.

"I'd always heard that Gladys Luume was a witch," his wife said. "But I didn't know she could buy warts."

"Maybe it's something she just lately picked up," Virgil replied.

"But it works," his wife insisted. "Maxine went to see her. Gladys rubbed each wart with an owl's thigh bone and paid Maxine two cents apiece for them." His wife paused to salt her stiff mashed potatoes. "A week later, every wart was gone."

Virgil had to think about that for a minute. He had seen Maxine the day before. They never spoke, but she had looked different. "Didn't she have three or four big warts right between her eyebrows?"

"She sure did," his wife answered. "But not no more. Her skin's as clear as it was when she was a baby—except for the moles."

"Gladys Luume don't buy moles?" Virgil asked.

"She told Maxine she didn't have the right bone for moles."

Of all the many things that were wrong with his wife, Virgil had to admit she was not a liar. Long ago, he noticed that her inability to lie was closely linked with her stingy way of looking at the world.

His wife sucked her fork a few moments; her eyes seemed pulled out of focus by the force of the suction. "But there must be something wrong with the whole business."

Virgil looked at his wife. Her face had outgrown the hair bobbed above the ears and banged halfway down her forehead. Before she had time to get it combed down in all the right directions, it looked as if it grew out of a central hole in the top of her scalp. Virgil hadn't minded, long ago, when she suggested they'd both sleep better if they got separate beds. He'd always suspected that their son had given her the idea. That night, in his bed on the far side of the room, Virgil kept thinking about Gladys Luume.

Virgil oiled his machine and—before he could catch himself—Kelton's machine. The boy had a degree in geography or geology, Virgil wasn't sure which, but he didn't know anything about oiling boring machines even though Virgil had explained it to him a dozen times. Virgil enjoyed climbing up on the bed of the machine and squirting the oil into the small holes that lubricated the drills. His machine had four vertical drills housed in five-foot steel sheaths. The sheaths were movable. With this machine, Virgil could bore screw holes for almost any piece of furniture, from two-inch-square brace blocks to a seven-foot bed rail. Once the drills were locked into place, he could turn the speed up on the bed until it was fairly bouncing. If Kelton didn't interrupt him, Virgil could bore forty-eight holes a minute, loading the machine with his right hand and emptying it with his left.

For the last week, though, his pace had been off because the jokers were on his mind. Today would be different because he had his plan. After work, Virgil was going to visit Gladys Luume. A woman who could buy warts might be able to do something to people he didn't like—even if it was nothing more than giving them warts. He'd feel satisfied enough if he could see three or four large warts pop out on Mick Blybone's nose. With his wife going to her Lottie Moon Circle meeting at the church, she wouldn't be home to notice his coming in late.

Virgil admitted to himself that he wasn't exactly certain how he felt about his plan. No doubt, Gladys Luume was a shady character, but all night long, Virgil had thought about what he had to do. He was sixty-three years old. He had been at the factory for forty-three years. It was too bad he couldn't just walk over to Mick, kick his ass, and jerk out his tongue. That would make him feel better, but Virgil knew if he tried the direct approach the joke would just get bigger.

If his helper, Kelton, had any pride, he would have gone after Mick, but that boy simply lacked backbone. Virgil looked up from adjusting his drills to see Kelton walk up. Since the boy had started working in the factory, he'd worn the same outfit: a black sweatshirt, blue jeans, and motorcycle boots. Kelton rode a motorcycle. Virgil had seen him several times, plowing along the highway, the wind slapping the boy's thick dark hair against his skull as if trying to beat some important truth into his head.

Kelton wasn't much taller than Virgil, but he was built solid. At first, Virgil was glad the boy was quiet. But like a lot of college boys who came to work in the factory, Kelton slipped into the habit of singing and talking to himself after the newness of his job wore off. Virgil saw that his reflexes were pretty good—good enough to where he didn't have to watch the boy all the time. He had seen him wince that first day. All of Virgil's assistants were shocked by his missing fingers. He always told them the story about how he lost them—not to the boring machine but to a buzz saw back when he was seventeen, then again when he was nineteen, working at the sawmill. Still, Virgil got uneasy when Kelton got wrapped up in singing to himself. Frequently, the boy would have his eyes shut and his head would be rocking back and forth. A couple of times, Virgil pointed out to Kelton that those drills were deaf and blind so the man running the machine had to watch what he was doing.

More than Virgil resented Kelton's lack of backbone, he wanted to know what he was getting into if he went to see Gladys Luume. Sounding as casual as he could while he set up Kelton's drills for the table braces he'd be drilling, Virgil asked, "What d'you think about women who buy warts?"

Kelton, always slow to answer, leaned one elbow on the bed of the boring machine. "I never thought about it," he replied, still not looking as if he were thinking about it.

"Well, do you think it's wrong?" Virgil studied the boy's triangular face.

"I suppose somebody has to do it." Kelton's black eyebrows flattened out in straight lines above his brown eyes. "People buy mushrooms, and they're as bad as warts."

By the time Virgil punched out at four-thirty, the footprints had been chalked in front of his machine five times: two less than the day before. Virgil still wanted the joker's hide, but he'd settle for warts. Maybe she could put a dozen or so on Mick's tool. If she did that, though, Virgil realized he wouldn't get to see them. No, it'd be best to put them all over his face. On his tongue. Stuff his nose with warts until he suffocated on them.

Gladys Luume lived beside the Saucy Seas Fish Camp. When Virgil slid his way out of his finned green Chrysler, he could smell fried fish blowing from a vent in the side of the fish camp. His stomach grumbled. He hadn't expected Gladys Luume to live in a sparkling white cottage with aquamarine shutters and trim. The small front yard was filled with cherry trees. Despite the bare limbs, Virgil's mouth watered. He could eat cherries all day long.

When he got to the front porch, the smell of fish disappeared, dissolved by the odor of two cedar trees growing on each side of the porch. Virgil had expected a sign in the front yard or hanging down from the roof. Every palm reader and faith healer he'd ever seen had some kind of advertisement stuck out in her yard. The woman who answered his knock was not what he expected either.

This woman, with her neat, gray hair, her smooth skin, and her round cheeks, could just as easily be selling Tupperware or encyclopedias. She was short, even standing in front of Virgil's stooped figure. Virgil wouldn't have considered asking her if she bought warts except for the odd way she was dressed. She was wearing some kind of muslin robe. To Virgil, it looked African, with its broad strokes of gold, red, and black. Although they hadn't spoken, the woman was smiling through the storm door at him. He touched the bill of his baseball cap and cleared his throat.

"Are you Miz Luume?"

"Yes," the woman replied. The word blended with the smell of the cedars.

"My sister-in-law came to you a while back." Virgil pressed his elbows against his ribs. "She had warts."

"Do you have warts?" Gladys Luume opened the door for Virgil.

Three steps closer to her, Virgil noticed that her gray hair had a purple hue to it, like a cloud at sunset. He also noticed that her left shoulder was lower than her right shoulder. "I've got another kind of problem. I'm not sure if it's the kind of thing you can clear up with a bone and two cents."

"Let's sit down and talk about it." Gladys Luume led him down a small hallway. She limped slightly.

Her living room made Virgil think of spring, full of yellow and pink. The couch, the chairs, the coffee table seemed smaller than life; their legs and arms were curved in happy directions. Gladys Luume sat on the couch and held out her hand, as if she were holding a tray, toward a chair. Virgil sat down. From where he was sitting, he could see two pink suitcases beside the couch.

"Going on a trip?"

Gladys Luume leaned over so she could see what Virgil was looking at. "No. Those are my display cases. I'm getting ready to be a Brenda Bryte distributor."

"Brenda Bryte?"

"Brenda Bryte Cosmetics." Gladys Luume stroked one of the cases. "They're made for the more mature woman."

"Have you stopped buying warts?" Virgil began to doubt he had any hope for satisfaction.

"I do that as a public service," Gladys Luume answered. "Besides, I've also gotten to know lots of women with skin problems." As she spoke, she tilted her head to the right and studied Virgil's narrow face. "If you've not come to get rid of warts, what is your problem?"

Virgil explained to her his torment at the factory. Somehow, he found himself explaining how his marriage had led up to his putting the shoes on the wrong feet. He explained how his son had grown up so smart and independent he no longer listened when Virgil tried to give him advice.

"It's like I'm shrinking," Virgil concluded. "And everybody is glad of it."

Gladys Luume had listened to him without saying a word. Her light green eyes hadn't moved from him as he spoke. Virgil had felt her attention through them. Three times, she had tilted her head one way, then the other, clearly taking some kind of measurement that only she knew how to take. The only other movement she had made as he talked was to trace small circles on the cushion of the couch. Virgil was convinced that her mind was working in those small circles, working on his problem. What kept him talking for so long was the certainty he had that she was going to help him. For a few moments after he finished talking, they sat silently. Evening came into the small room like a load of coal dumped through the window. Gladys Luume produced a small handkerchief from somewhere and wove it through the fingers of her right hand as she stared at Virgil. Her breathing quickened.

"It's been ages since I've performed the kind of services you're talking about." She shook her head crookedly. "It takes so much—"

"Well, I've got money," Virgil interrupted. "I ain't rich, but I want to get out from under these jokers bad enough to pay whatever it takes."

"I'm not talking about money." Gladys Luume leaned toward Virgil. "It's one thing to take warts away. All you need is a lot of sympathy. That's always been my specialty." Gladys Luume crumpled her handkerchief. "But sending out warts takes something else."

"I'd do anything you asked me to," Virgil replied.

"I was just never any good at that other sort of stuff. It always went against the grain—"

"I know how that feels." Virgil's voice sagged, uncovering a discolored corner of his disappointment.

Gladys Luume got up and turned on a small lamp across from where Virgil was sitting. She limped to the window and looked out. Virgil knew he should go home, but he felt weighed down. He realized that every muscle in his body was tight, wrapped around every word and gesture of Gladys Luume. At the same time, he felt as if something were wrapped around him, tightening slowly. The sensation made him hate Mick Blybone all the more.

Still, Gladys Luume stared out the window. Her hands gathered folds in her robe, then smoothed them out. "I can do it. Some of that feeling is there. You've got enough of it, maybe, for both of us." She turned to face Virgil. "But there's always the danger of a backfire."

"You mean I might get the warts?"

"Or something worse." Gladys Luume smiled for the first time since Virgil had come through the door.

"What's it going to cost?"

"I can't tell you right now. It depends on what it costs me. But the one good thing about this business is that it never takes more than you can afford."

Virgil got home very late that night because he had to listen to Gladys Luume's detailed instructions. He had to spread a gray powder over the places where his enemies stood as they worked. She warned him to be careful about being seen. The powder was never to be placed in direct sunlight or near a water fountain. Her instructions also covered how to meditate. For at least an hour each day, Virgil had to concentrate his attention on Mick Blybone and the humiliation he had made Virgil feel that day. "Pour it all out," Gladys Luume said. "From your heart through your head, see those warts growing from Blybone's face."

His wife was waiting for him when he got home. She was finishing off what was left of the fried chicken. The only light in the room came from the television. Her face, in the blue skittering light, resembled a balloon filled with detergent. Her eyebrows were so dark they cast her eye sockets into a perpetual shadow. Her chewing was vindictive, her teeth clopping together, her lips pressed grimly into a struggling cord across her face.

After watching her eat half of a chicken leg, Virgil went to the kitchen and fixed himself a bowl of Grape-Nuts. It was easier to talk to her if he didn't have to look at her. "Looks like I missed a good supper."

"Looks like you had something else to do. Or did you forget the way home?"

Virgil felt calm. He was out of reach of his wife. In fact, he felt safe enough to tell her the truth. "I've been talking to Gladys Luume." He settled down in front of the television.

Virgil's wife started laughing. She had to put the chicken breast she'd just taken a bite from in her lap and cup both hands over it to keep from jostling it onto the floor.

"I'm getting her to help me fix the jokers at the shop." Virgil ignored his wife's snorts and wheezes of amusement.

"That's foolishness," his wife gasped as she wiped tears away with the back of her greasy hand.

"You didn't think it was foolishness when she bought Maxine's warts."

"Warts is one thing." His wife scooted up in her chair. "Casting a spell on a whole factory is something else. Them kind of women was burned a long time ago up above New York somewhere." His wife pulled herself out of her chair, laughing once more, and swayed to the phone. "I've got to tell Maxine what her warts have started." She took three deep breaths to calm herself. The laughter shot up from her throat and bounced off the roof of her mouth. She swallowed hard so she could talk.

She was still talking when Virgil went to bed. She'd called their son and recited the same story that she'd given her sister. Virgil wondered, as he took off his pants and carefully arranged his shoes, if he could include his wife in the wart curse. Then he remembered: he'd have to see her every day. Besides, she already had warts.

A week passed and nothing happened. Every morning, Virgil got to work early and spread the powder around where Mick and his cronies worked. Every evening, he shut himself in the bedroom and chanted his hate for the people drawing the chalk footprints. Still, they kept appearing whenever he left his machine. Virgil even pretended to be over his mad spell so he could get close enough to Mick to see if he had the beginnings of any facial warts. He didn't even have a new freckle that Virgil could see. On Thursday, the sickening thought struck Virgil that perhaps Gladys Luume was playing some kind of joke on him.

Friday evening, after depositing his check at the drive-in window of the First Bank of Boehm, Virgil stopped by the white house with the aquamarine trim. Next door, the fish camp was churning out the odor of fried fish. Virgil noticed that the smell seemed to have a tougher texture to it, like maybe the fish they were frying was shark. When he got on the porch, he noticed that bagworms were dangling from the cedar trees on either side of him. White smudges appeared on his knuckles when he knocked on the door.

Gladys Luume greeted him with a smile that showed irregular teeth. They leaned toward the right and were crowded together. Her eyes were bloodshot, and her hair was pressed severely to the left side of her head—as if she'd been sleeping on it. She held her left hand in her right hand, both pressed to her stomach.

"I know nothing has happened yet." Gladys Luume led Virgil into the living room. It was littered with jars and scraps of paper. On the coffee table was a small black pot filled with dried leaves and what looked like coffee grounds. "I'm working on it. I even missed the weekly meeting with my Brenda Bryte sponsor." Gladys Luume's voice had turned raspy.

"I've spread the powders and meditated." Virgil looked around the room. It still reminded him of spring, but it was now the kind of spring where rivers get swollen and septic tanks have to be pumped out. "Maybe you need some fresh powder."

"It's not the ingredients," Gladys Luume said heavily. "It's me. This just isn't my kind of show. Give me more time." She stirred the contents of the black pot with her finger. "Has it been hard on you this week?" She gave Virgil a direct gaze.

He sat down in the chair that was the least cluttered. The paper in it was light brown and thick, like the skin of an animal. He had to sit on the front edge of the chair. "The jokers are still working on me, but I've been able to get back up to forty-eight holes a minute because I've had hope."

Virgil explained his boring machine to her. He showed her his hands and told her about working at the sawmill when he was fifteen years old. Four years and five fingers convinced him to get away from saws. "A drill ain't nothing compared to a buzz saw." He told Gladys Luume how his wife had taken him seriously once, and she had become pregnant. Afterward, she treated him like something she wouldn't watch on television. Eventually, his son had picked up her attitude. Gladys Luume listened and listened. When Virgil got home, he'd missed supper again.

Another week passed. Kelton Mims finally learned how to oil his own machine. Virgil even let him set up the drills for the order of bedposts the boy wanted to drill. It took him an hour, but he finally got the measurements right. Now that his assistant was getting hold of the job, Virgil felt he could spend more time meditating. He thought it might help Gladys Luume if he meditated twice, once at the regular time in the evening and once while he was at work in close range of his victims.

Virgil had started eating lunch with Mick. Sometimes at this meal, Virgil could get within a foot and a half of Mick's face when he lit his cigarettes for him, but no wart appeared. The jokers went without blemish. Whenever Virgil felt discouraged, he thought about Gladys Luume stirring her black pot, skipping her weekly meetings with her Brenda Bryte sponsor, digging up all the warts she had bought through the years, trying to find the right words that would spray them over Mick and his friends. At home, he ignored the references his wife made to warts. He ignored the phone conversations when she'd look in his direction and laugh, fueled for another thirty minutes of describing his foolishness.

Instead of going to visit Gladys Luume on Friday evening, Virgil waited until Saturday morning. The Saucy Seas Fish Camp was cleaning its oven and grills—a black smoke was billowing through the vents. It smelled of dead whales and disasters at sea. Virgil was just barely able to see Gladys Luume's front yard. The whole door rattled when he knocked on it, and two or three flakes of aquamarine paint fell from the door frame. The sight of the shriveled cherry trees brought a bitter taste to the back of Virgil's tongue.

Gladys Luume had to lean against the door when she opened it for Virgil. Her hair was white and stringy and hung down into her eyes, which were the color of scorched cream with algae just starting to form in the center. Her gray, splotched skin reminded Virgil of snails. As he followed her to the living room, he noticed that her limp was worse, her shoulders more uneven.

She spoke in a voice that sounded like a drawer full of broken kitchen utensils. "Nothing works. You don't need to tell me." She coughed and looked around her left shoulder at Virgil. "The factory is too strong for me. We have to get ugly. We have to get some serious supplies."

Virgil felt suffocated in the small room. The curtains were closed. Only a candle burned, tilted over the black pot so its gray wax dropped into the dark contents. Virgil didn't want to sit down because he kept hearing the rustling of small animals all over the room.

Uncomfortable as he was, he stayed with Gladys Luume all day. He found himself asking her question after question. He discovered that he was as interested in listening to her as he was in having her listen to him. She'd had polio, had lived in an iron lung for years. She'd read hundreds of books, turning the pages with a pencil held between her teeth. Somewhere in her reading, she'd learned how to be sympathetic, how to buy warts, and how to collect herbs. From her reading, she'd learned how to breathe on her own again, then how to walk, then how to do income tax returns. And, most recently, how to apply makeup on more mature faces.

That night, when Virgil left her house, the air was clear, and he had all his hope back. Without a doubt, he and Gladys Luume were in business together. In her dark and rustling living room, he had felt a power—not quite ripe, but gathering, pulling itself up like a wave from the ocean. All he had to do was wait for it to arrive.

If he could get some token of power from the factory, Gladys Luume had told him, they could most certainly hurry up this thing that was brewing between them. When he'd asked her what the token would look like, she answered, "Just watch. You'll know. It'll pull you to it."

All day long on both Monday and Tuesday, Virgil looked for hints of the token until his eyes were watery. He knew that Gladys was still at her pot, believing in him, waiting for his discovery, sitting in the dark, wanting to help him find peace.

On Wednesday, Kelton told Virgil he was getting tired of boring holes in the bedposts. Virgil offered to let him switch machines so he could do the bed rails, but Kelton shook his head. Ordinarily, Virgil would have taken Kelton's restlessness as a sign that he needed to be watched, but instead he found himself unable to think about anything except Gladys Luume. Once or twice during the morning, Kelton's singing would catch Virgil's attention. The boy was also trying to incorporate a few dance steps into his vocals.

About four o'clock in the afternoon, Virgil felt a warm spray flit across his left cheek. He thought Mick had snuck up on him with a water gun, but when he turned to see who was squirting him, he saw Kelton clutching his right hand, staggering back against a load of bedposts. His face was white. His eyes looked as large as cue balls. He didn't seem to know where he was. Then Virgil saw the small red puddle at Kelton's feet. He'd cut his finger. Virgil rubbed his cheek. The spray he'd felt had been blood.

"It's gone," Kelton whispered when Virgil got beside him. "My finger is gone." He was gripping the injured finger so tightly that only a few drops of blood were oozing from the raw nub above the first joint.

"You're not so bad." Virgil led him through the factory, a throng gathering behind them.

The plant nurse assumed that the drill had chewed off the whole top inch and a half of Kelton's index finger. That was what Virgil thought too until he returned to the boring machines to clean them off. As he was sweeping the sawdust out from under Kelton's machine, he found the top inch of the boy's finger. He held it between his clawlike right thumb and fourth finger. A warmth flared inside him that had nothing to do with the boilers or the machines in the factory. He glanced around to make sure he wasn't being watched. Then he stuck the finger in an empty cigarette pack and rushed to Gladys Luume's house.

Driving to the north side of town, Virgil got caught in a sleet storm. In minutes, the road was glazed and slippery. He practically had to crawl up the porch steps. The house was gray, encased in ice. The cedar trees were drooping with ice. The cherry trees looked like nothing more than barren veins in their jagged sheaths of ice. The only odor that came to Virgil as he waited to be let in was the smell of the fish camp's overflowing Dumpster.

Virgil's hands were still trembling when he unwrapped the finger for Gladys Luume. The house was darker than it had been on Saturday. Above the heavy rustlings, the sleet could be heard as if it were made of lead. For a few moments, Virgil had the sensation that it *was* lead, piling up outside, shutting off the house from the rest of the world.

"This might be what we need." Gladys Luume held the finger cupped in her hands as if it were an injured butterfly.

The living room had a sooty fireplace in which a gloomy fire sputtered. The black pot was suspended above the flames. "All the omens are right." Gladys Luume stirred the pot. "Don't be disturbed by what happens when I throw the finger into the pot."

Virgil spread his legs and leaned against the wall. "Should we shut our eyes?" He watched Gladys Luume's hand trembling above the concoction.

"Yes. Do."

"You be careful, too."

She looked at the pot, then back at Virgil. He could almost see her bones through her skin, the fire glowing beside her like it was. He started to ask her if he could throw the finger in, but he knew what the answer would be, just as she knew he had almost asked her the question. He noticed that he could hardly breathe. The room was tightening around him, pushing him toward this stooped woman leaning toward the fire. With one small motion, her hand opened and the finger dropped into the steaming pot.

Virgil hadn't meant to look. He expected to be blinded and deafened. That didn't happen. The finger plunked into the foamy broth, floated to the surface, and bobbed on the agitated currents. The sleet slacked off. The clouds broke. Still Virgil and Gladys watched the finger putter around in the pot. Finally, the fire went out. The room grew cold. Gladys Luume wearily stood up.

"That's it." She leaned against the wall next to Virgil. "They've beat us, Virgil. Nothing is going to happen. We could boil every finger, hand, arm, and body of every person in that factory, and nothing would happen."

Virgil took Gladys Luume's hand. Her voice reminded him of the way she looked squatting in front of the fire. "I need to move around a little bit," he said. "Get the circulation going in my legs."

They took the pot out of the fireplace and rekindled the fire. Virgil helped Gladys Luume clean up her living room. They worked side by side, often touching shoulders and hips. They burned the heavy pieces of paper and the herbs. In the soft glow that came from the fire and in the spicy smell that filled the room, they became so enchanted with each other that they paid no attention to the warmth that went so deep it straightened their spines and shrank their shame.

Rather Than Seem

Nora Knowling, plant nurse, disposed of the bloody gauze she had used to control the bleeding of Kelton Mims's severed finger. For half a second, she thought about taking the stained mesh home with her but quickly dismissed the idea. The time for collecting mementos had come to an end. Seeing Kelton blanched and shaking made her realize that the phase of her silent adoration was over. After years of watching him, making friends with his relatives, and following his development, Nora knew she was now ready to approach him.

In a corner of the wastebasket was the hypodermic Nora had used to give Kelton morphine. As far as damaged flesh went, Nora had seen worse: Bullis Mullinax, who had the cutoff saw go through his hand up to his wrist, Walt Haigler, whose lathe threw out a spindle that lodged in his eye. But none of them had shaken her as much as when Kelton came through the door, hunched over his finger. He had entered the realm of accessibility.

Even before Nora got the bleeding stopped, Kelton had recognized her. By the time the ambulance arrived, he had summoned up her name. That was one of his charms; he never forgot anything. In the four years they went to high school together, they'd spoken only once. That was nearly ten years ago, but he could still recall her name. Nora had to sit down on the examination table to steady herself. Her chance had really come. She and Kelton Mims were finally sharing a common ground. He was clearly in need.

In high school, he had been an absolute to her. When everyone else was wearing bleeding madras shirts, Kelton wore his blue oxford cloth. When paisley shirts were the rage, Kelton still stuck to his blue oxford cloth. That long ago, Nora had been struck by his calm self-possession, his understated confidence, his serene intelligence. Even that far back, Nora knew his memory was photographic.

Throughout their senior year, Kelton had been on the high school quiz team. Every Friday afternoon, the team competed with other groups from rival schools on a local radio program called Tri-County Quiz. Nora never missed it. During one program, the Quizmaster asked, "What is the North Carolina state motto?" Kelton was the first to press his buzzer, and the Quizmaster said, "Kelton Mims from Boehm." Then there was a pause in which Kelton was supposed to give the answer. Instead, there was only silence. So the Quizmaster repeated, "Kelton Mims from Boehm." More silence. Approaching exasperation, the Quizmaster said, "Kelton, if you don't answer, I'll have to give the question to the other team." By this time, Nora's heart felt swollen and hard as a basketball.

Then she heard Kelton's calm voice ask, "Do you want it in Latin or in English?" The Quizmaster stammered, his authority pulverized, and Nora knew this was exactly what Kelton wanted. He was buying time while his infallible though not instantaneous memory burrowed back to the freshman Latin class she'd had with him. And he found it before he could be penalized for his delay. Over the air came Kelton's raspy baritone: "Esse Quam Videri."

Back then, Nora kept her passion to herself. Kelton seemed too magnificent. She told no one about her devotion because even in her secrecy she felt humiliated by it. When the time came to vote for senior superlatives, Nora had circled Kelton's name for Most Likely to Succeed until her pen went through the paper. With that compulsive circle, she confessed to herself that he was on his way to Chapel Hill and she was on her way to Boehm Community College. He was on his way to distinction; she was on her way to being an R.N.

However, college didn't agree with Kelton. One of his aunts, who was studying cosmetology at BCC, informed Nora that Kelton had come home one weekend riding a motorcycle. Then his hair got long. His beard grew. Later came the rumors of drugs and drunkenness. He dropped out of college several times to work in a Mexican restaurant called Tijuana Fats. All along, he was majoring in geography. During his troubled years—six of them while he worked on his B.A.—Nora saw him only once. He was riding his black motorcycle through town. Although his helmet had a black face cover, Nora knew it was Kelton because looking at him she felt she was pressing her body against a thick piece of glass and she could feel her heart beating up and down every inch of her skin while her lungs ached, full of stale air. She'd also learned from one of Kelton's cousins, who was in automotive mechanics, that Kelton's bike was a 750 BMW.

Nora locked up the first-aid room. Ordinarily, she would have walked through the shipping room and out the gate to where she was parked. But she had decided to dispose of the gauze and the hypodermic. She didn't want the clean-up man handling the evidence of Kelton's injury. To get to the boiler room, she had to go through the small room where Wanda Dey hand-painted the expensive furniture, through the canteen, and through the machine room where Kelton had lost part of his finger.

She knew it was morbid, but Nora found herself drifting over to the site of Kelton's accident. Virgil Rummelhart had done a good job of cleaning up—no evidence was left that blood had been spilled or sprayed around the machine. Since Kelton had started working in the factory, Nora had forced herself to avoid him. She couldn't help but think of him as being in exile. But apparently it was an exile that he had chosen and probably had been in the process of choosing for six years.

Nora studied the concrete floor, the corrugated steel roof, the cinder-block walls that yawned away from her, the huge steel machines full of blades, saws, and sandpaper—the whole plant there for the purpose of cutting, drilling, planing, smoothing—and she realized that, threatening as the place was, it was less dangerous than Kelton was to himself. She clearly saw that he was in the process of reducing himself, like a patient who deliberately stops eating or taking his medication because he is tired of living, tired of the complications he must endure to survive.

While adjusting to this thought, Nora noticed a leather jacket hanging from the side of a wooden box filled with drill bits. It was the same shade of brown as Kelton's eyes, and it had the husky texture of his voice. Nora stroked it. A logical progression was unfolding for her. First, Kelton had come to the factory where she worked. Second, he had come into her first-aid room. Now, she had a reason to visit him. The jacket had to be returned.

In the boiler room, Nora tossed the gauze and the hypodermic into the fire. Then she took off her coat and slipped Kelton's jacket on. It was almost the right size for her because Kelton was short. Instead of walking back through the factory, she went outside from the boiler room and walked around the building to where her car was parked. The lining of the jacket was warm and intimate, like the inside of a mouth; the leather, heavy and protective, enclosed her.

Before she could get out of the parking lot and headed for her house, her Pinto was filled with the smell of the jacket much the way her head had always been filled with Kelton. "He's like a gas," Nora said aloud, "a rare gas. And he must be contained, maybe even compressed."

At first, Nora was tempted to take the coat directly to Kelton's cabin on Lake Rhodhiss. The thought of finally confronting him with his jacket—and her desire—puffed up her pulse until she felt her elbows throbbing in rhythm to her heart. Her training in trauma prevention guided her through the temptation. Tonight was too soon. She needed to sleep on her resolution to get it flexible enough. And Kelton would be drugged anyway.

Her house was just outside of town, about fifty feet beyond where the sidewalk stopped. It was one of the five poured adobe homes built in Boehm. The other four were unoccupied, cracked, consumed by weeds. But Nora worked constantly to keep her walls cemented together, her stucco in place, her window and door arches properly plumbed. She didn't argue with friends when they told her that the adobe looked like concrete. What mattered most to her was that it was the most Spanish-looking small house in town.

Short of having a dirt floor, Nora tried to make the interior look as Latin American as possible. She was striving for a particular Latin-American look: the one that prevailed in the movies of the forties. Peeking from behind large ferns, potted palms, and dwarf banana trees were large framed pictures of Carmen Miranda as well as posters from the thirteen movies she appeared in, from *Down Argentine Way* to *Scared Stiff.* Underneath a poster of *That Night in Rio* where Carmen Miranda poses with Alice Faye and Don Ameche, Nora had attached an embroidered statement she'd read in an old review of another Carmen Miranda movie: "How Miss Miranda gets around—and all the time standing in one spot!"

Her interest in the Brazilian Bombshell dated back to that one conversation she had with Kelton Mims. The spring of their freshman year, Kelton had told her that she looked like Carmen Miranda. Then, the only response Nora had was a giggle which seemed to confuse Kelton. For weeks, Nora was tortured with regret, but over the years she discovered that regret works as a preservative of the other emotions.

That was part of how she explained, to herself, her faithfulness to a man she'd never gone out with, never touched, never really talked to—only giggled at. She'd taken up her study of Carmen Miranda because it appeared to Nora as her most direct avenue into Kelton's life. If Kelton remembered her name, inevitably he would remember her resemblance to Carmen Miranda. And Nora knew that men never got over their infatuations with movie stars.

To a certain extent, Kelton had been right. She did look like Carmen Miranda, only on a slightly larger scale. Nora's face was a little wider, but she had the singer's wide, well-shaped lips, her slightly fleshy nose, her slanted eyes, and her high forehead. Once, Nora had even tried to learn the rhumba but finally gave up. Syncopated movement didn't fit in with her practical talents. However, she had succeeded in learning the words to "Chica, Chica, Boom, Chic," and "I'yi, Yi, Yi, Yi."

Driving out to Rhodhiss Lake the next evening, Nora tried to keep her mind blank. She wanted this meeting to be as spontaneous as the one in the first-aid room. She had her dark hair pulled back tightly because Carmen Miranda usually wore hers that way. She was also wearing what she called her Miranda Red lipstick, very red and glossy. Instead of her heavy coat, she was wearing an alpaca poncho she'd bought in Tijuana for just such an occasion.

The road that circled the lake was unpaved and practically washed away in places. Nora had to creep along to keep from knocking out the bottom of her car. From Kelton's younger brother, who was taking a first-aid class at the community college so he could be an ambulance attendant, Nora had learned that this cabin on the lake belonged to the family. Through the shingly trunks of the black pines along the shore, Nora could see the khaki-colored water catching the nervous light from the January sunset. On the opposite shore where the trees were less disturbed by cabins, oaks and maples cast thick shadows over the water. Nora pulled the leather jacket into her lap and leaned over her steering wheel to search for the cabin, which Kelton's brother described as "kind of a houseboat that never learned to swim." On a ridge that overlooked a muddy cove stood a cabin, not much more than a box made out of planks, with a 750 BMW parked beside it.

Nora hoped that whoever had brought the motorcycle to Kelton wasn't still around. As a rule, Thursday night was not a very sociable night in Boehm. The factory workers wanted to be home, storing up their energy for Friday night. Nora didn't blame the workers, who liked to gamble and drink. Boehm wasn't geared for any other forms of entertainment. But Nora had learned from one of Kelton's cousins that since he'd returned to town, Kelton kept to himself. He stayed in the cabin.

As she approached the door, painted a thick woodland green, Nora observed that the light in the cabin was very bright. Through the window, she could see Kelton sitting on an oddly shaped couch, his back to the door. After she knocked, she saw him lean his head back and rub his eyes with his index finger and thumb of his left hand. He stayed in that position for several seconds, as if deliberating. Nora felt her composure begin to ossify. If he didn't want company, she'd sense it and be as ineffective as she'd been as a freshman.

Then Kelton came to the door. Behind him, Nora saw that he'd been staring at a bare light bulb—at least two hundred and fifty watts. He carried his bandaged right hand stiffly across his stomach as if it were a weapon he didn't quite know how to use. Instead of his black sweatshirt and jeans, he was wearing a blue oxford cloth shirt, dark blue pants, and white tennis shoes.

The cabin was sparsely furnished but clean. The few pieces of furniture were old: the coffee table with the bright light on top of it in the center of the room, the metal-and-Formica kitchen table next to the rudimentary sink, two faded sling chairs. The only piece of furniture that caught Nora's attention was the couch where Kelton had been sitting. It was a fiberglass canoe with one side missing, raised on a plywood platform.

"Go ahead, try it," Kelton said when he noticed she was staring at the canoe couch. "It's a lot more comfortable as a couch than it was as a canoe."

"This is yours, I hope," Nora said, handing him the jacket. "If it isn't, you'd better be careful where you wear it."

Kelton took the jacket and hung it in a large wardrobe wedged into a corner that looked too small for it. The top looked as if it was being used to hold up the ceiling. Kelton took several seconds to get the jacket on its hanger. Nora pretended not to notice the difficulty he was having. Instead, she shuffled through the collection of magazines spread out in the front of the canoe. She felt a mild exhilaration when she found that all the magazines dealt, in one way or another, with geography: *National Geographic, Smithsonian, The Americas, Demography Today, Geographer's Gazette.*

"You must be the only person in the factory who reads such

magazines," Nora observed, hoping the admiration in her voice would put Kelton more at ease because he clearly had a look in his face that indicated he didn't know what to do. He wasn't exactly uncomfortable—he was too collected for that—but he was clearly perplexed.

"Well, I've offered to swap magazines with some of the other guys, but they don't seem too interested," Kelton replied, sitting down in a sling chair on the other side of the coffee table.

Nora had to put her hand over her eyes in order to see him. "That's an awfully bright light you've got there."

"Yeah, after being in the room with it for an hour, I frequently get the feeling that the front of my head is melting." Kelton switched on a cooler fluorescent overhead light, then switched off the large lamp.

"Are you using it to heat your place?" Nora asked, holding her hands out toward the large bulb.

"It's part of my home entertainment," Kelton responded. "See that Viewmaster viewer there to your left in the canoe?"

Nora lifted a black piece of silky cloth. Under it was a brown Viewmaster and innumerable boxes of Viewmaster reels. The entire back end of the canoe was filled with the yellow boxes, all of them neatly stacked. Some of the boxes were so old that the cardboard was fuzzy, with no trace of color, while others looked as if they'd just been bought. Each box was also carefully labeled. The set of reels with the top off dealt with towns and villages of the Amazon.

"That set just came today," Kelton pointed out.

"You want to go there?" Nora asked, looking into the Viewmaster.

"Not especially," Kelton answered, switching the lamp back on. "Travel is an inconvenience. . . ."

"An impurity, almost?" Nora ventured.

"A difficulty. . . ."

"A complication?" Nora suggested, raising one eyebrow in a way that emphasized the tilt of her eyes. Not to seem too intense in her observation of Kelton's response, she looked back into the Viewmaster. "This water is muddy," she observed. "And the houses are all on stilts."

Kelton was slow to answer. He was rubbing his upper lip with the middle finger of his injured hand, sniffing the bandage on his index finger. "That's the floating village of Belen," he said, as if surrendering the information. "It has a kind of migratory population. When the river level drops, people move out, stay with relatives in Iquitos, until the wet season brings the river back up."

"Now that sounds inconvenient," Nora said, looking back into Kelton's eyes.

"I wouldn't want to do it, but their culture is patterned more on cycles than ours, more agricultural, so they have more adjustments to make, but their sense of social rhythms tends to be broader—"

"And that makes them like to move?" Nora asked, suspecting that Kelton was getting lost in his total recall.

"To them, it's not like moving because they know in five or six months they'll be back on the river or back with a relative. To have the sensation of moving, they'd have to get outside their cycle. That's when the change gets uncomfortable." Kelton was gradually allowing himself to look at Nora for longer periods of time.

She shifted to a more provocative position in the canoe. She smiled—one she had picked up from Carmen Miranda in *Week-End in Havana*. "You get pretty uncomfortable around changes too, don't you."

For a moment, Kelton succumbed to the slouch of his sling chair. He pulled his legs under the seat until only his toes were touching the floor, crammed against the green linoleum. He crossed his arms over his chest, being careful not to jar his bandaged finger. "Did I thank you for returning my jacket?" he asked.

"No," Nora replied, stretching her arms along the side of the canoe that served as the back rest. She thought she should take off her poncho, but the cabin was cool. She crossed her legs, letting her skirt drape where it may. "But the happiness on your face was thanks enough."

Kelton seemed to be trying to remember what his expres-

sion had been. "I didn't thank you for the morphine either or for
stopping the bleeding."

"It does sound like you really owe me, doesn't it?" Nora
replied, lowering her voice to a historical murmur.

"Seems that way," Kelton agreed, his tone keeping a re-
spectful distance from the presence occupying the canoe.

"Of course it was only a matter of pressure points, gauze,
and a syringe. We're not talking transfusion, organ donation, or
intensive care," Nora admitted. "Not in this particular case."

Kelton looked around the cabin. "You know, I've been trying to simplify my life, so I don't have much to give in the way
of reward."

Nora followed his roving gaze. He seemed to be searching
through the contents of the cabin in an earnest attempt to find
some offering. Despite the chilly room, Nora felt an impatient
heat rise up her throat and fan out along her chin and cheeks.
She held the Viewmaster up to the light and advanced the reel
to a scene of an Indian village, a man in the foreground wearing
a grass skirt holding a blowgun twice as high as himself.

"You could let me borrow your Viewmaster," Nora suggested, keeping the viewer to her eyes. She expected the silence
that followed.

"That one's kind of an antique," Kelton finally responded.
"I've had it for fifteen years."

"I took care of you," Nora answered. "I can take care of your
Viewmaster . . . and your slides." She bit her lower lip, wondering if maybe she hadn't begun to apply too much pressure,
because Kelton's eyes were fixed on the floor.

Nora inspected the Viewmaster proprietorily, keeping an
eye on Kelton, who was blending more and more into the canvas
of the sling chair. Slowly, Nora pulled the dark cloth off the
entire collection of boxes. She tapped her red fingernails on each
box as if testing each one's ripeness. She'd have to take the polish
off before going to work in the morning, but she liked the way
the red emphasized the suggestive curve of her nails.

Kelton's voice sounded as if it came from beneath a heap of
used bandages. "I guess you could take it for a day or two."

Nora looked at Kelton full in the face, catching his eyes just as they ascended from the floor. "Or you could let me come back here and look through it."

"I could even fix you supper," Kelton suggested, sounding relieved.

"Not every night," Nora replied, "but four or five times would be nice."

"This is beginning to get complicated," Kelton said, pulling himself up straighter in the chair.

Nora stood up and smoothed her poncho. She smiled, drifting toward the door. "Have you ever thought that amputation is a kind of simplification?"

Kelton covered his eyes with his bandaged hand. "By the way," he said when he heard Nora open the door, "did you know that Carmen Miranda died in 1955?"

Break Time

At seven o'clock in the morning, Kelton had already been up for two hours, even though he wasn't going to work. He'd only been working at the factory for three and a half months, but habits had always formed easily for him, like sleeping with the baseball glove on his right hand to protect his injured finger. After two nights, he was already used to it.

Getting used to the poorly heated cabin was taking a little longer. Since the middle of December, the windows of the cabin hadn't thawed once. The warmth oozed out by the small gas heater disappeared through some secret passage that Kelton had never been able to discover. Miserable as the place could get, though, the cabin did serve an important service to Kelton: it kept people from bothering him.

The routine of the factory work, itself, had also helped Kelton isolate himself. People who remembered him as the high school valedictorian stayed away because he seemed tainted with failure. People who remembered him as a hell-raiser in college stayed away because he worked eight to ten hours a day—sometimes seven on Saturday—and slept the rest of the time. People at the factory stayed away because he had been caught during lunch break, sitting on a pile of unsanded table legs, reading one of his *Smithsonians*. Reading during lunch, Kelton had discovered, put him in a category slightly above child molesting and slightly below people who spit their tobacco into the drinking fountain.

The loss of his finger could be used as a filter too. This idea had come to Kelton while the doctor had been sewing up his wound. He held the bandaged hand up to the window. Dawn was beginning to gather strength far away behind the Blue Ridge Mountains. Vapor was rising from the lake in whisps and fragmented swirls. Kelton turned his hand slowly, following the motion of the vapor. He could see the woods across the lake through the gray place where the top two finger joints should have been.

Nora Knowling had been right when she told him that amputation was a form of simplification. Now there was nothing but landscape where his finger used to be. He didn't feel ready to deal with her—not the way she pushed into his cabin last night, telling him he owed her, pretending to want his Viewmaster just so she could get invited back. Kelton knew what all this attention implied.

He leaned his head against the back of his canoe couch. "Ask not for whom the belle trolls / She trolls for thee," Kelton said aloud. He could see his breath as he spoke, the vowels coming out in diaphanous ferns and toadstools that dissolved before they could get halfway to the dark rafters. Kelton turned on the bright lamp and picked up his Viewmaster. The most effective antidote for the acidity of his personality had always been looking at places whose populations were exotic and remote.

Before he could catch himself, Kelton inserted the reel that Nora had been looking at the previous night. A Yagua woman was standing on the ladder stairs leading up to a bamboo hut. Below her, a man was braiding together palm leaves for the roof. Both the man and the woman had large round bellies. Nora Knowling would, no doubt, point out that they were suffering from poor nutrition. She wouldn't notice how the clouds over the jungle behind the hut curled themselves like banana leaves and palm fronds.

Kelton had to put down his Viewmaster and take a blanket from his bed to wrap up in. His hands had started shaking, and it was awkward enough having to push the reel advance button with his middle finger without having to deal with chills. His gas heater sputtered its blue flames, sending its warmth along on some journey that only the gas company was aware of.

As he paced around the heater, Kelton thought about Nora's poncho. Last night, he had been freezing, but she appeared completely comfortable. He had remembered her from freshman Latin: she had reminded him of Carmen Miranda when he was going through his Carmen Miranda phase, catching her thirteen movies on the late show. Like most girls, Nora didn't know how to talk—or be talked to—as a high school freshman. Somewhere along the way to being a nurse, she'd learned how to talk.

Soon, Kelton had to face the fact that the cabin was too cold for Viewmaster viewing. Up until today, he had always been able to withdraw into the world rotating inside his Viewmaster, but this morning, the frigid air—or something else—wouldn't let him forget where he was. Kelton got up and put on his jacket. Through the smell of the old leather, he caught a whiff of Nora, the perfume she'd been wearing the night before. He sniffed the sleeves, shoulders, back, front, and waist of the jacket. The scent was all over it, not as if she'd sprayed the perfume on it, but as if she'd kept it close to her. The flowery smell wasn't in the leather but clinging to the outside.

Having no other choice if he wanted to get warm, Kelton slipped the jacket on and zipped up the front and sleeve zippers. Because his fingers were feeling stiff, he also put on his riding gloves. Putting on the right one took a long time because he had to work his injured finger in with excruciating care, breathing all the time as if he were standing on a very narrow ledge. Kelton held his gloved hand in front of him. Eventually, he supposed, he'd have to get the glove's index finger trimmed down to fit his amputated finger. He flexed his fingers. The injured one quivered, unable to curve like the other four. "O earth, who knows what losses you have seen?" Kelton quoted, remembering a red-headed philosophy major who loved Rilke and now drove a truck, trying to blot out the terrors of Wittgenstein.

If he were going to be cold, Kelton decided, he might as well be on his motorcycle. Life was reduced to its most basic elements on a motorcycle: momentum and balance, the purity of motion allowed by two wheels. Kelton had once thought about looking into the possibility of putting a motor on a unicycle. He'd even gone so far as to feed the information into a computer during one of the computer classes he took to fulfill his science requirements. The machine told him that momentum, after a certain point, needed a separate wheel if balance were to be maintained. "You can't have your speed and sit on it too," Kelton said aloud as he kicked the starter.

The first few minutes on his bike always stirred up the memories of his wild years. He had worked very hard to destroy all the expectations people had for him, expectations that clouded the first two years of college. "Other people are hell," Kelton declared as he bounced along the dirt road that led to the main highway. He stopped before pulling out on the pavement and put on his helmet. He had trouble getting it tightened up. Twice, his injured finger bumped against the strap and brought a lump to his throat each time. He'd have to see about getting something for the pain. The doctor had given him only enough to get him through yesterday.

Lacking his usual flare with the throttle, Kelton chugged out onto the highway. He could feel the strain on his hand from having to compensate for his missing finger. This was a complication he hadn't counted on. Neither was the appearance of Nora Knowling at his place last night. Unexpected complications were the worst kind, he acknowledged.

"Disasters are like bananas," Kelton recited above the roar of his motorcycle. They come in bunches. That was what he learned in Disaster Geography. The problem, the idea of disaster is a matter of population, not of place. An earthquake on the moon is not a disaster, Kelton remembered. People have to be shaken up, buildings have to fall down before it's a disaster. Disaster, by definition, implies human consequences.

Kelton pulled up behind a school bus and had to slow down. Several prepubescent faces stared out from the back window. Through the obscurity of the dirty bus window and Kelton's black face shield, all the children looked identical. They pointed at him. One face, with pigtails, pressed its lips against the window while the others laughed. Kelton dropped to second gear and slid around the bus without checking the oncoming traffic, without wanting to check it.

During a disaster, he reasoned as he edged back in front of the bus barely in time to avoid becoming a bug screen for a Lincoln Continental, caution becomes a liability. Resolution, loyalty, pride—all suspended for the duration of the tremors, the tidal wave, the tornado. A few horrible seconds of simple response, reduced to—overwhelmed by—pure sensation, the baggage of memory dropped, the furniture of duty abandoned. Kelton tightened his legs against the motorcycle and leaned over the handlebars, opening the throttle slowly, wanting to get out of sight of the bus as quickly as the cramp in his right hand would let him.

No sooner had Kelton left the first bus behind than he came upon another one, stopped on a hill, its blinkers flashing urgently. The lights called to Kelton's mind the oranges and apples he had carried to school, the stoplights he had waited at, the headaches he had suffered. More grapefruit-sized faces stared at him. Kelton had never noticed how stiff his brake lever was, but this morning he was having trouble holding his motorcycle back. His front wheel was almost under the back of the bus before he got fully stopped.

He could feel the kids looking down on him and was glad that eyeballs didn't drool. He put the bike in neutral and let it roll back. His hand was severely cramping now, and he couldn't get a tight enough grip on the brake. Looking over his shoulder, he saw a car coming up behind him. It was one thing to get smashed head on, quite another to roll back into some accountant in a station wagon who was driving to work listening to Living Strings on the radio. Kelton backed as easily as he could off the road and into a ditch lined with broomstraw, which helped him lose enough momentum to jump off the bike. He had to let it drop on the ground because his right hand was gnarled in pain and he couldn't hold the entire weight of the machine with his left hand.

Although the bus was pulling away, Kelton was sure he could hear hoots of derision. His face and armpits burned. Sitting down on the frozen ground, Kelton massaged his aching hand. He left his helmet on so he wouldn't have to return the stares of the people who drove by. He felt too close to these witnesses of his humiliation. He had wrecked before, but this was the first time he'd ever lost control while being stopped. Despite the heat given off by his motorcycle and the bank of sunlight he was sitting on, Kelton felt as cold here as at his cabin. A dozen buses passed by while Kelton sat rubbing his hand. The tendons felt raw and shrunken.

Most of the glances that passed over him, Kelton knew, were indifferent, at most curious. But he also felt people looking at him sympathetically—elementary school teachers, probably, who had sons ruined by motorcycles. Innocent boys who grew up into egomaniacs, beer drinkers, and dirty joke transmitters. They were embarrassments, balding disappointments. But not exactly disasters. Populations were not displaced by those wayward sons. Cultures didn't cave in. Besides, all of them eventually gravitated, as Kelton had found himself doing, to a job. Settled down. Kelton closed his eyes and pictured sediment drifting to the bottom of a lake, becoming the foundation for a swamp, then a jungle populated with natives carrying blowguns, killing the parrots.

When he was once again able to flex his hand, Kelton got back on his motorcycle, regretting that he'd come out, but he was unwilling to return to his cabin. He felt migratory but out of season. Beneath his wheels, the pavement whined as if with longing, a long uninterrupted pull on his ears while the wind struck him with oblong flirtatious blows.

Kelton passed the open, rolling fields that separated the town of Boehm from the lake. The lake, in turn, separated the fields from the steeper slopes of the Great Smoky Mountains. These mountains were to the north and west of Boehm. To the east of town were the Brushy Mountains, which came down to the very city limits. Kelton had never figured out why the town had spawned so many furniture factories. The nearest large city was seventy miles away. Since Teddy Roosevelt, most of the mountain forests had been part of the national park system so the tons and tons of wood used by the factories had to be brought in by rail. The town didn't work on logic, and that was why, Kelton admitted to himself, he could never leave it.

That was why, Kelton realized, he had gone to work in the factory. It made very little logical demands on a person. You had to be there at seven o'clock in the morning. You worked at your machine until nine, when you had a ten-minute break. Then you had lunch at twelve. Another ten-minute break at two. The work wasn't stimulating. After two months, it got extremely boring, but Kelton subjected himself to the boredom in the hope that it would be a purifying experience. During one year when he'd dropped out of college and worked part-time at Tijuana Fats Restaurant, he'd joined a motorcycle gang. That was when he thought he had pent-up aggression that needed to be released. The wildness had left him dissatisfied and scarred, with a large collection of knives and guns—none of which ever came close to replacing the affection he felt for his Viewmaster viewer. The gang had let him drop out without the usual rite of degradation; he wasn't ridden out backward to a nearby cow pasture where his clothes were pulled off and he was rolled in cow manure. The gang had been too fond of Kelton's ability to remember the names of the towns and the numbers of the roads that they encountered while on their trips. He further impressed them by being able to remember the number of points each gang member had on his driver's license. Secretly, he thought of himself as the gang historian. The feeling of relief that Kelton experienced when he got out of the Asphalt Knights was what started him on the path of simplification. He had learned that the less one belonged, the clearer one saw.

With this knowledge, he had gone into geography because no other course of study could make him feel more detached than geography. When he read about other places and other populations, he was free from the danger, the trap of belonging. He had taken as his philosophy of life a lesson he had learned from Abbott and Costello. Abbott says to Costello, "I can prove that you aren't here." Costello says, "Go ahead and try." Then Abbott says, "Okay, you're not in Chicago, are you? And you're not in St. Louis, are you? So if you're not in Chicago or St. Louis, you must be somewhere else. And if you're somewhere else, you can't be here."

By the time Kelton got around to studying local geography, he had disciplined himself enough to feel detached even when he did computer research on population distribution in counties that were in the process of changing from agrarian to industrial production. This assignment, done for his senior thesis, had brought him a job offer from North Carolina Cablevision Company. Kelton thought about that offer every time he rode by the Boehm Cablevision office, a subsidiary of N.C.C.C. The offer had confused him. The starting salary of twenty-five thousand had frightened him, threatened him in the same way that Nora Knowling's attention threatened him. Both demonstrations of interest interfered with his search for clarity.

Kelton had been skirting the edge of town in order to avoid having to use his brakes. This route soon brought him to the furniture factory section. Over the rumble of his motorcycle, Kelton could hear the drone of the gigantic fans that sucked the sawdust out of the machines and through pipes painted yellow, suspended from the factory ceiling. Every few seconds, Kelton heard the screech of a cutoff saw hitting knots in the lumber being trimmed.

The morning air drooped in discouragement over the smokestacks. Around the outer edges of the smoke trapped over the factories, the sun was the color and consistency of pus, making Kelton think once more that he'd like to have something for the pain in his finger. But he didn't have time to think about the sky or his injury because he'd gotten close enough to the factories for the road to be littered with slivers of veneer and blocks of wood. The wind was brown with the smell of varnish and stirred-up sawdust in dingy clouds. It was the desolate spell between seven and nine o'clock, between punching in and break time, when the workers, Kelton knew, were unable to believe that the day would end.

Kelton parked his motorcycle in front of the white aluminum kiosk that barely contained the bulk of the security guard, Strother McSorely. To get out through the door of the guard-house, McSorely had to press his clipboard tightly against his chest. After he had squeezed his way out the door, he was disappointed that he'd gone to the trouble of struggling into daylight simply to greet an employee instead of an official visitor who'd have to sign in and receive directions. Then, when he saw who the employee was, after Kelton took off his helmet, McSorely's face brightened.

"Let's see your hand," he ordered cheerfully.

Kelton held up his gloved hands. "I'm not armed," he said, unzipping his jacket and holding it open. Accidents weren't that common in the factory, but even if they were, the victims would still be called upon to display their mutilations. The workers relished being shown what their machines could do. They were always interested in extremes.

"Not armed?" McSorely said, his face going blank. Then one side of his mouth curved up, pulling his nose out of alignment. "I thought you just lost a finger." He approached Kelton, patting his clipboard against his thigh. "Let's see how much damage you did."

"The biggest damage was done to my soul," Kelton confessed, looking toward the sky. "I'm not the same man, Mac. You wouldn't believe how much of your inner life is attached to a few inches of skin and bone. It's like something has died, like a light has gone out, like a radio has been unplugged—"

"Let me see the finger," McSorely said.

Kelton slumped against the cyclone fence, pulled off his left glove, tossed it to McSorely, then began easing off the right glove. McSorely moved closer. He was a man for whom weight was an asset, perfectly in keeping with his other values. He looked like he needed the wide leather belt, which held up a tiny holster and an even smaller pistol.

"How many stitches did it take?" McSorely asked.

"Eight, I think," Kelton replied. "I was looking the other way while they were being put in."

"There's worse things to watch," McSorely pointed out.

"Yeah," Kelton agreed, "like watching the drill bore through my finger." He pulled off the glove as if performing a magic trick. "But I believe what you say, Mac. If you let me know the next time you lose a finger, I promise to come and watch them sew up the nub. I'll even take pictures—color slides—so on holidays instead of watching football we can pull out the projector, hang up a sheet, and relive those manly moments in the emergency room."

"Hold it up so I can see how much is gone," McSorely responded. "If you move it over a little to the left, that number four smokestack fits right in where the top half of your finger was."

When Kelton started walking toward the plant, McSorely walked with him. "You know you get three thousand dollars for losing that finger," he said, his voice bland but firm as a two-by-four.

"You've got me there, Mac," Kelton replied, walking faster. "I admit it is a good year to lose fingers. How much would I get for a whole hand—five fingers . . . and a wrist? Let's throw in the wrist so the insurance people can be sure they're getting a complete hand."

McSorely increased his pace too and pursed his lips, sipping his memory. "A whole hand is ten thousand dollars. A couple years ago when Bullis Mullinax let the cutoff saw rip up through his ring finger and up to his wrist, he thought he'd get ten thousand because he lost a lot of the use in his other fingers, but all the insurance would pay was seven thousand. There was most of his hand still on the end of his arm, they said. Bullis thought about going to court but backed out. Shit, a factory man don't have any business in court. I told him we could just wait around awhile and then catch the insurance agent and maybe back a truck over his hand a couple of times."

Casting an exaggerated glance over his shoulder, Kelton asked, "Aren't you supposed to stay at the gate?"

"It's almost break time," McSorely said, checking his watch. "I can get some coffee and see the kind of reception you get. Nobody's expecting you back this soon."

Instead of going in through the front entrance, Kelton followed the railroad tracks along the rows of stacked lumber until he got to the back entrance. If he was seen before the break buzzer went off, he'd have to spend the entire break time talking about how it felt to lose a finger. They'd probably ask him and Bullis Mullinax to stand up and sing a duet of "Nobody Knows." Then he'd have to tell everybody what he planned to do with the insurance money.

"Why you going in the back way?" McSorely asked.

"I just want to stop by the boilers and get warm," Kelton answered. "I could still go into shock. Don't let this get out, Mac, but I'm not good at losing parts of my body. Never have been. They used to have to blindfold me to cut my hair. I still have to take a couple of drinks to cut my fingernails."

McSorely snorted. "Maybe it'll be easier now that you've only got nine to trim." He patted Kelton on the shoulder. "But you oughtn't let it get you down." He took his hand off Kelton's shoulder and put it behind his back where his other hand was waiting for it. "How long you going to keep the bandage on it?"

From where he had positioned himself in front of the boiler, Kelton could see only the outline of McSorely's figure against the brightness of the open loading bay. Kelton slowly rotated in the damp heat. "Think it needs some air, Mac?"

"If it's going to heal, it's got to have air," McSorely replied.

Kelton paused, facing the fire in the boiler. His injured finger tingled with restored circulation. The break buzzer cut through the other noises of the factory. McSorely shifted impatiently from one foot to the other. Kelton fingered the small flesh-colored clamp that held the bandage in place.

"I'm kind of awkward, Mac," he said. "Come over here and help me unwrap this thing."

Despite his eagerness, McSorely was slow in getting the bandage off because Kelton would let his other fingers get tangled up in the loose gauze. He wanted to make sure that everyone had time to get to the canteen.

"Well, you did lose some of it, didn't you?" McSorely exclaimed at last. "Nice job of stitching, though. Looks neat as a cat's ass."

"Can you tell how many stitches?" Kelton asked.

"Light's kind of bad," McSorely complained, leaning his face close to Kelton's finger.

Kelton gritted his teeth and pushed his finger into

McSorely's eye. He thought his arm would explode.

"Son of a bitch!" McSorely yelped, staggering back into a stack of broken tabletops.

Kelton had already turned, running through the temporarily deserted factory, holding his throbbing hand by the wrist. He met Nora as she was coming out of the first-aid room, transcendent in her white uniform.

"I need something for pain," he declared, holding his unbandaged hand up for her to see.

She took his hand and kissed the nub. Kelton winced but didn't pull away.

Factory Hand

In the eleven months that Zerle Kitcheloe had worked in the sanding room of Chalfant Furniture Factory, she had picked up eight splinters, not counting the tiny white slivers that barely went deeper than the fine wrinkles of her palm. But the eight she had counted were nothing compared to the piece of timber that split off from the drawer siding she was sanding and sank itself, straight down, into the center of her palm. As she stood on tiptoe, waiting for her vision to clear, she knew she had not experienced splinters until this very moment: two-thirty Friday afternoon, August twenty-seventh. In about ten hours, she was supposed to be on her way to the beach. That's what she had to think about: the beach. Driving her 4-by-4 Toyota through the night to Carolina Beach, Lydia and Kelly beside her, singing along with her Alabama tape. Then Saturday night, their boyfriends would meet them. The Sea Oats Motel. Zerle didn't want to think about that part of the trip. Too much guilt. But she and Max had agreed to go ahead and do it. The thought didn't help ease the pain in her hand. Better to think about her black truck all shined up, the mag wheels polished a painful whir of chrome.

In a few seconds, Zerle felt in control enough of the pain to turn to the man she worked with and hold up her injured hand. "Stewart. Picked up a splinter."

Stewart Prevette straightened up from the stack of drawer sides he was arranging on the push truck beside the sander. He pressed his hands against his lower back and stretched. Then he shuffled over two steps so he could study the palm that Zerle held level with his nose. Stewart moved slowly, not because he was old or dim-witted but because he was meditative. What Zerle both appreciated and despised about Stewart was his deliberation, both in movement and conversation. As a rule, the sanding room was one of the more hectic sections in the factory. For every single drawer made, sixteen sides had to be sanded. Consequently, all the sanders lagged behind the shapers and finishers.

"Looks pretty deep." Stewart took hold of Zerle's wrist, disregarding the man from the machine room, who pushed another load of unsanded drawers right up against his back.

Eleven months ago, Zerle would have been embarrassed to get caught with an older man like Stewart holding her hand up, studying her palm. The man from the machine room held up his own palm, kissed it, and rolled his eyes. If it had been any time but Friday afternoon before Labor Day vacation, Zerle and Stewart would have been kidded for several days about what was really going on behind those stacks of drawer sidings. Now, Zerle didn't care much about what other people thought. She knew the kidding was just a way of passing the time, greasing it up so it passed more easily.

"Can you get it out?" Zerle respected Stewart's delicate touch, an extension of his unhurried personality. She was also comfortable with Stewart because he was a preacher. Some of the other workers told her he could be a thumper and a stomper when he got into the pulpit, but except for his praying over his chili in the canteen, he never tried to mix his religion with his job. Had he been the type to sermonize at work, Zerle figured she could have put him in his place. She had debated in high school—much to everyone's surprise. She liked to argue when the other person irritated her enough. And she was also larger than Stewart Prevette. Her father had been telling her since she was twelve that she was a big girl, healthy looking. That was his favorite phrase. She argued a lot with her father.

"I'll give it a try." Stewart reached into his overalls pocket. "But this one is deeper than I like to go." He opened up a Case knife with a three-inch blade. Even under the filmy blue gleam of the fluorescent lights, the metal sparked brighter than Zerle's mag wheels. The blade had been sanded down so much that the point was as narrow as a toothpick.

Zerle found the sharpness comforting. Her palm was throbbing. She was afraid to flex her hand, afraid the splinter might come zinging out the other side. She knew Stewart wouldn't hurt her anymore than he had to. It took pain to neutralize pain—especially where splinters were concerned. "Try to get it out in one piece. I want to have this one framed."

"Sit down over here." Stewart moved to the wooden toolbox where the spare sanding belts were stored.

For a moment, Zerle hesitated. This was serious. Stewart had never asked her to sit down before. He'd always joked with her about how strong she was. As she was settling herself on the toolbox, she realized that no one in the factory had ever called her fat. That was definitely one thing she liked about the men in the factory. They appreciated a woman for being a woman. She didn't have to be slim or graceful or talented. Not one man in the factory had struck her as stupid or as silly as some of the boys she'd put up with in high school. From what Lydia told her about college boys, they didn't sound much different from high school boys: one more reason why Zerle was glad she'd gone into the factory right after she graduated. Lydia certainly wasn't having much of a time. Still, she planned to return, starting back the week after Labor Day.

"Whatever you do," Stewart said, "don't jerk." His grip on her wrist was actually painful.

"Don't you jerk either." Zerle gripped the toolbox with her free hand. Her last thought before Stewart sunk the point of his knife into her palm was that she might wear a bandage on the drive down to the beach, just to shock Lydia and Kerry. She never went into the ocean anyway. Then, all she could think about was not jerking her hand away from the blade, which had suddenly turned red hot and at least a foot wide. Two huge tears ballooned from the corners of her eyes and spread across the whole factory. Then all she could think about was how much she hated Stewart's slowness. He didn't have to poke around like this, and although she couldn't see clearly through the second set of gigantic tears, she was certain that Stewart was twisting that machete of his. "Don't whittle!" Zerle yelled.

Stewart pulled back, leaving her hand in midair. "Better take that to the nurse."

"I don't like the nurse." Zerle inspected her hand. She expected the skin to be pulled back in strips. Extending downward from the hole made by the splinter was a shallow cut about a fourth of an inch long. "It felt like you were scraping the bone."

"I never dig that deep." Stewart wiped his blade on his thigh.

A bright thread of blood lined the cut that Stewart had made. "I'm supposed to leave for the beach tonight." Zerle stood up, wondering why she wasn't bleeding any more than she was. "If it's in so deep why isn't there more blood?"

"A big splinter'll draw the blood." Stewart moved back to the sander. "That's why you ought to get it out soon as you can. Once the splinter swells up, it festers."

Zerle sat back down on the toolbox. "Okay. Let's get it out." She held her hand out to Stewart.

"No. I'm through digging." He pulled a canvas work glove out of his back pocket. All of the fingers were cut off. Zerle had tried wearing such a glove, but she hated for her hand to be sweaty eight or ten hours a day. "You'll wear a glove from now on."

"I won't. My hand would rot off if I wore one of those things."

For a few seconds, Stewart stared out over Zerle's head. Gradually, he shifted his gaze around the sanding room until he'd made a full inspection. Satisfied that no one was close enough to hear, he stooped beside Zerle and said, "If you won't go to the nurse, go over to the rough end and get Greer Efland to dig it out."

"I thought he was retarded." Zerle did not want to take her

splinter to Greer Efland in the rough end. She'd heard other people talk about how good he was with splinters, but she'd never let that oddball cut on her hand.

Stewart pulled off his glove and held his palm up for Zerle to see. It had more scars than the surface of the moon. "Some of these scars I got from letting the nurse get splinters out. Some of them I gave to myself. But you can't see where Greer worked on me because he knows what he's doing." Stewart put his glove back on. "I wouldn't call him retarded. He's just not ordinary."

Zerle went to the bathroom to wash her injury. It wasn't quite fifteen minutes before three. She knew the bathroom would be empty until three o'clock. At that time, the other women in this part of the factory would come to make themselves ready for the three-thirty whistle. After she washed her hands, Zerle sat down on the deacon's bench, which had been culled because the arms had been chipped in the packing room. She took the metal clips off her shoes. She couldn't stand to wear leather-soled shoes like most of the other people in the factory wore.

Her first week of work had been miserable because every fifteen or twenty minutes she would get a jaw-locking static electrical shock. Her crepe soles insulated her instead of letting the electricity ground itself on the floor. She'd actually lost five pounds that first week because of the shock treatments. On her own, Zerle had figured out that all she had to do was snip off the hooks of two coat hangers and bend one over each shoe so the metal could touch the floor while she worked. That remedy had made her feel good about being in the factory.

Very carefully, she tried bending the fingers of her right hand. She held her palm rigid. The fingers bent without difficulty. Zerle wiped the perspiration from her forehead and tried to relax her palm. As it slowly curled, Zerle began to feel the splinter, first as a stiffness, then as a throb with jagged edges, and finally as a single sharp stab. She uncurled her hand. Splinters were supposed to work themselves out. That was common knowledge around the factory, but Zerle couldn't think of anyone who had actually waited around for it to happen.

The plant nurse was supposed to be pretty good. From all

the evidence that Zerle had seen, though, the plant nurse was a flake. She lived on the outskirts of town in a stucco house that she tried to make look Mexican or something. When Zerle was a junior in high school, the plant nurse had come to her Spanish class to tell them about Carmen Miranda. She had admitted to the class that Carmen Miranda was her idol. Zerle had never before heard one woman talk about another woman—a dead one, no less—with such sticky emotion. Even if the nurse had been a normal person, Zerle would have been reluctant to take her hand into the infirmary. Medical science in general made her uneasy. She didn't like to think about her body. It was too big and she had no control over it. She liked her skin, which was smooth and olive. She hated her hair, which was wiry and brittle. Her eyes were green and looked good against her dark skin. That was about all of her anatomy she could stand to deal with.

She refused to consider Greer Efland.

"Okay," Zerle said, pulling into the parking lot of a Krispy Kreme on the south side of Charlotte. "I got us through the big city. One of you has to take over."

Her two friends were silent. During the day, they were travel demons, but at one o'clock in the morning, eighty miles from home, both of them preferred to be passengers. Zerle remained silent against them. She'd made the mistake of letting her father dig for her splinter. He had cut deeper than Stewart but still hadn't found it. He had further compounded the damage by insisting that she pour peroxide into the hole he had excavated. She had really needed the bandage she wore around her hand. If she drove with her fingertips, she didn't feel too much pain. Shifting gears brought tears to her eyes. For the hour she had been driving, all she could think about was that if she had gotten the splinter in her left hand, she could hang it out the window. Now that she had navigated them through the big city, she wanted to get in the passenger's seat and let the wind blow across her injury.

"Come on. I got us through the hard part." She leaned against her door so she could browbeat her two friends. "I need to rest. I've worked eight hours and I'm carrying a stake in my hand."

"I've been working all day too," Kelly replied.

"How many bottles of perfume did you sell today?" Zerle asked with the smile she could never control when Kelly started talking about her job at the Belk's cosmetics counter.

"Spare me," Lydia said, pushing against Zerle's shoulder. "Let me chauffeur my two moral superiors through the dark state of North Carolina. Guilt will keep me alert."

Walking around the front of her truck, Zerle caught a whiff of doughnuts drifting from the Krispy Kreme. She pointed her bandaged hand stiffly at Kelly. "I'm riding beside the window, so get comfortably scrooched up against Lyd while I buy some doughnuts."

The wind did soothe her hand. Zerle wanted to sleep. She knew that Lydia would be dozing off before they got to 211 in Lumberton. Kelly was already asleep, chin heavy on her chest. The high heels wore her out. Zerle had tried to get Kelly to work in the factory, but Kelly preferred waiting on people to getting sweaty. Working in the factory might be a grind, but working with shoppers made a woman into a servant. When Kelly got to work a full week, she barely made half of what Zerle brought home. All she could afford to drive was a beat-up Ford Pinto that didn't run three-fourths of the time.

Lydia didn't have any kind of car. Probably wouldn't have for another three or four years. Zerle was convinced that college would ruin her. She was already getting thin lips from worrying. When she got out, she'd be an elementary school teacher not making much more than what Kelly made at Belk's. Zerle was fairly certain that education was a fake, a way of putting off going to work. Only hourly wages were real. Before the weekend was over, Zerle knew, she'd have to lend Kelly and Lydia money. She didn't mind.

Once the lights of Charlotte had disappeared behind them, Zerle felt that the trip had finally begun. She poured Lydia a cup of coffee from the stainless steel thermos. Lydia took the cup without taking her eyes from the road. Zerle had to admit to herself that Lydia was becoming a stronger person. Last year, she had absolutely refused to drive after midnight. Zerle felt sad, seeing her friend change, even though Zerle also needed to change, to stop clinging to her parents the way she did. In another year, Zerle figured she might be able to move out on her own. She'd still have the truck payments—three more years of them—but in a year she'd be making enough to afford a small place. In a year, she could be married. This trip would probably be what Max needed to make up his mind.

Max worked in the veneer plant across town from Chalfant Furniture Factory. He tailed a splicing machine. The operator fed in two pieces of veneer. The splicing machine heated up the glue that had been sprayed on one edge of the wood. By the time the two pieces came out the other end, where Max pulled them out, they had become one piece of veneer. It wasn't much of a job, and Max hated it, but until he finished his computer courses at the community college, he would have to stay there. Max was, in some ways, like Kelly. He couldn't feel good about himself unless he was dressed up. And he wanted to be dressed up all the time. Once he got out of the factory and into a bank or an insurance company, he'd settle down and be satisfied. Until then, Zerle knew it was up to her to keep Max soothed. Max needed someone to assure him that he was worth something even before he graduated from the community college. This was the weekend when the solid assurance began.

"How's your hand?" Lydia drained the last of the coffee from the Styrofoam cup.

"The wind hides the throb." Zerle tipped her hand, causing her whole arm to rise on the air current rushing by the truck.

"Will it mess up your weekend?" Lydia kept her eyes on the road. Zerle could be terribly sensitive about questions concerning her and Max.

"You tell me," Zerle replied. She didn't like how weak her voice sounded. She cleared her throat loudly. "You and Russ have been going at it since Christmas vacation."

"There's nothing to be afraid of." Lydia glanced at Zerle.

Zerle couldn't deny she was afraid. She couldn't admit it either. Not to Lydia, who just a year ago seemed so dense. Now she could drive after midnight and at the same time let Zerle know she understood exactly what she was feeling. "So much is going to be changed after this weekend," Zerle said.

"You seem pretty convinced that it's going to be a bad change." Lydia handed her cup to Zerle. "Give me another dose of that coffee."

The warm thermos jug made Zerle's injured hand tingle. "Max and me have just reached a point where we've got to get in deeper." She was sorry she had let Lydia trap her into talking about Max. She knew Lydia didn't really like him, even though he and Russ were good friends. Max had always treated Lydia as if she were Zerle's younger sister. Thinking back, Zerle realized that all through high school and this year, Lydia had been pampered. Maybe Kelly didn't want to hold a real job, but at least she was working. Zerle ran her left hand over Kelly's honey-blond hair. It was damp with perspiration. For a moment, Zerle thought about turning on the air conditioner, but she wanted to check her gas mileage and she wanted to hold her hand out the window.

"If you weren't in that factory, you wouldn't be worrying about this weekend." Lydia slowed down behind a tractor-trailer carrying a load of pigs. The smell filled up the small truck like a soiled blanket.

"Pass, pass," Zerle ordered. She could tell that Lydia was afraid to pull around the huge truck. It was one thing to drive after midnight, something else to pass a big truck crawling along the highway. Before Zerle could give Lydia a second order to pass, the big truck pulled into the parking lot of an all-night diner. Lydia immediately speeded up as if she had done something. "Life is too easy on you," Zerle complained.

"It could be easier on you," Lydia said. "You don't have to work in a factory."

"Once you get used to it, the factory isn't so bad." Zerle tried to bend her hand. The splinter felt larger.

On bad mornings, when she hadn't slept but three or four hours, she hated the factory. When she was drowsy or when she had a cold, her eight-hour shift dragged on and on. Stacking drawer sidings seemed to be the dullest work in the world. In another six months, she might get her own machine. Then somebody else could stack what she sanded. In another year or year and a half, she'd be married. That would give her something to do. Give Max two years to get set up and prospering and she could quit work. The truck would be paid for by then.

"Honest, Zerle," Lydia said. "You can do better for yourself."

"You don't know what you're talking about." Zerle pulled her hand inside the cab and held it palm up in her lap. It felt hot, like anger. "I didn't make the grades to get into college, and I won't ever have the money to waste on education. Look at me, Lydia. The factory is all I'm fit for. I'm not smart like you. I'm not pretty like Kelly."

Hearing her name, Kelly pulled herself up and stared around groggily. "My turn to drive?"

"Not yet," Zerle replied. "I'll let you know when I get that hungry for thrills." She leaned across Kelly, who was already settling back to sleep, and asked Lydia in a low voice, "Why don't you try to improve Kelly's life?"

"Not much room for improvement." Lydia shrugged her shoulders and yawned.

No further explanation was needed. Kelly's life was already arranged. She and Danny were getting married in December. They had a trailer picked out. By then, Danny would be finished with his insurance training program. They'd been dating since their sophomore year. Since their junior year, Kelly and Danny had been sneaking around, having sex. Zerle figured that even Kelly's parents were getting tired of pretending that she and Danny were behaving themselves, so the wedding was going to relieve a lot of people. Zerle was fairly certain that Kelly would be one of those girls who disappeared into marriage the way some travelers disappeared into an unexplored jungle. Zerle vaguely disliked the idea of jungles, of disappearing. At least when you worked in a factory, you knew who you were. You didn't have to worry about waking up one day to find yourself completely changed. Changing was another way of disappearing.

"You're going to have to drive for a while." Lydia pulled into a service station. "And we need to get gas." She reached under the seat for her pocketbook. "Do we take turns paying for it?"

Before answering, Zerle rolled out of the truck and slammed her door solidly. "I'm paying for the gas. You and Kelly keep your money for the beach." Zerle felt good being able to say this to Lydia. All her friend Lydia had were ideas and a big opinion about how independent she was. Zerle shook her head as she filled up the tank. What she liked about Kelly was that she had never worried about being independent. The furniture factory had taught Zerle that independence wasn't a way of life. It was a momentary sensation. It was the way you felt Friday evening, walking across the parking lot to your truck. It was the way you felt taking your check to the bank. Nobody was independent more than ten minutes out of each week.

Soon after Lydia got settled on the passenger side of the truck, she was asleep, her head tilted sideways, resting on the door. Her short hair swirled in the wind. Zerle wanted to play some music, but she also liked having her two friends asleep. They made her feel strong. In about an hour, they'd be passing through Council. From there, the beach was less than sixty miles. She could get them there by six o'clock. Kelly and Lydia could go play in the sand while she took a long nap. Max had told her to expect them around five that evening. He would be concerned about her hand. They would have to be careful. She'd noticed when she put the gas in the truck that the soreness was spreading.

Of course, that kind of soreness helped keep her awake. Whenever she started feeling groggy, all she had to do was squeeze the wheel with her bandaged hand. The pain worked better than music to get her mind back on the road. It was a good thing she didn't go running to the plant nurse. Now she didn't have to worry about needing to pull over and sleep.

Her hand was getting worse. If Max couldn't get the splinter out, she didn't know what she'd do. She would have to choose between a doctor and Greer Efland. The doctor meant missing a day of work. He'd want to know how she got her hand all cut up. She'd have to sit there, suffocating in the smell of clinic and sickness, and tell about her father's clumsiness. Zerle hated the kind of interruption a visit to the doctor caused in her normal life.

Then again, she didn't relish the idea of visiting Greer Efland in the rough end. The rough end was made up of four different sections: the planing section, the ripsaw section, the cutoff section, and the gluing section. Zerle didn't mind the planer or the saws, but the glue section always made her nervous. With the exception of the finishing room, the glue room attracted the most deformed types of workers. The men in that part of the rough end were somehow less human than the other men. They were rougher. Zerle thought of them as less evolved than the other factory workers. She knew that part of her opinion came from the type of machinery used in the glue room.

All they had were two short conveyor belts, which carried strips of wood across a revolving drum coated with pink glue. The men picked up the strips of wood and clamped them into the glue reels. They were the most primitive machines in the whole factory, resembling a large Ferris wheel that had been stomped nearly flat. Where the seats should have been were six metal arms, each one fitted with an adjustable clamp. Three men worked on each reel. They arranged the glued strips of wood in a particular width, then tightened the clamps. To make sure the strips were as flat as they could be, the men had to pound on them with metal mallets. When each man had flattened his square of wood, he would step back. Then one of them would pull back the bar on which the ends of the metal arms had been resting, allowing the reel to advance to the next set of arms. By the time one set of arms had made the full circuit of the reel, the glue had dried; the squares of wood were removed and carried to the planer, where they were smoothed and made ready to be cut in specific shapes.

Zerle wasn't sure what kind of power turned the reel. On all the other machines, she had seen motors, generators, or belts giving life to saws, drills, sanders, and lathes. But the glue reel moved mysteriously, silently, except for the clank of the bar being pulled out from under the arms and the clank when it was pushed back under the next set of arms as they swept around.

Of all the deformed men who worked around the glue reel,

Greer Efland was the most distorted. He had extremely long legs which seemed to get thinner as they approached his lumpy torso. His body was much too short for his legs. Although no one could call Greer fat, his stomach did droop, pulling flesh away from his chest. Through the thin fabric of his old shirts, his shoulder blades flared like the fins of a '57 Chevrolet. Except for his shoulder blades, his torso resembled a pillow badly in need of fluffing.

From his waist up to his shoulders, Greer Efland tilted forward, still growing thinner. His shoulders were narrower than his hips. As if to counterbalance the slant of his spine, Greer's long neck, gnarled with an elongated Adam's apple, tipped back. His jaw was always dark with beard stubble. The lower half of his face was broader than the upper half and looked heavy, like a thick coffee mug. His forehead was sloped and rounded, dipping into deep eye sockets. His eyes were brown with long, curled lashes. They would have been his most attractive trait if they hadn't been tinged with yellow and looked so feminine.

After sunbathing most of the day, Lydia and Kelly were bright pink and subdued as they sat beside Zerle in the crowded lobby of the Red Lobster, where they were to meet Max, Russ, and Danny. Zerle had spent most of the day trying to sleep, but she had been worried about her hand. By the time they had checked in at the motel, Zerle knew that her hand had started to swell. The bandages were noticeably tighter than when she left home. Now her whole palm was tender, and, in addition to the throbbing, a buzzing deep down in the flesh had commenced, as if a small wasp had begun building a nest in the center of her hand.

When she hadn't been worrying about her hand, Zerle had worried about Max. More than anything, she dreaded the undressing. That would be awkward. For the last six months, Max had been assuring her that her body appealed to him. After all, Max himself was large. Down the road, Max expected to lose weight. The business world preferred slim men. One of the teachers at the community college had passed along this secret to Max. Fat might float, but it didn't rise in the business world. Zerle wondered how many times in a four-hour period Max referred to "the business world." From what Zerle had seen of managers, she wondered if Max would be able to fit in.

"There they are." Kelly suddenly came to life, standing up and waving. Her turquoise sundress was a jersey material that shimmered over her movement.

"Relax," Lydia said, leaning down to Zerle's ear. She smoothed her saffron sundress, stirring up her perfume. It was called Cinnabar and made Zerle think of Russian tea.

For the first time since they'd left their motel, Zerle noticed that her two friends had spent much more time getting dressed than she had. She had worn her favorite outfit: her blue jeans, her mariachi sandals, and her green Izod shirt with the tail out. If that wasn't bad enough, Max, Russ, and Danny were also more dressed up than usual. Max even had on a tie and a new pair of white patent leather loafers with tassels. Zerle had brought a dress for this occasion. She had taken it out of her suitcase and hung it up. But then she had stretched out on the bed, holding an ice cube, hoping the swelling would go down and the pain would ease. When Max was only a few feet away, she stood up, wondering why Lydia and Kelly hadn't said anything to her about not dressing up.

Then Max was hugging her, crowding out Lydia's perfume with his Old Spice and Juicy Fruit. "You should have seen us trying to change clothes coming down the interstate. They let me have the back seat to myself. The pants are the hardest to change."

"You ought to try it with your foot on the accelerator," Danny said, sliding onto the bench and pulling Kelly onto his lap.

Although Zerle felt as if she had left her stomach back at the motel with her dress, she let her friends persuade her to buy lobster. The only seafood she really cared for was deviled crab, but everybody else was having lobster to celebrate the special occasion. When Zerle asked them what they meant by that, Max quickly explained that all of them being at the beach together was the special occasion. For the rest of the meal, she kept her eyes on Russ and Danny. If she saw one smirk, one crooked smile, one raised eyebrow, she would throw the table at them.

Too many people were at the beach. Too many people were in the Red Lobster. Too many people were sitting at her table.

Perhaps because she was watching her friends so closely, Zerle noticed for the first time how much Lydia and Kelly changed when they were with Russ and Danny. Kelly became almost an invalid, drooping her eyes, leaning against Danny's shoulder. Her voice got softer, and she stopped speaking in complete sentences. Somehow, she made her eyes larger. That could have been makeup, but they were also more watery.

If Kelly got softer around her boyfriend, Lydia got harder. Her lips grew thinner. Her back got straighter. Her shoulders grew sharper. She wouldn't let Russ finish anything he started to say. About the only time Zerle could understand a woman acting so nasty was when she tried on those stiletto heels in Belk's. Despite Lydia's sharp tongue, Russ would laugh and nip her neck. Zerle didn't taste a bit of her lobster.

The conversation during supper centered primarily on how long the drive from home to the beach seemed. Zerle could tell that Russ and Danny wanted to get back to the motel where the fun would really begin. Max was the one who continued talking. Zerle knew he wanted to steer the topic around to "the business world." He had new respect for Danny because he was about to become a full-fledged insurance agent. Under any circumstances, Max liked to control the conversation, but tonight he seemed particularly determined to make people talk to him. He was acting as if he didn't want to leave the Red Lobster.

Zerle realized that he might be as nervous as she was about what they were planning to do. Her own reasons for being nervous were clear to her. She was doing her duty. She was giving him proof of her own serious interest in him. All she had asked him to do was be in charge of the protection. Because she had asked him to buy the protection, Zerle had felt obliged to make her own contribution to their first night together. She had gone shopping for a negligee. She had tried on two. Then she had decided that any piece of clothing that had a French name would never look right on her. Anything transparent and lacy made her look like a poorly decorated Easter egg. If Max wanted a negligee, he would have to wear it. On the other hand, maybe he was nervous about getting naked. With a tiny pang, Zerle noticed that Max was probably the least popular person at their table. His clothes were a large part of his personality.

"Let's go see how the ocean looks in the dark." Zerle stood up. Her injured hand came up slower than the rest of her body. She had barely flexed her fingers, but she felt the splinter.

"I think Russ and I will explore the boardwalk." Lydia picked up their check and handed it to Russ.

Kelly was yawning. "We're going back to the motel so Danny can help me put on some moisturizing cream. My skin's starting to feel like tissue paper."

"Well, do you want to meet at the pool after we all get back?" Max searched through his plate one final time to make sure he hadn't overlooked any edible part of his lobster.

"No," Russ said. "Let's just call it a day."

"We'll get together tomorrow and maybe hunt shells." Lydia patted Max on the back. "Watch out for your hand, Zerle."

"What's wrong with her hand?" Max slid around in his chair to confront Zerle.

"A splinter," Zerle said.

"You'd better let me take a look at it." Max pushed himself from the table.

"Let's wait till we have some privacy," Zerle said, moving a couple of steps back. "People are trying to eat in here." She didn't mind going back to the motel as long as Max had something else to occupy him.

Walking back to their motel, Max kept Zerle squeezed against him. Side by side, they took up about two-thirds of the sidewalk. Max didn't notice how they were forcing people to step into the road. Although the night was cool, Zerle could feel her left side, pushed up against Max's right side, beginning to sweat. He had never held her this tightly before. Off to her right, on the other side of the bars and arcade games, Zerle could hear the waves breaking and foaming to shore. One of the new sensations in her bandaged hand reminded her of foam—small clear bubbles of pain fizzing at the end of her arm.

For a moment, Zerle had the idea that if she could run down to the beach and soak her hand in the salt water the pain would disappear. But Max was holding too tightly. He was rushing her back to the motel, no longer reluctant about getting what he wanted. Back at the restaurant, he wanted to appear casual, as if this trip were not something he'd been suggesting for the last three months. Zerle could feel each one of his fingers pressing into her skin. He was hustling her along. Since she had agreed to sleep with Max, Zerle had not been expecting romance. She wasn't the kind of woman who had romantic experiences. Max wasn't the kind of man who provided romantic moments. She hadn't expected to be rushed, though.

"Why are we walking so fast?" Zerle stopped, letting Max's momentum pull his arm from around her.

"Well, don't you think it's time we were alone?" Max crossed his arms and took a couple of steps back to where Zerle was standing. "This is an important night for both of us." He spoke in his quiet voice, the one that made Zerle feel awkward and guilty.

"I know it's important, but jumbling along like we were hurts my hand." Zerle meant to lift her hand, to remind Max that she was injured, but as soon as her forearm muscles tightened, the splinter sent her a sharp warning signal. Tears came to Zerle's eyes. "I can't even raise my hand anymore." She pulled her hand against her stomach.

"All the more reason to hurry," Max said. "I'll get the splinter out. Working with veneer, I have to pull out four or five a day."

Zerle walked up to Max and let him put his arm around her. "This one is awfully deep."

"If it's in too deep, I'll just get it out from the other side." Max gave Zerle a gentle shake. Her hand translated the motion into a wave of nausea.

"Don't do that," Zerle said.

Two more blocks along the oceanside street, then Zerle and Max turned left, past the Twin Dolphins Department Store, past the Mad Mouse Roller Coaster, past a bingo pavilion that took up a whole block, past a park filled with scraggy pine trees and children's rides, all the time the ocean at their backs, sounding more and more like people exchanging rumors.

When Zerle had been in her motel room by herself, it had felt comfortable. Now that she had to share it with Max, the room felt cramped and hot. As soon as he had chained and bolted the door, Max began pulling off his clothes, pulling his shirt loose, unbuttoning it, revealing the waistband of his underwear, which rode up about four inches higher than the waist of his pants. He hung his shirt on one of the thief-proof coat hangers, beside Zerle's dress.

"You should have worn this tonight," he said, fingering the thin fabric of the dress.

"I meant to, but this splinter has started to make me absent-minded." Zerle began picking at the bandage, trying to put Max out of her mind. She didn't really know how badly she was hurt because she had spent too much time worrying about this beach trip. If she had stayed at home, she could have paid more attention to her hand.

Max paused long enough to pull off his tasseled loafers. Then he walked resolutely to where Zerle was sitting on the bed. "Let's take care of this business, then." He dropped down beside her, sending a quake through her hand and her stomach.

"Don't bounce around." Zerle allowed Max to take her hand and finish taking off the bandage. The last layer was stuck to the wound by a mixture of blood and pus.

"You should have taken this to the nurse."

"I've never trusted her. She acts like a foreigner."

"As messy as this hole looks, I don't know if I should go digging around in it." Max started to place Zerle's hand back on her lap.

She leaned back on the bed and gazed up at the ceiling. "Until I get this splinter out, I won't feel like doing anything but keeping still. I can't even lean back without my hand making me sick."

To get at her hand, Max had to sit on the foot of the bed. Like all good factory workers, he kept his knife sharp and with him at all times. At first, Zerle was optimistic because Max was less delicate than Stewart but more precise than her father in the way he probed her palm. Zerle knew better than to look. She kept her eyes closed and concentrated on breathing deeply.

The pain in her hand turned into a nest of worms with teeth of broken glass. Then they turned into round hacksaw blades pumping up and down through her hand. Occasionally, one would pump up the length of her arm and drill into her armpit. At those times, she held her breath. Big wobbly tears grew out of the corners of her eyes and tumbled down the side of her head, pooling in the whorls of her ears. Max never spoke. His grip on her wrist kept tightening, and Zerle was glad because it numbed her hand except for the sharpest pains.

Coming through the pain was a new sensation: the scrape of the blade against something hard in her hand. She wasn't sure if she was actually feeling it or if she was only imagining it. She could see the blade turning, moving deeper into her palm. Max seemed to be bearing down. She could tell he was all concentration because his breathing was shallow and rippled, a fish's scales. He was panting. Often when he breathed that way, his tongue stuck out from under his mustache like a large pink snail. Zerle didn't dare open her eyes. She wanted the splinter out. She didn't want the nurse.

But she could tell that Max, despite how deeply he had dug, was not going to get the splinter out. Stewart had been too afraid; her father had been too clumsy. Max was too eager. He wasn't really looking for the splinter. For that reason, he would never be able to see it.

Zerle pushed herself up on her left elbow. She opened her eyes. They felt filmy and thick, as if she had overslept. "Forget it, Max." She saw that he had managed to get a few drops of her blood on the bedspread.

He didn't look up. Two drops of sweat fell from his forehead on either side of Zerle's arm. "I'm almost there. I have to be."

"You're not even close." Zerle reached over and gripped Max's wrist. She pulled the blade out of her palm.

"I could take you to the emergency room. Carolina Beach must have one." Max jumped from the bed and grabbed his shirt.

Ignoring him, Zerle got up from the bed and went to the bureau to check her suitcase. All she'd unpacked was the dress. She didn't want to take it back home with her. The idea of the long dark drive back home made her feel good for the first time since she'd picked up her splinter.

By Tuesday when she went back to work, Zerle's hand was swollen up to her wrist. The skin was tight and smooth. Her fingers were no longer tapered, and her knuckles were no longer visible. Luckily, her parents had gone to the mountains for Labor Day, so she didn't have to put up with their questions. With them gone, she could let the phone ring itself off the hook. She hid her truck just in case Max or Lydia or Kelly tried to visit her. She didn't want to talk to them. She wouldn't be able to talk to anyone until she got the splinter out. Sitting in her dark house, she had concluded that only Greer Efland could help her.

He was always the first person to arrive at the factory because one of his jobs was to mix the glue used by the men in the glue room. Zerle was leaning against the conveyor belt in front of the glue reels when Greer shambled in. He was wearing a pair of olive-drab fatigue pants spattered with the pink glue he worked in, mixing it, then applying it eight hours a day. The older the glue, the less pink it was, darkening to stiff patches of varying beiges. His shirt, a faded green Hawaiian pattern, was also punctuated with the spattered glue.

Because his body diminished in size as it stretched from his feet to his head, Greer seemed much taller than he really was. His expression was always remote. The factory was quiet this early in the morning, but Zerle heard herself raising her voice when she spoke to him. "I've got a splinter."

Greer Efland scrutinized first Zerle's face, then the hand she was, with difficulty, holding out for him to see. "You're from the sanding room," he said, taking her hand but not looking at it. He tossed his lunch sack on a load of wood waiting to be glued into rough cores.

"Belt sander," Zerle said.

"Then the splinter come from a drawer." Greer reached into one of his baggy pockets. From it, he pulled a Hawkbill Barlow. The blade was at least five inches long. He pulled it open with his teeth while he studied Zerle's palm with his faraway feminine eyes. "This is a yellow mess."

"People tried to get me to go to a doctor, but I don't trust them." Zerle braced herself against the conveyor belt.

"I don't either." Greer slumped over, closer to Zerle's hand, but he kept his knife held out from his side. "First there's buzzards, then there's doctors." He brought the hooked blade up above Zerle's palm. "You've got strong hands." The point of the blade dipped.

Zerle focused her attention on the glue reel. Her view of the arms was slightly askew. Instead of parallel rows of metal arms, Zerle saw a stunted forest of bare trees, a harbor full of dwarf sailing ships. She felt the blade cutting through her tight inflamed skin, parting the flesh as if it were water. This pain was blue and cool, a breeze cutting through a fever.

Then for an explosive moment, the red pain flared behind Zerle's eyeballs, the glue reel swayed like a willow, and Zerle knew the splinter had been pulled out. Before she could turn her head to thank Greer Efland face to face, she felt another sensation, wet and soft, warm and inquisitive, pressed against her palm. Greer had pressed his mouth to her cut hand. He was sucking the splinter hole. When he finished, he pressed Zerle's hand toward her, against her stomach. Zerle waited for him to turn away and spit out the blood and pus, but he didn't.

Slowly, Greer looked up from her hand and into her eyes. "That ought to be better in a couple of days."

"It already feels better."

"Want the splinter?" Greer raised his knife. Stuck on the point was a sliver of wood a fourth of an inch long.

As Zerle reached for the splinter, another wave of relief washed through her. All of her was coming back to life. The sweet smell of wood from the lumberyard filled the rough end. Zerle could almost see the wisps of odor drifting in through the double doors that led to the dry kiln where the wood was treated. A darker odor, like an undercurrent, drifted in from deeper inside the factory, the odor of the finishing room, the dark aroma of the varnish. For the first time, Zerle smelled the machines themselves, the fragrance of oil, electricity, and metal. Beyond the sanding room, there would be the odor of the shipping room, railroad tracks and distance. Sitting in the center of all that distance was the furniture factory. Zerle never wanted to leave this place again.

Greer Efland clicked his knife shut and leaned against Zerle's shoulder. "With hands like you've got, I bet you have your own machine by January. You was made for factory work."

Lady Luck

Lennis Murr only watched as his three buddies threw Alka-Seltzer tablets up in the air while the sea gulls wheeled and tried to catch them. The four men were on their September weekend beach trip, sponsored by Chalfant Furniture Factory where they worked. The rest of their group had gone to one of the Myrtle Beach bars, but Lennis and his friends had decided to stay at the motel and begin an early card game. Reluctant to gamble without drinking, they'd discovered that the ice machine on the fourth floor was broken. Huitt Percy had suggested feeding the gulls Alka-Seltzers until room service brought up their bucket of ice.

Actually, Lennis was the one who mentioned having seen what happened to a gull when it ate Alka-Seltzers. Now he was feeling guilty for what the other three men were doing. He was about to suggest that they go back to the air-conditioned room just as a gull managed to snag one of the tablets.

Randal Bolon pointed at the bird. "He got it. Keep your eyes on him."

For a few moments, the gull looped and dipped like his companions. Then his flight stuttered. His wings stiffened. He dropped out of the aerobatics and turned toward the ocean. Before he had flown twenty yards, a red ribbon unfurled behind him, dissolving as it stretched into the air. Lennis knew that this was the hemorrhaging. The bird's insides were exploding. The ribbon turned darker. The gull folded one wing and spiraled down to the Holiday Inn parking lot.

Kirby Pardue, who was the foreman of the cabinet room where Lennis, Randal, and Huitt worked, leaned out over the balcony to see where the bird crashed. "One of us ought to retrieve that gull."

"Not me." Huitt opened a second bottle of Alka-Seltzer. "I told my wife I'd bring her back some shells. She wouldn't know what to do with a dead bird."

"She does pretty well with yours." Randal unzipped and zipped his pants with a strumming wrist action.

"We don't want the manager jumping on us for littering up his parking lot." Kirby looked up and down the outdoor hallway.

"Kirby, it's not like we're knocking these birds out of the sky by the hundreds." Huitt pulled his Bermuda shorts up over the hump of his lower abdomen. Once his clothes felt stable, he dumped five tablets in his hand and threw them in the air.

Another gull caught one of the tablets. Lennis felt his stomach knot. He'd been working in the cabinet room for five months, and this was his first trip with these men. Although he had spent at least eight hours, five days a week with them, he'd never suspected them of heartlessness. While he was learning to put on the furniture hardware and staple on the back panels of chests, dressers, and armoires, these same men had been patient and instructive. They had a tolerance Lennis assumed they had learned from the tedium of factory work.

Lennis had learned that repetition was a purifying act. Certainly he got tired of screwing on the handles, knobs, and hinges of all the furniture that daily and hourly glided in front of him on the conveyor, but after an hour or two of restlessness, the boredom itself took on a texture and rhythm that fascinated him. It was a sensation very similar to being lost in fog. If you're trying to get somewhere in a hurry, the fog irritates you, cuts you off, and blocks your progress. But if you aren't in a hurry, that same fog rubs against you like nostalgia or a pleasant dream half remembered.

What Lennis had learned since he'd dropped out of college was that he couldn't live with long-range plans. His natural state of mind was hazy. He hadn't been able to make the clear-cut, quick decisions that the college teachers wanted him to make. One history professor had even suggested he try a stint in the army. Some of his buddies had gone into the army out of high school, but as far as Lennis could tell, the army wanted people who could make clear and quick decisions. That ability was one, Lennis thought, which he had yet to develop.

When Lennis looked out over the parking lot, he saw that a third gull had swallowed an Alka-Seltzer. He also saw that a bony woman in a floppy blouse and long skirt was running across the parking lot toward where they stood. She was shaking her fist in their direction. "Stop it! Stop it!" Lennis heard her yelling. "You cruel bastards. I'm reporting you!"

"Report this while you're at it." Randal shoved his arm up in the air with his middle finger sticking out of his fist.

"Let's get in the room." Kirby pushed Randal away from the rail, obviously trying to keep his face turned away from the woman.

"They're just sea gulls." Huitt threw another handful of Alka-Seltzer tablets, then tossed the empty bottle halfheartedly at the retreating figure of the woman. The bottle fell very short, but when she turned around, Huitt ducked behind the rail and duckwalked to the room.

Much to his shame, Lennis found himself hiding behind the rail. And he knew that, despite their bluster, the other three men felt equally humiliated by the woman's threat. From what Lennis had seen in the factory, the only time a man got defiant was when he felt very close to humiliation. Lennis's defiance took the form of an urge to run after the woman and try to explain to her that his friends were cruel out of innocence. For them, the rights of birds was an abstraction on the same level as an appreciation for the Rosetta stone.

"All gulls do is eat garbage." Randal pulled the cellophane off a deck of cards.

"They're not anything but tall pigeons, if you ask me." Huitt opened a box of Brach's Chocolate Stars. "Just pests. I bet the town has to kill off two or three hundred every year to keep the sidewalks clean."

Kirby settled down at the octagonal table under the elaborate light fixture and picked at his nails. "Well, that woman thought they were something precious, and we don't want trouble."

"She was wanting trouble." Randal shuffled the cards.

"Who'd she think she was, calling us bastards?" Huitt handed Lennis the box of chocolate stars.

"She called us cruel bastards." Lennis took six or seven stars and handed them to Randal.

"You don't get anything but trouble from bony women." Randal passed the candy to Kirby without taking any.

"Probably all she does is walk up and down the beach looking for people she can criticize." Kirby rested his elbows on the table and scratched his head.

Randal looked up from his shuffling. "Lennis, are you and Huitt going to pout for the rest of the weekend, or are you going to lose your money to me and Kirby?"

As they settled in around the table, Huitt said, "She wouldn't know what real meanness was if it bit her on the ass."

"She'd probably think it was love." Randal began dealing.

"I don't think of myself as a mean man." Kirby picked up his cards before they stopped sliding across the table, catching them with a cupped hand, the way some men catch flies.

"You've got to be the meanest one here or you wouldn't be a foreman." Huitt reached across the table and retrieved his box of chocolate stars.

"Kirby don't have to be mean to be a foreman. He just has to be early. First one there to get the belt cranked up." Randal picked up his cards and tapped them on the table. He noticed that Lennis was watching him. "If you tap your cards before looking at them, you're supposed to give yourself a better hand."

"I didn't know that." Very early in his career as a factory worker, Lennis had learned that the men he worked with, from the smartest to the dumbest, wanted to instruct. From the sweeper who cleaned up shavings and spilled varnish to the plant's personnel manager, all of them would give you every consideration if you'd just let them tell you something you didn't know. Lennis had decided that maybe the factory was where he should have started his education all along. The information these men fed him stayed with him much easier than what he'd tried to pick up in college.

"I don't care what anybody says, killing a bird is just about even with killing a snake." Huitt slurred his declaration because of the chocolate melting in his mouth.

Kirby fanned out his cards and leaned back. "Didn't use to mean anything, killing a bird. Used to kill two chickens at a time when I was a boy. Sometimes five at a time when we had a lot of company."

"That's what I mean," Huitt said. "I've chopped off more chicken heads than I can remember and never once felt mean doing it."

"When is that ice going to get here?" Randal arranged his cards. "All this talk about killing chickens is making me thirsty."

"We ought to be careful about answering the door. If that woman reports us, might be the police knocking." Kirby loosened his belt. His stomach was only slightly smaller than Huitt's, but he tried harder to contain it.

Lennis was conscious of his own slimness as he pulled his chair closer to the table. Both Kirby and Huitt were fat. Both were in their late thirties, but Huitt acted as if he had been fat for fifty years. He never dressed to accommodate it. His shirts were either too large or too small. The larger his shirts, the fatter he looked. The smaller his shirts, the fatter he looked—with his hairy midriff spreading above his belt like half-solidified lava. At least Kirby kept his navel to himself. Many of the lifers in the factory had let their stomachs dominate their anatomies.

Then there were others, like Randal, whom Lennis could only classify as thick. His bulk was not confined to his stomach; he seemed more solid than men like Kirby and Huitt. Maybe these younger men seemed more threatening to Lennis because they were closer to his age. They were not as predictable as the older men. That touch of wildness in the younger workers kept

Lennis uneasy because, whatever act of stupidity they were capable of, Lennis knew he had the same capacity.

"Anything wild?" Lennis asked.

"Just that woman out there protecting sea gulls," Huitt replied.

"Nothing wild." Kirby leaned toward Randal. "Come on, dealer, make it a man's game."

"Let's keep them tame." Randal studied his cards as if calculating the next solar eclipse.

On those Saturday mornings when Lennis had worked overtime with these men, he had watched them play poker during break. This was probably the most abstract time in their lives. Certainly, the money in the pot meant something to them, but they also loved the game because it allowed them to delve into possibilities. To them, this kind of risk was a luscious fruit. Gambling was a tropical jungle to them. On the surface they seemed to be nervous and anxious, but Lennis had watched them closely enough to know the aggressiveness that came out in these games was excitement, an excitement they didn't trust because when they submitted to it, they gave up the dull control they had over their thoughts. But the change went even deeper, almost as if their insides were being rearranged.

Huitt shook out another handful of chocolate stars and wedged them in his mouth. His fingertips were too large for his fingernails, nearly three sizes too large, as far as Lennis could gauge. The undersized nails made Lennis think of an English saddle on one of those five-hundred-gallon barrels of a horse. And Huitt handled his cards with the top joint of his finger, even when he was arranging his hand. Now, for the first time, Lennis saw that each man handled his cards as if they were a bouquet of wilted flowers whose petals would fall off if they were held too roughly.

"To simplify this game," Randal said, coming up from studying his cards, "why don't all of you just let me have your billfolds and I'll take the money out as I need it."

"I just wish Huitt hadn't thrown that empty bottle at the woman." Kirby tossed a dollar in the pot.

"I didn't come close to hitting her." Huitt pulled himself up in his chair and braced his elbows on the chair arms. "Sea gulls don't make that much difference. They didn't have to snatch up those Alka-Seltzers."

"Oh, come on, Huitt." Randal threw in a dollar when the betting came back around to him. "And raise you two. Why don't you just go ahead and admit that you hate birds. You'll sleep better tonight."

Lennis watched Huitt's face. Huitt was a man who did not like to be accused of anything, even as a joke. Like many men who spent the day isolated in his particular assembly-line function, he was overly sensitive to intrusions in his private world. However, instead of immediately denying that he had any kind of feelings for sea gulls, one way or the other, Huitt surprised Lennis by shutting his eyes and stroking his nose thoughtfully with his cards.

"I had an uncle who was mean to parakeets. He killed his wife's parakeet. It was a nasty little green bird. My aunt kept it in a cage beside the kitchen table. And it couldn't keep still, always jumping around in its cage and squeaking to itself. Couldn't help but make a person nervous. Finally, one day, my uncle took all he could stand. He started feeding that little bird saltine crackers while his wife was down in Wilkes visiting her family. I remember it was a Sunday because my daddy and me went over and tried to get my uncle to go fishing with us."

Lennis had never credited Huitt with having much of an attention span, but Huitt had cocked his ear to his own voice and seemed to be interested in what he was saying. He had never heard himself explained—not by himself.

Huitt paused when the betting came to him. He rubbed his stomach and considered his cards. "Don't want to put too much faith in the first cards of the night."

"It's not how they're dealt. It's how they're played." Randal thumbed his stack of one-dollar bills.

"Finish about your uncle." Kirby, who wasn't made for vinyl motel furniture, had slid down in his seat and was having trouble breathing. He wiggled into a more upright position.

"My uncle didn't want to go to the river with us, but he did let us feed a couple of crackers to the parakeet. I couldn't have been more than twelve, but I could tell the bird was stuffed. It could cheep, but it sure couldn't jump around the way it usually did. When my aunt came home and saw how stiff her bird looked and how empty his water dish was, the first thing she did was to give him fresh water. Soon as the water hit them crackers, that bird swelled up; its feathers sparsed out until it looked like a pine cone gone to seed. Then it fell onto the floor of its cage, fell flat down, like you'd slap down a half dollar for a cigar. And when it split open, it didn't have no more insides than a banana. Just that cracker mush that had filled up its insides." Huitt smoothed his cards with his bulbous fingers.

"Well, I think you can be inhumane to parakeets." Kirby slid against the padded arm of his chair and braced his leg against the table leg.

"Need a rubber mat for that chair?" Randal asked. "Maybe it's got a seat belt."

"Just worry about all that money that's fixing to slip out of your pocket." Kirby wedged himself harder against the chair arm but then realized that with his back partially turned toward Randal the young man might be able to see his cards. He slid back to the center of his chair. "Any kind of animal you keep in a cage is your responsibility. A man shouldn't mistreat something he's responsible for, even if he does hate it."

It would be like Kirby to make up that kind of rule, Lennis thought. In a wooden kind of way, Kirby was the best man at the table. Lennis could tell that he felt responsible for his poker partners. The foreman held his cards nervously. His hands were pale, more angular than Huitt's, and they fidgeted with the cards like some sea creature building its nest.

"Meanness is what passes between two people." Kirby licked his index finger, tapped the fanned top of his cards even, then locked his armpits over the top of the chair. "If you overfeed a parakeet or starve your dog, that's not being mean. That's being inhumane."

"To show everybody what a sweetheart I am," Randal announced, "even though I take all your money, I plan to pay for the gas on the way home. Nobody walks when I win the pots."

Huitt shoved the box of chocolate stars into Randal's face.

"Eat some of these stars and give your mouth something to do besides worry us."

If Lennis hadn't seen these men play poker before under the overworked fluorescent bulbs of the cabinet room, he might have believed that the yellow and orange light from the motel chandelier over the table was giving his card partners their deeper skin colors and smoother complexions. But their bodies always improved when they played cards—even in the smoky café called Gruber's Grill. Despite their arguing and threats, Lennis could feel them being drawn together. Through the beers and whiskey and cigars, through the talk of deer hunting and fishing and football, Lennis had sensed a vulnerability being exchanged among the cardplayers. Although he wasn't much of a cardplayer himself, he had felt that sensation of submission to the game, as if throwing in part of his salary in some way made him accessible to a force outside himself.

"I knew a man who worked in the machine room years ago whose wife got terminal sick. A tumor in her head." Kirby let his fingers sink below the table where he was holding his money in his lap and retrieved a bouquet of green bills. "She declined to the point that she couldn't work, so she started drawing disability unemployment. Everybody told her to get a nurse or a housekeeper to help her. Some of her relatives did what they could, but they couldn't be there all the time. Then after listening to all these people advising his wife to get her some house help, her scoundrel of a husband told everybody that he could nurse his wife as well as any nurse or housekeeper. Since he was staying more at home, he took some of his wife's insurance money and bought himself a CB radio to keep himself from getting too bored with his wife's company. He was the kind of man who never had much to say to his wife, but then when she got sick, he all of a sudden felt the urge to talk to somebody at night."

Kirby's fingers played around the edges of his cards. They reminded Lennis of a fish he had once seen in a pet store aquarium: kissers, or something like that. They hung onto the side of the aquarium with their mouths and moved slowly up and down the glass, licking off the algae or fungus, Lennis supposed. The fish looked like small catfish only more translucent. All the people that Lennis knew in the cabinet room had skillful hands. Some of the men in the machine room, like the guys who ran the band saws, also had to have good coordination, so Lennis knew when he was looking at skill. What came out in those hands during a card game was something else. He saw delicacy in the way Kirby felt of his cards—and caution, as if each card had a razor edge.

"The inside of their house got to looking more and more like a barn because the old man didn't do any kind of cleaning and the wife finally reached a point where she couldn't move around much. The summer got hot, and the sick woman asked her husband if they had enough of her insurance money to buy her a little air conditioner, one that would cool their den, where she spent most of her time making pillow covers. He'd never heard of anybody who was dying needing an air conditioner, so he bought himself a big antenna for his CB. One of those big double-V quadrabeam antennas. Laid out a bunch of money to get that thing mounted on his roof and calibrated." Kirby stroked his cards. When he brought his hand down to the table, his fingers curled in on themselves.

"Let's wake up and play cards," Randal said to Kirby as he picked up the deck. "How many knots for your stomach?"

"If the game is going to get serious, shouldn't we be playing with chips?" Lennis scanned his cards. His mind was too fuzzy for him to be a good cardplayer. He had three queens. Maybe he could draw to a full house or four of a kind.

"Playing with chips is like kissing your mother." Randal rested his elbows on the table and smiled at Lennis from under his cards. "It's not the real thing."

Lennis pinched his two discards and watched as Kirby once again pushed himself up in his chair. The foreman glanced at his card partners, unsure if he should continue with his story. Kirby was a foreman because he knew when to duck his head and let the business at hand take its own direction. He didn't necessarily have to swallow his pride, but he did have to swallow his personality pretty regularly. Lennis knew that to a certain extent all factory workers had to swallow their identity if they expected to get through their eight- or ten-hour shifts week in and week out, but the foremen had to be masters of it. They had to be so good at it they could persuade other people to swallow their personalities too.

This was a vacation, though, and Huitt was taking a long time to study his cards, so Kirby continued. "The old woman went downhill fast. Got so she couldn't walk *or* make pillow covers. Her husband still wouldn't spend any money on a nurse, so my wife started going over three times a day to feed the woman and clean her up. That's how I found out about how her husband was treating her. All the woman wanted to do was watch television, but they didn't have one in the bedroom. So she asked the old skinflint if she could have a little portable black-and-white. Well, he was the same about the television as he was about the air conditioner. He didn't think his wife was alert enough to get much use out of a television, especially when what he really needed was a power booster for his CB. A big antenna ain't much more than a lightning rod if it doesn't have a power booster squirting more electricity through it so that signal can spew out all over the countryside."

Huitt discarded. "Give me three." He added the new cards to his hand. As he went through an elaborate rearranging process, he asked Kirby, "Did the woman ever die?"

"Yeah. She just about had no choice, what with the drugs, the tumor, and that sorry husband."

"Did the woman get around to forgiving her old man?" Randal tapped the deck to remind Kirby that he had to kick off the betting.

"No." Kirby adjusted one card. "It's hard to forgive pure meanness, especially when it's directed at you. It's like knowing the person is a little crazy. And after he's mean to you once, you can't ever know when it will happen again. All you know is that it will happen."

"I don't believe in forgiveness." Huitt leaned back in his chair, his knit shirt creeping up over his navel. Instead of pulling his shirt down, Huitt covered his exposed stomach with his cards.

"Some things just can't be forgiven," Randal replied. "And you're one of them, Huitt."

While they talked, Lennis observed that each man kept shuffling his cards, which were as crisp and clean as a fish's gills. Their movements were that subtle and necessary. Fat and smart-assed, they still struck Lennis as graceful. Gambling elevated them. He saw when he discarded that his movements were also liquid and marine. His cards flicked across the fake marble table like two rays gliding across a sun-printed ocean floor. A man couldn't gamble without changing, Lennis realized. It wasn't his normal state of mind—or body. That was why he always felt this flutter of energy. That was why these other men sometimes raved and talked about things they didn't even think about when they were working.

"People who can't forgive are people who don't understand the situation around them." Kirby slumped behind his cards. His voice was murky. Lennis couldn't tell if he didn't believe what he was saying or if he had just lost interest in the conversation.

"I get so tired of people who think they can dig up explanations for everything that goes on." Randal fanned his cards closed, propped his elbows on the table, and rubbed his forehead with his poker hand. "All the real trouble in this world comes because people like lawyers and doctors try to figure out what's going on between and inside people."

"So you don't think we should try to figure out why those folks down in the lobby ain't sent up our ice?" Huitt stuffed the last six chocolate stars into his mouth.

"You don't need to start drinking until you start losing." Randal slid his cards down his nose and over his lips. "Give us a bet, Kirby, or drop your ass out."

"See if you boys can swallow five in your nuts." Kirby dropped the bills in the pot, his fingers wavering like the fins of a tropical fish.

They reminded Lennis of his mother's fingers when she sprinkled flour in a pan: that same casual but calculated motion. Every time he played cards, even back in college, he had found himself thinking about his mother's fingers. Handling cards brought out the feminine in men. Even Randal's fingers curled maternally around his cards. One of his fingernails was dark blue where he'd dropped a dresser on top of it, but now that he was gambling, his large knuckles resembled the eroded ridges of a very old seashell. Lennis leaned slightly to his left, trying to catch a glimpse of Randal's palms. Surely they would be pink mother-of-pearl.

Seeing that Huitt had pulled his cards up for another close inspection, Randal leaned back in his chair and stared at the ceiling. "I used to run around with this guy who got hooked on a girl. He didn't have enough sense to close his mouth in a room full of flies. If brains were spit, he couldn't lick a stamp. But he managed to snag this real babe. Her family had money. She had a chest you'd have to carry in the trunk of a Cadillac and legs like cold water down your spine."

"What kind of legs is that?" Huitt lowered his cards and sucked on the chocolate dissolving in his mouth.

"They give me shivers just to look at them. Long and perfect. I got knee-jerk lust for them legs of hers." Randal shook his head. "I might have tried something with her, but Travis knew he had to make his move before she got to know him too good, so they got married. And before long, she got pregnant."

"Five and raise three." Huitt kept his eyes on Randal while he made his bet.

Pressure in the room had increased, as if they had dropped into deeper water. Lennis massaged his scalp. The pile of bills in the center of the table was small, but it took on a new importance in his eyes. The four of them were contributing to its growth. They were gambling against one another. The game was like an outer wall they had built, a shell to protect the money they were trying to give to each other. This was the generosity of nature but necessarily wrapped in this membrane of chance to filter out sentimentality. "Eight and raise you five." Ordinarily, Lennis wouldn't have made such a bet, but he wanted the pot to grow. He was proud of himself for not even checking to see what his two draw cards were.

Randal glared at Lennis. "Are you trying to cut your vacation short by a week or two?" He leaned close to the table to check the size of the pile.

"We're in this together," Lennis answered. His cards pulled at his fingers as if they contained shallow tides.

Now Randal hesitated.

"Did Travis's wife leave him finally?" Kirby asked.

"What happened was, when she was about seven or eight months pregnant, Travis took her for a ride up in the mountains. Her daddy had just given them a jeep. It might have been for Travis's birthday. Travis felt pretty good about the jeep, but I'd noticed how, the more pregnant his wife got, the more spiteful Travis got. Maybe it was because he couldn't get any from her because she had complications of some kind."

"How'd you know about the complications?" Huitt slowly pulled the candy box apart.

"Travis told me the day the doctor cut him off. About the fifth month, his wife got some kind of . . . it don't matter. What was eating, really eating at Travis, was all the attention his wife was getting."

"Jealous of his own pregnant wife?" Kirby jacked up his eyebrows and cocked his head toward Randal.

"You know how people treat a pregnant woman." Randal put his cards face down on the table and leaned toward Kirby, spreading his elbows to include Lennis and Huitt in his revelation. "This girl glowed with that baby inside her. And she was rich. Maybe her vitamins made her the way she was. She took good care of herself, and everybody in her family took good care of her, to the point that Travis felt like he wasn't much more than a tractor for his balls. Even his own family ignored Travis when his wife was with him. They couldn't do enough for her." Randal picked up his cards but stayed with his elbows spread on the table. "While they were riding along on this back road, Travis's wife said she could feel the baby kicking but it made her want to use the bathroom. Then she asked Travis to find a place where she could get out and pee. Up ahead, Travis saw this washed-out lumber trail, so he pulled off on it. But instead of slowing down, he speeded up, started bouncing his wife all over that front bucket seat. What I think is that he just got tired of her thinking she was so special. See, he wanted to humble her by making her pee on herself. Anything to bring her back to his world. But he kept the shaking up too long, the idiot. The trail got rougher and rougher, but he kept on going with his wife screaming and begging him to stop—"

"And she lost the baby." Kirby closed his fist around the cards.

"Yep." Randal glanced at his cards once more. "See your bet and raise another five. She came close to dying herself. Travis had to leave town. Nobody would have anything to do with him. As much as I hate to say it, I think Huitt is right. There's no such thing as forgiveness."

Lennis slid forward. His wrists hummed down to his fingertips. Time to show. He wanted this game over before something happened. In no other game had he felt this exposed, so aware of how fragile that shell of their gamble could be. But thinking back, he had felt this way watching his mother in the kitchen. The kitchen walls were just another sort of shell, keeping out the night, which could sometimes be as strange to him as the ocean. Lennis could tell that his poker partners were also caught up in the same anxiety to save the game.

But the knock on the door caught Kirby just as he pulled himself up in his chair to spread his cards on the table.

In the few seconds Lennis took to walk to the door, ignoring the conflicting advice shouted in whispers from the other three men, his stomach had time to turn sour and cringing. The policeman, backed by bright sunshine and a slim woman, took the doorknob out of Lennis's hand and moved inside the room, his hand resting noncommittally on the handle of his pistol. Lennis took a few steps back.

"Are these the men you saw?" The policeman directed his question to the woman behind him.

The woman rested her hand on a large camera hanging from her shoulder. Standing behind the policeman with the stainless sunlight attached to her back, the woman didn't look as floppy as she had when she yelled at them from the motel parking lot. Despite the bun that pulled her hair tightly against her skull, Lennis could see that the woman could hardly be more than twenty-five. She was thin, but not from lack of love. She wasn't hungry from the denial of dieting or from disgust with food. She wasn't starved for anything. And her eyes were round and moist, not flat and dry like the eyes of some of the teachers from which Lennis had fled. Her gaze, far from the brittle insect that Lennis expected it to be, slipped over him, not defiant or angry, not afraid, but inquiring.

Lennis turned to see what she had found in the room. There sat Kirby, Huitt, and Randal. Then Lennis knew that he was seeing them through the woman's eyes. In fact, everyone in the room had begun to trade shapes with what they saw. Lennis saw his friends: fat, ignorant, cruel, but trapped, stunted by the darkness in their natures, some days suffocating by their inability to match the beauty they occasionally glimpsed when they drove to work, but magic in their ability to draw comfort from long hours on their feet, keeping pace with the conveyor belt weighted with half-finished dressers and coffee tables until finally their souls took root rather than wing, not healthy but strong, not beautiful but reliable, not kind—but not cruel either.

"If you want something done about the sea gulls, you'll have to file a formal complaint." The policeman motioned for Lennis to move over to the table with his poker partners.

The woman hesitated, breathing in rhythm with the four men she'd come to accuse. "No. They're too much to pity." She moved toward the door, giving her back, then her shoulders, then her face to the sun. "I'd rather forgive them."

The policeman gave the four men some parting advice, cautions that could have come from a manual. Even as the policeman spoke, Lennis, Kirby, Randal, and Huitt were already settling back to their game, too relieved to feel threatened by what the policeman was saying. Beyond the relief, they felt soothed. The woman had given them assurance.

When Lennis spread his cards, he wasn't surprised to see that he was holding five of a kind: queens of hearts, diamonds, spades, clubs, and another queen—queen of luck, a suit the shape of hope, the color of forgiveness.

When Loads Shift

Trucks wreck when loads shift. And when trucks wreck, the cargo is bound to be damaged, especially when furniture is the cargo. Although the loading dock is not part of the production process, many plant superintendents know that the profit margin funnels down to those large doors where the trucks and boxcars are parked.

Like any other department in the furniture factory, the loading dock has its blend of humanity. Men who will not last, who are not born to lift and stack the boxed tables, chairs, and bed parts, quickly conclude in the summer that there are easier ways to get sunstroke and, in the winter, that pneumonia doesn't need to be complicated with a hernia—such men represent the foam of the loading dock crew. A perceptive foreman can detect the foam as soon as it appears in the shipping department, and he begins to assign the foam worker all the heaviest jobs because his only worth is that he serves as a recess period for the more substantial loaders.

The main body of loaders consists of men who have a high degree of mechanical and geometric skills because the largest part of loading is done with forklifts, and a man must be able to visualize the most efficient way to stack whatever merchandise is about to be shipped out. Every load is different, because boxes were not designed for truck trailers and trailers were not designed for boxes. Men with such talents could do well in any problem-solving job, but they prefer to load trucks and boxcars because they enjoy the challenge of packing space as tightly as possible while being paid to bounce around on a vehicle that reminds them of a carnival ride.

Mixed with this main body of loaders are a few men who would have to be considered the pulp of the loading dock. In the cloudy fluid of the factory's dependable workforce, the pulp men stand out as being more dense than their buddies. What they lack in manual dexterity and organizational insight, they compensate for by having strong backs and, if not always a cheerful disposition to work, at least a well-lubricated awareness of how well suited they are for their manual labor. They are there to perform the minor adjustments the forklift operator requires if he wants his load to be neat and stable.

Of all the pulp employees, Neb Fredell was best suited to toss a fifty-pound box into a stray space twelve feet off the ground or to climb a stack of tabletops and dislodge a crate that was wedged against the ceiling. Aside from the enjoyment derived from the pure physical exertion, Neb loved his work because he drew comfort from the dark air that he breathed while loading trailers and boxcars. The staleness pleased him the way semisweet chocolate pleases certain cravings for a flavor that is neither sweet nor sour but intensely bland.

When Neb stood sweating or shivering inside a trailer, waiting for the forklift to bring a pillar of boxes that he would have to push and twist into place, he always had the vague but comforting suspicion that he was inside a body that was closely linked with his own well-being. As far as Neb was concerned, his wages flowed from the trailers and boxcars rather than from the factory's business office. During breaks and lunch, Neb preferred to squat inside the trailer he was loading and gaze at the blank drive-in movie screen across the road instead of fighting the crowd that crammed into the canteen. Had Neb been less bulky or more verbal, his co-workers would have found his preference for boxcars and trailers a source of ridicule and practical jokes. But Neb was such a part of the large awkward boxes he handled that even the most dedicated joker saw little advantage in trying to humiliate him.

Neb had a broad forehead, wide-set eyes, and a nose that barely raised itself above the two mounds of his cheeks. His hair, blond and fine, had receded enough to give his forehead a domed shape, almost an intellectual vault, but no one on the loading dock thought of Neb as anything more than a box shover. In other departments, Neb's dull blue eyes, slightly bowed legs, and bashful habits would have made people suspect that he was dim-witted, but the men who worked with Neb had too much respect for the large man's lumbering efficiency. In a way that perplexed them, the other loaders respected Neb's disdain for forklifts. Most new workers on the dock jumped at the chance to drive or ride a forklift, but from his refusal to take forklift classes and his disinterest in them even when he shared a boxcar with one, Neb struck the other loaders as a man who was somehow more self-sufficient than they were.

Whether or not Neb was a moron was not what people on the loading dock discussed when they found themselves trying to establish the intelligence of the people they worked with. Usually, such discussions cropped up after someone had made a stupid mistake like misreading a route card and loading up half a truck before realizing that the card was saying drawers to Atlanta instead of dressers to Atlanta. Then the half-loaded truck had to be completely unloaded, the dressers had to be re-stored, and the drawers then had to be loaded.

But Neb never made such mistakes because he never ventured to suggest where and how a load should go. He simply stacked. He'd stack as long as the forklifts brought him boxes. He'd stack when the temperature was a hundred and four degrees or when it was ten. In the summer, he wore faded short-sleeve shirts with floppy collars. No matter how hot the day was, Neb never took off his shirt or even unbuttoned it. Sometimes he'd sweat so much he'd be dripping through his shirt, and his pants waist would be wet all the way down below his pockets. In the winter, he wore long underwear under his short-sleeved shirts and a zip-up sweatshirt with the hood puckered and tied around his round face.

When the need arose, Neb would help speed up the loading process by using a hand truck. He was the only man in the whole plant who could wheel two full-sized dressers at once using only a hand truck. His strength was, of course, a factor, but the other men ascribed Neb's sense of balance to a peculiar sort of concentration on his part. Nothing seemed to distract him. General opinion held that it would be easier to snag the attention of a bowl of vanilla pudding than to distract Neb. At least once a month during lunch in the canteen, the dock workers would agree that Neb was certainly the least distractable man they'd ever met, but what they tried to figure out was what you couldn't distract Neb *from*.

"To me, Neb looks like a man who thinks about professional wrestling." Morris Groves tried to open his microwaved hamburger without burning his fingers.

"Just because a man looks like a wrestler doesn't mean he's thinking about them." Dwight Bumgarner stirred his ravioli. He had mistakenly pulled the cheese-filled brand out of the machine. "I look at Neb, and all I can think of is balloons. I think when an idea goes into Neb's brain, it expands and just fills up his head, but when that happens, the idea stops being a thought and turns into stuffing."

Cecil Vickers looked up from adding mustard to his ham sandwich. He contended that mustard helped prevent food poisoning. "I know what you mean, Dwight, but I've known Neb longer than anybody here, and I think his brain isn't a matter of too much space and not enough ideas." Cecil added another squiggle of mustard to his sandwich. "What makes Neb so concentrated is too many ideas and not enough space. He's like a closet stuffed with clothes. After they all get jammed into a tight space, they stop being clothes. All mashed together, you can't tell a shirt from a sweater or a pair of pants. Neb's got ideas, but they're all so bunched up he can't tell one from the other."

"It don't matter how long you've knowed him." Roger Sherrill paused, deciding whether to start on his pimento-cheese sandwich at one corner or along one edge. He resembled a man deliberating a pool shot. "Neb's been loading trailers so long that all his brain is packed like a shipment of furniture. I wouldn't be surprised if he didn't have little doors in the back of his head. If you'd open them and tilt his head back, all these little cardboard boxes would come sliding out."

"He does live in a trailer." Walt Etheridge crumbled crackers into his tomato soup and poured in five packets of sugar. "But I think a man like Neb has to spend most of his time trying to keep straight the names of his kids."

The other three men laughed. Nobody who just worked beside Neb would suspect him of having seven kids—or even one child. When the other men wanted to talk about their wives, the whole loading dock was invited to submit opinions and criticisms. Although a man was unlikely to receive clinically sound advice, he might come away from the dock at the end of the day with a sense of perspective. Neb, however, never offered complaints or advice.

"No, Neb's worked out a system for remembering all those children's names." Cecil licked mustard off his thumb. "All their names come from *Gunsmoke.*"

"Who're they named after on *Gunsmoke?*" Dwight sliced open one of the ravioli squares and frowned. The cheese leaked across his plastic fork.

"Let's see. I went over to his place right after his last kid was born. It was a boy because his wife had stuck a blue ribbon out on their mailbox. That was their sixth boy: Dodge, they called him. The one before that was a girl—Kitty." Cecil shifted his sandwich to his left hand so he could count with his right. "The first boy was named Matthew. Then Chester was second. After that, they had Festus. Newly came next. Then Doc."

"I just never took Neb for the type who'd be a fan of anything." Dwight was trying to eat his ravioli without getting any of it on his tongue.

Morris Groves was almost finished with his hamburger. "If he's got seven kids, he must be a fan of at least one thing."

Walt Etheridge, hunched over his tomato soup, rolled his eyes up to the top of his head and frowned at Morris. "I stopped liking *Gunsmoke* after Miss Kitty's face started getting puffy."

If any of the men had thought to ask Neb why he watched *Gunsmoke* or why he named his children after the western characters, he probably couldn't have given them any answer except to say that the TV show made him feel full and warm. Even on the more savage episodes where Matt was bushwhacked or Miss Kitty was abused, Neb came away feeling as if he'd eaten milk and powdered doughnuts with his kids. Something about *Gunsmoke* made Neb think about drive-in movies. Much of *Gunsmoke*'s landscape was raw and hostile, but with the TV screen between him and the rain, snow, mud, and wind, Neb could intensely appreciate the comfort of his crowded living room. He had his wife, Eula, and his kids around him too. They kept him warm and reassured. *Gunsmoke* showed him how lucky he was to have seven kids and a wife and a double-wide trailer. *Gunsmoke* showed him how rough life could be without a safe job and a big family.

As Neb waited in the parking lot for the Friday evening traffic to thin out, he thought mostly about the smell of his van. Like his home, it smelled of his family. It was cluttered with baby blankets, toy guns, mismatched socks, and popcorn boxes. What came to Neb's nose was the smell of faintly sour milk, the musty odor of old popcorn, and the scent of bodies—sweat, feet, hair. Occasionally, someone who knew Neb would hold up traffic and motion for him to pull out into the road. In response, Neb would wave, smile dreamily, and shake his head. He never felt hurried, even though Friday night was his night to have sex with Eula.

As they had more children, their regular Friday night schedule had stopped being regular. Tonight, though, Matthew and Chester were spending the night with a buddy from school. Festus, Newly, and Doc had agreed to spend the night with Eula's parents. Neb nodded to himself. They would have a good time with their grandparents because Eula's mama and daddy lived close to the Catawba River. The boys would talk their granddaddy into fishing all evening and then most of the morning.

Of all the kids, Kitty was the hardest to fool about Friday nights. She was more interested in what Neb and Eula were doing—all the time. Neb hadn't, after three years, learned how to respond to his daughter's curiosity. With the boys, all Neb had to do was take them outside and run them around until they were exhausted. While they napped, he and Eula got together. The youngest—Dodge—was happy and content to be by himself as long as he had a bottle of Coke to suck on. This evening, Neb planned to use the same tactics with Kitty that he had used with her older brothers. They would walk around the trailer park until she was ready to drop. Then maybe he wouldn't have to worry about her peeping into their bedroom at the wrong time.

Normally, Neb didn't think of his three-bedroom trailer as being crowded. He drew comfort from having everyone so close to him: Matthew and Chester shared a room; Newly, Festus, and Doc shared a room; Kitty and Dodge slept in Neb and Eula's room. Dodge was no problem. He preferred his crib to his parents' bed. But Kitty expected to sleep with her mama and daddy. On the rare Friday nights when she fell asleep watching television, Neb and Eula were able to have their Friday night fling, but Neb stayed nervous through the whole match. He worried about Kitty waking up and running into their room. More than fear of getting caught, Neb struggled with a dread. In the back of his mind, he thought that his daughter was too exposed, too alone when she sprawled out on the living room couch. With her brothers away, Kitty would have two bedrooms to choose from. Her older brothers never let her wander freely through their rooms, although she wanted to be exactly like them. This would be her chance to pretend to be her brothers. Neb knew she'd welcome the chance to surround herself with Matthew's and Chester's guns and GI Joe toys. Matthew's record player would occupy her enough to spend the whole night—with the door closed—listening to her brothers' records. They would be upset, but Neb would make it clear to them that Kitty was in their room with his permission.

The traffic thinned out. The afternoon light settled on the drive-in screen across the road. The silver dust from the parking lot gravel was thick and high in the air. Even in the winter, the glittering dust settling over the highway and across Neb's windshield gave him a moment of warmth. In the spring, particularly in May, the dust reassured Neb that he was where he belonged, rolling along a road he had traveled since he'd been born, surrounded by brick and metal buildings that were, in turn, surrounded by lumber hacks and parking lots, and them surrounded by foothills that were surrounded by the Blue Ridge Mountains.

The Cardinal Trailer Park was built on a low hill of five long terraces landscaped to give the impression that the trailers were perched in some alpine meadow instead of in a soggy field with huge powerlines sagging through the middle of the park. Neb's trailer was located in the third terrace, halfway between the highway and the woods that loomed over the trailers at the extreme edge of the park. Neb had trouble believing that people actually paid more for those end lots than he paid for his middle lot. He liked to think about the wagon train circled up against the night and the Indians. Living in the very middle of the trailer park was like camping in the middle of those circled wagons.

Eula's shift at the paper plant started at five o'clock in the morning, so she always got home at least two hours before Neb arrived. As soon as Neb stepped inside the trailer, he knew she was fixing salmon cakes, slaw, and hush puppies. That meal always meant she'd bought groceries and they'd have sex tonight.

Dodge and Kitty were in front of the television. Dodge sat in the crank-up swing, which hadn't cranked up since either Matthew or Festus had broken the spring while taking care of Newly. Kitty was lying on her back under the swing, pushing the baby. Her toes pointed toward the screen where GI Joe was throwing a grenade into a COBRA machine-gun nest. Neb paused for a moment to look at Kitty and Dodge and to see if any of the COBRA soldiers escaped, but Eula called to him from the kitchen.

"Can you eat seven salmon cakes?" Eula's voice reminded Neb of pine sap. It had an edge to it like turpentine and seemed to stick in the air, but it was a clean sharpness. Neb always wanted to breathe deeply whenever Eula was talking.

"Depends on how much slaw you fixed." Neb sat down at the kitchen table. Eula was still wearing her jeans from work. Small threads of paper stuck to the seat of her pants. Eula worked on the sealed air machine, gathering the meat pads as they whizzed out of the processor. When she had gathered a handful of pads, she would cram them into a box. After she filled up the box, she slid it down a roller to a guy who taped the boxes, stacked them, and finally loaded them onto a truck. Neb liked to think of Eula sitting on a stool, making neat stacks of meat pads—yellow ones for chicken, blue ones for fish, and white ones for beef and pork. Frequently, the processing machine would get out of alignment and seal the plastic crookedly onto the tissue paper. Usually, a hundred or so pads would come out defective. Eula would bring these home. On days when the machine was really out of adjustment, Eula might bring home three or four boxes of the defective pads. They'd use some of them for napkins or paper towels. The rest they'd sell at the flea market.

Eula carried an iron skillet over to Neb. "I fixed you some fried squash."

"Where'd you get squash?" Neb half stood to peer into the pan.

"Food Lion had a pile of it." She picked a crisp squash chip out of the pan. "Blow on it before you put it in your mouth."

This was how Neb wanted his life to always taste, a mixture of yellow squash, cornmeal, and the slight tang of pepper. Squash was like steady work, cornmeal was like family, and the pepper was like sex and drive-in movies. And nobody could slice squash as thin as Eula could, so thin they would fry crunchy all the way through in ten or twelve seconds and she didn't have to flip them over to cook both sides.

Neb squeezed his tongue against the roof of his mouth to mop up all the flavor of the fried squash, but he kept his eyes on Eula as she loaded up their plates. Her hips had widened with each child. Neb liked that. She was a comfortable armful. On Thursday night, she'd painted her fingernails and toenails red for Friday night's event. Neb liked for her to leave her glasses on when they made love because the lenses magnified her eyes to the point that half her head looked brown and swimmy with her irises. Neb's breath grew wavy just thinking about Eula climbing in the bed, wearing nothing but her yellow Myrtle Beach T-shirt.

All the boys had inherited Eula's silky black hair and brown eyes. No matter how much time Neb spent with them, they also adopted Eula's mannerisms: the way she walked with hardly a bend in her knees, her arms cocked firmly parallel to the ground; the way she preferred to talk out of one side of her mouth, her words working themselves loose as if she were ejecting marbles; the way she knitted the kids together with her swimming eyes, able to pull them closer to her wishes just by squinting.

The only member of the family who didn't squint, besides Neb, was Kitty. She was a version of himself that Neb had managed to slip into the echoes of herself that Eula produced through their other children. When Kitty backed into the kitchen, pulling the swing where Dodge sat with his elbows braced over the arms of the seat—exactly the way Eula braced her arms whenever she sat in the captain's chair in the van—Neb wanted to set his daughter on his lap and stroke her pudgy arms. Like Neb, the only call to supper that Kitty needed was the smell of food drifting from the kitchen. Tonight, Neb decided, he would give Kitty all the little drum-shaped bones that he picked from his salmon cakes. Usually, he shared half-to-half with her.

Midway through supper, Eula pushed her chair away from the table, angling herself toward Neb so her back was turned toward Kitty. "When we get to bed tonight, I think you'd better use one of them condiments."

Dodge was squirming on Neb's lap. For a second, he thought that Eula was trying to tell him something that another wife had said to her husband. He hadn't bought condiments in over three years. He didn't like to buy them. The druggist always looked at him as if Neb had just asked him to measure him up for one of them goober gaskets with the foreign names. They always made his pecker feel like it belonged to a mummy. One of them even sounded like the name of some dusty old Egyptian king. Neb had once bought a few condiments out of a machine in a filling station bathroom. When he mentioned to Eula where he'd bought them, she jumped straight up off of him. The girls at work had once told her that sometimes the men in the gas station would use those condiments, then put them back in the machine.

"I don't think I have any." Neb picked up two fried squash chips and tossed them into his mouth. He had to eat Eula's squash with his fingers because they were too thin to eat with a fork. Now they made his mouth feel dry and grainy.

"You can go to Eckerd's." Eula leaned forward, pushing her red fingernails toward him. "I want us to start being more careful."

"Careful about what?" Neb felt dread only when Eula talked with this metal band of certainty around her voice, especially when she was talking about their Friday nights together.

"We've got our family sized about as full as we can afford, Neb." Eula nodded toward Dodge, then wagged her elbow toward Kitty. "They don't make triple-wide trailers, and I wouldn't care if they did."

For a moment, Neb studied his wife's face. He'd always liked her full lips. They stuck out from her face as if her tongue were too large for her mouth. Neb could understand why Matt Dillon never got around to marrying Miss Kitty. It was because of those thin lips of hers. Neb wanted lips that made him think of Christmas candy. When Eula was feeling especially excited on Friday nights, she would wear a glossy red lipstick. On those occasions, Neb felt as if he had popcorn exploding in his pelvis. But as he tried to understand what Eula was talking about tonight, his blood felt about as lively as congealed pork grease. "Are you feeling crowded? Is that what you mean?"

Eula wiped the crumbs off the table in front of Neb with the side of her hand. "Not crowded." She spoke slowly, like a beginner laying bricks. "Poor."

Neb leaned back in his chair. Friday night was not the time to feel poor. Eula got her check cashed at the grocery store on Friday, but she always had at least fifty dollars left over. Usually, he didn't even have to cash his check until Monday or Tuesday. Of course, most of it was gone by Wednesday—and that was the day to feel poor. On Thursday, he could start thinking about getting paid on Friday. "What are we lacking?"

"Nothing right now. We get by just fine." Eula leaned closer to Neb. "But we're both over thirty now. We ain't saved a cent.

Have you thought about what'll happen when the boys get older? They'll want a car."

"Why, Eula, Matthew's only nine. He won't be able to drive for another seven years." Neb felt a momentary glow of relief. Surely his wife was trying to pull his leg before sex.

"That's what I'm talking about, Neb. In seven years, we're going to be exactly where we are right now if we don't start saving some money. Look, the year after Matthew gets his license, Chester'll get his. Think about what the insurance is going to cost us." Eula pulled herself back into her chair, her head tilted back slightly, a gesture that indicated she wanted Neb to think about what she was saying.

"Don't you think the boys'll want to work?" Neb felt a cloud descending over the Friday night sky. He knew Eula wasn't saying no to Friday night, but something she was saying made him feel denied.

"Maybe they will and maybe they won't. You know as well as I do that factory work is getting scarcer week by week. And my plant won't hire teenage boys." Eula picked her teeth with the red nail of her little finger. "What I'm saying is we can't depend on the children to help theirselves *or* us. When they're all seven years older, we will be too, Neb. That's what really worries me."

"You won't even feel seven more years, Eula." Now Neb did feel relieved. His wife was just worried about getting older, and seven years older at that.

"But look ahead, Neb." Eula's voice dropped to a gravel pitch. "By the time Dodge is ready to take off on his own, you and me'll be nearly fifty. Now tell me we won't be feeling fifty years. Somewhere along the line, one of us might need an operation. We've got to get ready for age and sickness."

"Fifty ain't that old." It didn't feel the least bit like Friday night to Neb. He didn't share Eula's fear, but he saw she was afraid.

"And I know you're going to say our health has always been good. But, Neb, we got seven kids whose health might not be as good as ours. Even if they are healthy, we got to think about accidents. They could get hurt or we could get hurt. You know what the morning and evening traffic is like in this town. In the kind of work you do, you could hurt yourself easy."

"I always watch myself." Neb wanted to get away from the table, away from Eula's fear. He wanted to grab up Kitty in one arm and Dodge in the other and go watch a Gene Autry movie or a Cisco Kid show. He wanted all three of them to eat powdered doughnuts until they fell asleep.

"Other people can cause you to have an accident, Neb. It's like driving in the snow. You know how careful you are and how good you can get around, but you never know what kind of fool is going to come sliding around the corner." Eula pulled a folded pamphlet out of her pocket. "A man come by the plant today with an insurance savings plan." She spread the paper out on the table.

Neb pulled himself up to the table and peered at the paper. He wasn't really interested in what it said, but he did want to reassure himself that all this fear was coming from Eula's brush with an insurance salesman. He knew that Eula was smarter than he, and when she thought something was worth being afraid of, Neb knew he should be worried. But he never worried about insurance. He had insurance at the furniture factory, and Eula had insurance at her job. "Did that insurance man tell you about how we was going to get old and have sick children?"

"No. That just come to me." Eula smoothed the pamphlet more insistently. "If you'd look past them trucks you load, you'd see that we've got to level off. We've been fat lucky, Neb. But down the road, we'll need more than luck. We need protection from getting mashed by the daily grind. It's going to get us. Even if all of us stay healthy, you and me are going to have the rug pulled out from under us when we're too old to jump off it."

"I don't feel the least bit mashed." Neb stood up from the table and pushed out his stomach. "I feel better now than I ever have."

"But we're not always going to have now. If you'll think for half a minute, you'll see that." Eula opened the pamphlet to the last page. "I know both of us are in good shape. That's not what I'm arguing. A time will come, though, when we won't be in good shape. Even if we stay healthy until the day we die, we still have to deal with our funerals." After a penetrating squint at her husband, Eula tapped on the pamphlet and motioned Neb to read it.

" 'Covers all funeral expenses, to be determined by the beneficiaries including the price of burial plots which may be selected up to twenty years prior to death.' " Neb lifted Kitty out of her chair but continued to gaze at the pamphlet. "That's talking about burial insurance." He backed toward the living room where the television played the theme song for *Magnum P.I.* Neb wanted to curl up on the rug with Kitty and pretend he was in the warm sand. He didn't want to think about Friday night. He decided he would be happier if tonight remained blank. Tomorrow, he could start all over again. They'd sell the meat pads at the flea market; then, that night, they'd go to the drive-in. Eula could twist up Friday night if she wanted to, but she wouldn't take the drive-in away from the kids.

As Neb expected, Eula didn't object when he asked her if they could go to the drive-in. The flea market crowd that Saturday had been large, thanks to the May weather, and they had sold every meat pad, mostly to fishermen who wanted something to wrap their Sunday catches in. Neb was amazed at men who could make plans for Sunday. Although he wasn't a regular churchgoer, he had enough Baptist in him to feel a certain awe for Sunday.

Eula even suggested, as the kids checked the paper to see what was featured at Drum's Drive-In, that they take a picnic to the movie. She fixed green bean sandwiches, biscuits filled with mayonnaise, pineapple sandwiches, cold fried chicken, and potato chips. She and Neb knew that before the third feature, Matthew, Chester, and Festus would be demanding popcorn from the concession stand. Eula had tried making their own popcorn, but the three oldest boys claimed it wasn't as good as what could be bought at the concession stand. Tonight, Neb didn't plan to argue with his sons about the popcorn because their feelings had been hurt when they found out that Kitty had slept in their room and played with their toys. Since they'd come home from their visits, they had refused to speak to Kitty. Neb hoped the movies and the popcorn would help the boys forget their father's betrayal.

Mitchell Drum had survived with his drive-in by being flexible. During the week, he showed pornography, kung-fu, and slasher movies. During the weekend, he showed kung-fu, cowboy, and science-fiction movies. Neb could watch any sort of movie as long as he could stretch out in the driver's seat of his van under the stars, but he was especially glad to pull into the terraced lot of Drum's Drive-In because the western tonight was *The Shootist*. While Neb firmly believed Matt Dillon was the best marshal in the world, he couldn't deny that John Wayne was the greatest cowboy. Part of the ritual of the drive-in was getting settled in. Neb cruised the entire length of each terrace, the older boys beginning to moan when he neared the far edges of the lot. They, like Neb, preferred the center parking spaces. As Neb approached each tiny concrete island with the two speakers attached to the pole, he slowed down so he could listen to the music coming out of the speakers. Sometimes, a speaker went bad; he didn't want to park in a spot with a dead or crackling speaker.

As soon as they maneuvered into a spot, the front of the van tilted slightly upward so Ned and Eula could lean back and take in the whole screen, Matthew, Chester, and Festus began collecting their pillows, sandwiches, and canteens of iced tea. When it got dark enough to hide what they were doing, Neb let his three oldest climb up on top of the van, spread out a blanket, and watch the movie from up there. That gave Neb and the rest of his family more room and more peace. If the boys stayed inside, they always wound up fighting during the kung-fu movie, which this particular night happened to be a genuine Chinese movie called *The Claw of the Dragon*. Neb had to give the Chinese credit. They could move quicker than anyone he had ever seen, but he still preferred professional wrestling to that dancing they called kung fu. Not a day went by, though, that one of the boys didn't kick or chop another one in the stomach or throat. Of course, that wasn't as bad as when they tried out pile drivers or atomic drops on each other.

The movie started at dusk, but real darkness hadn't settled

in until the kung-fu fighters had already begun their final attack. Generally, the last fight could last fifteen or twenty minutes. Neb allowed Matthew to crawl over his lap, pull himself through the window, then sling himself on top of the van. Chester went next. Both of them had to grab Festus's arms and pull him up because he still hadn't learned how to sling himself sideways from a standing position on the window ledge so he could hook his leg over the van's luggage rack. At first, Newly wanted to join his brothers outside. Then he realized that the next movie was *Invasion of the Body Snatchers,* and he decided to stay with Neb and Eula. When Neb explained to him that this was a scary movie, Newly stood behind Neb's seat and wrapped his arms around his father's neck. Doc, seeing his brother's uneasiness, took up the same position behind his mother, who was holding Dodge in her lap. Kitty climbed up in Neb's lap.

Neb wasn't much impressed with the plants that turned into people. Or, better yet, he wasn't sympathetic with how upset the plants made everybody. In fact, once someone was taken over by the plant, he seemed much calmer and more likable as far as Neb was concerned. Neb thought about the men he worked with. All of them would benefit from being taken over by those okra from outer space. He glanced at Eula. She might be easier to live with if she didn't get so feverish about getting old and not having a grave already paid for. For several minutes, Neb studied the women on the screen. One day they were nervous and frantic about what was happening around them. Then, the next day, they were perfectly satisfied and serene. Neb wondered if he could make love to Eula, knowing she was a vegetable deep down. The women up on the screen looked pretty inviting. Maybe their sex parts were like the inside of a cantaloupe. Neb could live with that.

Despite Friday night's disappointment, Saturday night was exactly how Neb wanted it—a pair of small arms around his neck, and Kitty resting in his lap. Occasionally, she would ask Neb to explain what was going on, but most of the time she let the flocks of light from the film splash across her face without questioning their meaning. From across the lot and the highway, the dry pine smell of the factory lumber hacks drifted into Neb's van. A train clanked in the factory rail yard, puffing forward, then backward, latching up the sealed boxcars that Neb had helped load, ready to pull them as far away as New York. And over it all hummed that black sky with its stars, as far away and romantic as Hawaii.

During the final chase scene, when the last two frightened, fully human people left in San Francisco were fighting to stay awake, Matthew, Chester, and Festus thumped back through the window. They knew only one more movie was left in this triple feature, and they knew the concession stand closed soon after the third feature began. Matthew was always the spokesman for his two brothers. "You said we could have popcorn since you let Kitty sleep in our room."

Kitty, who had been forced out of her father's lap when her brothers came through the window, resented Matthew's accusation. She tugged Neb's sleeve. "Make them take me too."

"No." Matthew gave his sister a push. "You had your fun last night. Just boys get to go to the concession stand."

Neb could tell that Matthew was in no mood to compromise. "Kitty, they'll bring you popcorn back. You don't want to go out in the dark."

"I won't bring her any popcorn." Matthew stuck his hand into Neb's pocket. "I bet she put our stuff in her mouth while she was playing with it."

Before Neb could think of more convincing arguments to keep Kitty in the van, Eula turned around in her chair, grabbed Matthew's arm, and gave him a shake. "Don't talk back. Your daddy brought you to this show, and Kitty didn't do any damage to your room. If you want any popcorn, you'll take her with you." Eula had a way of drawing a line with her voice. Matthew was quiet for a few seconds.

"Well, come on, then. But you'd better keep up." Matthew squinted at Kitty.

If the movie had starred anybody but John Wayne, Neb might have accompanied his children to the concession stand. He also knew that Matthew would have been further insulted if his father had gone with them. Neb didn't like the idea of making Matthew do what he didn't want to do. Forcing him to take

Kitty along wasn't good for the boy or for Kitty. Neb followed the silhouettes of his children as they ambled toward the concession stand. Newly had fallen asleep, so Neb could feel the night breeze around his neck where the boy's arms had made him sweat. The emptiness of his lap soaked down all the way to the pit of Neb's stomach.

Fifteen minutes later, the three boys returned. Neb leaned out his open door to see if Kitty was squatting beside the van, going to the bathroom. "Where's your sister?" Neb craned his neck back toward the three boys but continued to lean outside.

Matthew, Chester, and Festus exchanged glances. Matthew took a handful of popcorn. "She said she could keep up with us, but she didn't. I guess she must have got lost." He quickly stuffed the popcorn into his mouth, as if expecting Neb to knock the box out of his hand.

"My lord!" Eula whipped around in her seat so quickly that Dodge began crying. "You sit there eating popcorn and tell us you lost your little sister!"

All Neb could feel was his throat filling up with stomach acid. "I'll go look for her."

"Make these boys go with you!" Eula struggled to open her door.

Neb circled around to her side and pushed the door closed. "I want them to stay in the van with you."

The ground at the drive-in had always felt different from any other soil that Neb walked on. As far back as he could remember, walking around the drive-in was like walking on another planet. Outside his van, he could feel the dark sky. Neb looked up and realized that there wasn't really a sky, only outer space on and on. And it was always Saturday night in outer space. Tonight, though, that thought brought more acid up to his throat. This drive-in was just a tiny spot on the planet, and the planet was just a tiny spot in all that outer space. Somewhere, Kitty was lost in all that blackness.

First, Neb followed the route he figured the boys took up to the concession stand. Several people were hanging up their speakers and leaving. Sometimes, a driver would forget and turn on his headlights before he got to the exit lane by the outer fence.

Briefly, the picture on the screen would fade as the headlights swept across the projector beam. Horns honked, people stuck their heads out their windows and yelled. Neb saw that the air was full of silver dust, glittering like powdered razor blades. Whenever a car growled by him, he peered inside. But for everyone who passed by close enough for him to inspect, three or four more pulled away at some distant part of the lot.

Too much was going on for Neb to follow. He had to inspect every shadowy lump in the dark, and he had to keep track of all the cars that pulled out. Each car that was too far away felt like a year carved off his life. He stumped his toes on rocks, twisted his ankles on beer and drink cans, stumbled into small ditches, and nearly belly flopped twice when he stepped on slippery glass bottles that squirted right out from under his feet. In all his years at the drive-in, he'd never found the ground so contrary. He had waded in rivers up in the mountains and felt them pulling against him while the round rocks bruised his feet, but tonight he felt almost as if ragged hands were pulling at him, separating him further and further from Kitty.

At the backmost row of speakers, Neb saw a dark lump sitting on the small concrete island around a speaker pole. Kitty had her legs locked around the pole and was clutching a speaker against her chest. Whenever John Wayne spoke, Kitty yelled for Neb.

Somehow, being lost had made Kitty heavier, heavier than the approach of Sunday morning. Straining to lift her, Neb doubted if he could load her properly in the van. The weight had shifted down there with Eula and the boys. Neb sat down on the concrete island with his daughter in his arms, uncertain how far he could go now without tipping over.

Kiss the Button

The North Catawba Field Archery Meet turned out to be more of a carnival than a tournament. Ten different clubs showed up, six from North Carolina and four from South Carolina, but one of the clubs from South Carolina claimed that one of the other clubs wasn't really a separate club but just a bunch of their own former members who hadn't paid their dues and thought they could still come and shoot. Each archer brought his wife and children or his girlfriend and her brother. All the spectators followed the contestants, eating chicken or drinking beer. At practically every target, one of the officiating members of the North Catawba Archery Club had to call a halt to the shooting in order to yell at a spectator who had wandered down behind the targets.

Generally, Woodrow Redwine enjoyed walking the trails that led from one target to the next. As a member of the club, he was allowed to come to the range anytime he wanted to. He was surprised that the men had let him join. As far as he knew, he was the only Cherokee in the club. Because he wasn't sure how the other members of the club would respond to his shooting, he had put off taking part in other tournaments. But as the club grew larger, his evasion had become more difficult. At first, as long as he paid his dues and did his share of the work to keep the range in repair, no one minded not seeing him practice. Woodrow had noticed that archery attracted the more solitary kinds of people anyway.

At least, he had believed that until today. To get his mind off the crowd, he looked up at the leaves. They had just reached their full color. Their reds and yellows magnified the Sunday sun, which cracked through them with metallic intensity only to land in warm puddles on the ground or on the crowd's shoulders. Between the leaves and the shoulders—where Woodrow was gazing—the sun had a clarity that brought the taste of iron to his tongue. It was the same kind of taste he had in his mouth just after a perfect release and follow-through.

Although Woodrow had not had a chance to shoot, he noticed that several archers were giving him long glances. Before he could feel resentful, he looked more carefully at their eyes. They were really looking at his bow. He gripped it tighter, his Liquaflight Duoflex bow. A year ago, he had promised himself that the first time he scored 530 out of the standard 560 points on this range, he'd buy himself a Liquaflight. After he'd ordered it, he had to wait three months. The man at the store had taken every possible measurement of his arms, hands, fingers, chest, face, and back. Woodrow had the uneasy feeling, at the time, that he was being fitted for an artificial limb. To this observation, the man at the store responded, "There's nothing artificial about a Liquaflight Duoflex."

Erdahl Coffey, a member of the North Catawba Archery Club who worked in the shipping room at Chalfant Furniture Factory and who occasionally ate lunch with Woodrow, came up behind him and grabbed Woodrow by his black hair. "What you mean coming to this match with a bow like that?" he demanded in a voice much deeper than he normally used.

Woodrow grabbed Erdahl's small hand and squeezed it, causing Erdahl to yelp and rise up on his toes. When Woodrow saw whose hand he was crushing, he dropped it and put his hand on the skinny man's shoulder. "I didn't mean to hurt you, Erdahl," he apologized. "This crowd is making me nervous."

Erdahl put his hand under his armpit and bit his lip. "This might mean I won't win the tournament this year," he said, raising his eyebrows and stretching his jaw as he spoke, almost doubling the length of his narrow face. He pulled his hand out from under his arm and wiggled his fingers. "Good thing I was able to stop you when I did. Just a little more of a squeeze and you'd have sterilized me."

"I guess that would mess up your aim," Woodrow replied.

"If that's a sign of being sterile, then it's already happened, judging by my score on this first round." Erdahl pulled an arrow out of his hip quiver and checked its feathers. "I just don't practice enough with changing positions," he complained. "I won't ever shoot squatting down. The only time I squat in the woods is to shit—not shoot."

"Well, you got plenty of time to make it up," Woodrow said, checking his own feathers. People were bumping into him more and more as the crowd of spectators continued to grow.

"Ordinarily, I'd be the first to agree with you," Erdahl answered, "but here you are bringing in a Liquaflight, by damn." Erdahl leered at the mahogany-colored curves of the bow. "Looks like it's got a hell of a pull to it."

"Hundred thirty pounds," Woodrow replied.

"And you're using it in tournament?" Erdahl said, his voice going an octave higher.

"I've worked up to it," Woodrow answered, conscious of the tightness of his arms.

"Well, if you're going to put all this work and money into a bow, why are you shooting instinctively? Hell, you've got them stabilizers on there. You might as well have some sights on the thing."

"I don't like sights, Erdahl. If the target isn't in your head to begin with, the arrow won't find it no matter what kind of sight you're using."

But Erdahl didn't seem to hear what Woodrow was saying. He was searching through the crowd off to his left. "My sister just got here," Erdahl announced, turning his eyes back on Woodrow. "I told her I'd get you to wave at her. She's wearing the blue sweater and blue pants." Erdahl tossed his head in a vague direction.

Woodrow followed the direction and immediately saw the woman. She stood out in the crowd, slim and redheaded but somehow fresher than the sluggish strangers who milled around her. Woodrow felt his cheeks get very warm when he realized she was looking directly at him. Every time he saw her in the parking lot waiting to pick up Erdahl, she had looked at him just the way she was looking at him now. Her gaze made Woodrow feel on the verge of losing his sense of direction.

"Wave," Erdahl urged. "Wave just a little."

Before Woodrow could respond, he was called to shoot. The crowd had dwindled. Those who stood around were restless, waiting for their relatives to get it over with. Woodrow felt more comfortable with the indifferent audience. They seemed less distinct to him. To shoot properly, he had to force all these people—even the woman in blue—out of his mind and think only about his bow. He liked starting the match at thirty-five yards, shooting at the eighteen-inch target, three arrows from the same distance but shot from different positions.

Woodrow shot first from a standing position. The only vibration he could feel came from his own heart. The first shot was the only one he felt uncertain about, because to his way of thinking it had to open up the way for the other arrows. It struck the aiming circle with a moist *splat* and sank in up to its cresting. He shot his other two arrows from kneeling and squatting positions, pausing only long enough in his draw to kiss the small button of elkhorn that was threaded on the bowstring. Kissing the button enabled Woodrow to reproduce the same draw over and over. The button had to fit exactly between his pursed lips. Then the string would leave his fingers by a mutual agreement between Woodrow's eyes and the bow. As soon as the string slid from his fingers, Woodrow opened his left hand so his own imperfect body would not interfere with the movement of the bow. He wore a wrist sling so he wouldn't have to touch the bow at all when he released the arrow.

By the time he finished shooting, the crowd had lost its listlessness. All three arrows were embedded deep in the small sighting circle of the target. The spotter who had gone down to record the scores called out, "Redwine, perfect twenty." Even from thirty-five yards, everybody could see it was a perfect 20, but what held their attention was how closely grouped the arrows were and how all of them had sunk into the target to exactly the same depth. Woodrow could see in some of the faces that they didn't understand what he and his Liquaflight were trying to do. He was the instinct; his bow was the perfection.

The news of Woodrow Redwine's perfect 20 soon spread among the sprawling crowd. When he got to the next series of targets, several people joined his group to watch him shoot. This round was called the eighty-yard walk-up. Each man had to shoot one arrow from eighty yards, one from seventy, one from sixty, and one from fifty—at a twenty-four-inch target. Once more, Woodrow had to wait. Not even Erdahl came up to talk to him. He hoped it wasn't because he was jealous. Woodrow didn't like emotions to enter into his archery. As far as he was concerned, that's what archery was all about—escaping the torments of everyday life.

When his turn finally came, Woodrow stepped up to the eighty-yard stake. He drew the bow, felt the button between his lips, sighted—aiming just slightly above the inner circle of the target—and released, letting his right hand come back just far enough for his thumb to brush his ear. He held that gesture until he heard the faint thump of the arrow entering the face of the target. He had seen, just as the arrow left the bow, that it was a center shot.

When he got to the seventy-yard stake, he could tell that his first arrow was buried up to its cresting. Distance didn't seem to matter to the Liquaflight, Woodrow thought, as he released his fourth arrow from the fifty-yard stake. By this time, he could clearly see that all his shafts were inside the small sighting circle, all of them crest deep in the target. This time when the spotter called out, "Redwine, perfect twenty," he also added, "Two fletched out." This meant that two of his arrows had been so close they'd taken off the feathers of the other two. With each round, Woodrow expected to group his shots closer. He always carried a quiver full of arrows when he shot because he tore so many feathers off.

By the time Woodrow got to the last event, the fifty-yard walk-up, he had completely forgotten the crowd. He was down to his last four arrows, but that was all he needed to finish this round. He'd already won the tournament. Although he was shooting instinctively, his score was even higher than those of the men who were shooting in the sight division.

For Woodrow, the perfect shot was one that happened without thought. From fifty yards, he shot two arrows. When the second arrow hit the target, the crowd heard the squeal of metal against metal. More than feathers had been lost on the closeness of the two shafts. Woodrow didn't pause after the second arrow scraped beside the first. He walked up to the forty-yard stake and shot his third arrow. Once again, there was the squeal of an aluminum shaft driving its way beside another.

Then, when he drew the bowstring back for the second forty-yard shot, pressing his lips to the button, Woodrow felt a numbness of injury or intoxication. At the bottom of it was a sense of perfectness, of not needing to see or smell or touch or hear or feel. The string tugged from his fingers, his hand drifted back, his thumb brushed his ear. The taste of iron spread up from the back of his tongue. He was blank for a moment; then the crowd roared. From the target had come the sound of metal entering metal, a musical sound, like a guitar string breaking.

"Robin Hood!" the spotter shouted, bobbing up and down as if he were about to dive off the rock where he was standing. The assistant spotter jerked his binoculars out of his hands and also started bobbing. "Split it right in two!"

Woodrow left after the awards ceremony. After as much shooting as he'd done, he had to get back to his trailer and wax down his Liquaflight. He lived in the trailer park at the eastern edge of Boehm. Beside the trailer park was Gruber's Grill, and beside the grill was the forest. He needed to ease himself back into the Sunday afternoon, because in the morning he had to go back to work, spraying furniture. The way he was vibrating inside after seeing the split arrow, he knew getting back to his trailer and eating a couple of liver mush sandwiches would help him calm down. He had been careful to avoid Erdahl and his sister at the ceremony because Erdahl talked too much and Linda looked at him too much.

While the four rectangular slices of meat sizzled in the pan, Woodrow kept looking over his shoulder at the bow he'd just finished waxing. He had built a special table for it. The manual that came with it advised against keeping it on a rack, because over the years, such storage could cause weak points along the face. So one day the bow rested on its left side, and the next day it rested on its right side. The table was covered with a chamois skin so the finish on the bow wouldn't be irritated.

In the morning before going to work and in the evening when he got home, Woodrow would do his weight lifting in front of the bow. Woodrow was convinced that he got stronger by being close to the bow when he exercised. On the other hand, he didn't like to eat in front of the bow. Since it had arrived, Woodrow ate his meals standing up by the stove, with his back turned to the Liquaflight.

His sense of success was so strong he couldn't taste the liver mush or even the sharp mustard that he put on it. Between bites of his sandwich, he would sneak glances at his bow. He had always failed math, even in the high school on the reservation, but he could shoot a perfect 560. It didn't matter that he didn't fit in with the people who lived around him; today he had proven that there was a reason for his being isolated. He could shoot a perfect 560.

The next day, at work, Woodrow couldn't keep his mind on what he was doing. He started out the morning by mixing the stains too dark. The first three tabletops he sprayed came out looking like they'd been painted with very old tobacco juice. In the three years since he'd been put in charge of mixing the stains, he'd never made that kind of mistake. Before anyone could notice, Woodrow hid the tabletops under a packing crate. Later on, he could strip them. He wouldn't have been so angry with himself if it'd just been one table, but three had turned black right under his nose and he hadn't paid any attention.

He had to dump the five gallons of stain. You could make it darker, but you couldn't make it lighter. He had to clean his spray gun, too. This job took longer than usual because he kept forgetting if he'd cleaned the valve in the gun's nozzle. As he mixed the second batch of stain, he talked to himself constantly to keep himself reminded of what he was doing. He had known work would be different today, but he had thought it would be more exciting. It wasn't just that he knew people would be looking at him and talking about what he did. There was more to it. He had proven something. He wasn't sure what, though. He had not expected problems. But his mind felt like a piece of rotten cloth. When he tried to concentrate, it all just pulled apart.

Once the stain was mixed and he'd filled the tank attached to his spray gun, Woodrow slipped the rubber apron over his white Fruit of the Loom T-shirt and his jeans. He wiped the perspiration from around the lower half of his face and put on the rubber mask that covered his nose and mouth and anchored over his chin. Dressed in his protective clothing, Woodrow knew he looked like a pig pretending to be a butcher. His breath came to him moist and hissing, like an echo of the spray gun.

Usually, Woodrow could lull himself into a deep calm with the sound his spray gun made. The swish and the delicate spray that fanned from the nozzle were like layers of pleasant memories covering him up. By the end of the day, he could be so relaxed he had to pull himself awake as if from a deep sleep. But today the mask felt too tight; he was uncomfortably sensitive to how stiff and confining the rubber apron was. The hiss of the gun made something inside his ears squinch up. Never before had he found the back-and-forth motion of his work this tedious. After an hour, he could feel his arm getting stiff. It had never gotten stiff before. He'd never thought about its getting stiff.

He started missing places with the spray. The new boy who was rubbing was a hotshot who enjoyed pointing out Woodrow's mistakes. Each time, he and the boy had to carry the piece back to the spray booth so Woodrow could touch up the places he'd missed. By lunch, he didn't care whether he missed the places or not.

Woodrow took his liver mush sandwiches and his Jell-O chocolate pudding out to the shipping room. The days were still warm enough for the loading bays to be open, and Woodrow could watch the traffic pass by. Besides, Woodrow thought if he talked to Erdahl about the tournament he'd feel better, although he didn't usually like to have company at lunch. Erdahl wasn't like a real person.

Woodrow couldn't explain his dissatisfaction to himself, but he was somehow unsure of what he had done. It was like seeing the middle of a snake—he couldn't tell which end had the teeth.

As he'd hoped, the men in the shipping room were all positioned around the five large loading bays that opened out to the railroad track. About fifty yards beyond the tracks was the highway. Thirty miles north, the Blue Ridge Mountains glimmered. Woodrow found a space in one of the open doors where he could lean against the metal frame and face the mountains. This time of the year, the roads were swollen with people going to look at the leaves. They were the same people who drove up to the reservation to look at the Indians.

Woodrow took a restless bite of his sandwich. Those were the people who had pushed him out of the reservation, made him feel like he was in a zoo, like he was some kind of display. Very few of the Indians would cooperate with the businessmen who built their pink and aqua motels right up to the log gates of the reservation. The winos would agree to be chiefs and get their pictures taken, but if the souvenir salesmen wanted dancers, they usually had to hire Orientals who were students at Western Carolina University.

"Did your sandwich talk back to you?" Erdahl asked as he dragged up a tattered Louis XVI chair beside Woodrow. "You're biting on it like you aim to teach it a lesson." Erdahl pulled a sandwich out of his paper bag.

"I'm trying to figure out that tournament," Woodrow admitted.

"Hell, you won it," Erdahl said. "That's what it means when they hand you that great big trophy."

Dempsey Walsh walked up in time to hear Erdahl speak. He was carrying a Star Wars lunch box that had a small belt wrapped around it because it was stuffed so full that the latches would have to have been seven inches longer to work as they should. "Wood won a trophy?" he asked, pulling up a scarred commode with a chunk out of its top. When he sat down on it, all the joints groaned.

"One big enough to hold your lunch *and* supper," Erdahl replied, staring at the metal box that Dempsey had on his lumpy lap. "That's a nice lunch box, Dempsey," he said.

"It's my kid's. My damn brother-in-law took mine on a hunting trip over the weekend and didn't bring it back yet."

"Don't forget you've only got thirty minutes for lunch," Erdahl warned.

"Look, Dahl, I come up here to get away from that smart-ass Waters Blair." As Dempsey spoke, he was trying to unfasten the buckle of the small belt, but his fingers were too large. The struggle went on for a long time. Dempsey kept licking his lips, not looking up from his lunch box until the belt slid off. The lid popped open and four ham biscuits rolled into his lap.

"What've you got in there besides your laundry?" Erdahl asked.

"It just looks full because I brought three fried pies that my wife made last night," Dempsey answered.

"As full as that box looks," Erdahl observed, "I'd guess she left some of the tree on the apples."

"Wood," Dempsey complained, "you talk for a while. Dahl is so short he's talking out his asshole again."

"Yeah," Erdahl replied. "If I were an inch shorter, you wouldn't be able to see me from around that floppy stomach of yours."

Dempsey clinched the lunch box until the sides bent in. With one of the biscuits hanging from his mouth, he stooped over and placed the lunch box on the floor. Then he stood up facing Erdahl. Woodrow noticed that Dempsey's eyes were watery and not focused, although they were pointed toward Erdahl, who was holding his breath and pretending not to notice the bulky man looming over him. Dempsey clinched his right fist, a fist that was only slightly smaller than Erdahl's frail-looking head. Woodrow jumped up and, leaning over Erdahl, caught Dempsey's wrist. Dempsey went back to his ham biscuits.

After the three had eaten in silence for five minutes, Dempsey asked, "What kind of trophy was it you won?"

"Archery," Erdahl answered. "And he shafted everybody. A perfect five-sixty, and on the last target he split one of his own arrows."

"Sounds like you keep pretty close account of where your arrows go in," Dempsey said to Woodrow.

Woodrow folded up the paper bag; the brown taste of the liver mush and chocolate made his mouth feel grainy. He didn't care for Dempsey much, but there were times when the bloated lumberyard worker could settle down right on top of things. That was why, earlier in the fall, Woodrow had agreed to go to Sawmills Bog with Dempsey to look for deer trails. If you didn't mention Dempsey's fat, you could talk sense with him. Woodrow realized he had been keeping account of his arrows—the ones that found their way to the central spot, the aiming spot—on all the targets he'd been shooting at for the last few years. With the Liquaflight, he'd had more and more of those center-shot arrows—too many to keep track of. But even when shooting a perfect score, he realized that all he was doing was adding them up. The number was getting larger and larger, but he still didn't feel closer to that Liquaflight Duoflex.

"Archery's okay," Dempsey was saying, "but ain't it kind of like playing?"

"It's not playing—not the way Woodrow does it," Erdahl objected as he drained his coffee in one hurried motion. "That bow he uses is a hundred-and-thirty-pound pull."

"What's that mean?" Dempsey asked, eating into his second fried pie.

"That's how much weight you've got to pull to get the arrow drawed out full length. Usually a twenty-eight-inch arrow. That *is* what you use, Woodrow, a twenty-eight-inch arrow?"

Woodrow looked at Erdahl for a second. "Yeah," he answered. "Twenty-eight inches."

"Woodrow could go into business with how good he is," Erdahl continued. "All these years, I've been trying to get my sister, Linda, interested in archery, and she just turned her nose up. But after she saw Woodrow shoot yesterday, she started talking about taking some lessons." Erdahl paused to peel a banana. "And she wanted me to ask you if you'd be interested in helping her out."

For a moment, Woodrow imagined himself standing close enough to Linda to hear her breathing and smell her hair, but when he tried to picture himself and his Liquaflight giving lessons, using his bow to meet a woman, he could feel tiny compartments closing tightly inside his head. Using the Liquaflight for anything but shooting would be like eating liver mush sandwiches in front of it. This bow was not made to bring people together, Woodrow realized. It couldn't be disturbed like that. After all, in order for him to shoot his perfect scores, he had to forget that he was there, holding the bow, sweating, feeling the string bite into his fingers through the leather glove as the bow pulled against his muscles with its polished, laminated curves.

"Let me think about it, Erdahl," he replied. "She'd have to get her own equipment."

"I already told her she could use one of my old bows," Erdahl replied, the last of the banana distorting his right cheek.

"I thought if you had one of them high-caliber bows," Dempsey observed, "that you was supposed to go hunting. That makes a lot more sense to me than shooting at a target your whole life. That target is just practice—and still playing, if you ask me—and you practice so you can get good enough to do something real." Dempsey leaned back, propping himself on his right elbow and crossing his legs at mid-shin; the commode groaned again.

Woodrow stared at Dempsey. There leaned a man who was no good at tracking—they hadn't been in the bog more than an hour when Dempsey had stepped into a sinkhole and got sucked in almost up to his armpits before Woodrow managed to drag him out—but without ever having seen the Liquaflight, he talked as if he knew it better than Woodrow did.

Even Erdahl seemed impressed with Dempsey's insight. He could tell that Woodrow was taking it seriously. "How is it, Wood, that you learned how to track without actually hunting?"

Woodrow glanced at Dempsey, who had asked him the same question when they had gone to the bog. "Being on the reservation was like being on welfare. We weren't allowed to provide our own food. Besides, why spend the day killing a couple of deer and just have a couple of deer to show for it when you could take out four or five big-time hunters and get paid a hundred or two hundred dollars?"

"Well," Erdahl replied, "all you can do at the club is split more arrows. You sure can't improve your score. And once hunting season is over, you'll be able to teach Linda. I can get her used to the bow. That way, you won't have to start from scratch. But hunting does seem the right direction for you to take."

The advice sounded right to Woodrow. The Liquaflight was made for more than targets. He'd had the bow since July and hadn't realized that. Maybe, once he found out exactly what the Liquaflight could do, he'd be ready to face Linda. When the whistle blew at the end of lunch, Woodrow was ready to go back to work with his usual efficiency, but he was already thinking about the weekend.

All week long, Woodrow debated with himself about where he should go to hunt. Sawmills Bog was not a pleasant place for people. It was a dismal little valley running between Pine Mountain and Hibriten Mountain. Froney Keller, the old man who owned the land, was fond of telling people that it was haunted "from away back" and nothing would grow there but pine trees, moss, and crayfish. The trees were tall, scraggy black pine that looked as if they'd been exposed to poison gas. Each tree was heavily anchored in a dark green moss; otherwise, they might have been blown over years ago.

Part of Gunpowder Creek branched off into the bog, where it split into a dozen or more small springs. Along these springs, thousands of crayfish built their small Gothic towers out of mud and sand. Even the more daring boys of the community were intimidated by the endless rows of crayfish fortresses. Many of these structures were nearly two feet high and as big around as a man's forearm. Although Woodrow had been to the bog several times, he had never seen the crayfish. Whenever he had to weave his way through one of their settlements, he knew he was being watched by hundreds of stalked eyeballs.

The alternative to the bog was the Pisgah Forest. The leaves were still in full color, and Woodrow wouldn't have to constantly watch for sinkholes, but this time of year the forest would be full of men with beer and high-powered rifles. Since most of them didn't know how to stalk, the deer would be running a mile or two ahead of them. Then, there was always somebody who brought his dogs, or the fellow who wanted to see just how far into the woods he could get his jeep. The ones that scared Woodrow the most were the guys with the 30.06's who wanted you to drive the deer toward them so they could get those exciting head-on shots.

The one big advantage of the bog was that Froney Keller didn't allow guns there. He didn't mind slingshots or bows, but, in the past, one too many bullets had zinged across his back yard.

So early Saturday morning Woodrow parked his car off to one side of Froney's muddy driveway, took his bow and hip quiver out of the back seat, and hopped over the sagging barbed-wire fence that looked more like something that had sprung up from the bog than something a man would string up around his property. There was no path. Woodrow simply followed the slant of the hill, wading through coils of briars, swirls of broomstraw, and flocks of knee-high cedar saplings. At the bottom of the hill, the pine trees rose up, frozen in what looked like an attitude of ambush, some stooping from the previous winter's ice storms, some tilted at an angle that suggested underground activity.

Woodrow skirted the edge of the pines until he found the creek. He planned to follow the water as much as he could. When he had come here with Dempsey, most of the deer tracks he had seen were in the sandy soil around the springs. He hadn't pointed this out to Dempsey. A light rain began to fall. He had been walking for almost an hour, but the sky was still as dark as it was when he'd left his trailer. Woodrow knew this meant the rain would get heavier very soon. He pulled the billed hood of his poncho up over his head. The temperature was warm for October so he didn't mind getting wet, especially when he knew the rain would work in his favor. It not only covered up his smell, but, if it fell heavily enough, it would also cover up whatever small noises he might make.

He paused to check the fletching of his arrows. Even along the sandy banks of the creek, the undergrowth was thick, and Woodrow didn't want the briars to pull out the feathers. The hunting arrows were strange to him. He liked the clean simple lines of his target arrows, but the broadheads were different. The man at the store told him that the object of a hunting arrow was to do as much damage as possible. The main head, if the shot was good, should break two ribs as it entered the deer. Woodrow had nodded at this information, thinking about all the targets of deer that he had shot, not once associating the liquid thump of the arrow with broken ribs.

Then the man at the store had brought out a box filled with what looked like crescent-shaped razor blades. These are the inserts, he said. The inserts were fitted into the broadhead, forming two additional cutting surfaces. When the arrow enters the deer's body, these two edges break off right along here; he pointed to the outermost edges of the inserted blades. That forms a kind of reverse barb that will help scoop out vital organs as the arrow cuts through the deer's insides. You can't use an arrow like this on a bow of less than a hundred-pound pull. Even with your Liquaflight, I'd try to get within at least seventy yards of the animal.

Although Woodrow had felt uneasy with the arrows, the way the bow responded to them convinced him that he had been wrong to avoid hunting for as long as he had. A broadhead was more sensitive to the wind despite being heavier than a target arrow, and all the bow's added stability features actually worked better with heavier arrows. He had taken his new arrows out to the range and tried them out, careful to shoot only one arrow at each target and never shooting from closer than seventy yards. Always, they went dead center. Out of a dozen shots, seven went all the way through the target, splitting the wood stand that held the target up.

With the rain getting heavier and louder, Woodrow was certain that he could get closer than seventy yards. He had wandered through five crayfish settlements, waded three shallow springs, and eaten three sticks of beef jerky before he found deer tracks.

He followed the tracks slowly, although by now the rain was loud enough to drown out a chain saw. Woodrow was taking his time because he knew the deer would find a place to settle down at midday. That would give him a good chance for a still shot. But he was also feeling reluctant. He thought maybe the swamp was getting to him. Walking in the mud made him feel like mud. Soon he came upon deer droppings. He knew he was getting close. The tracks showed no sign that the deer was aware of him. His insides tightened up. He felt as taut as his Liqua-flight. When he nocked his first arrow, he noticed how well the wax was protecting his bow. Even in heavy rain, it didn't seem wet, just more shiny.

With his bow at ready, Woodrow moved through the trees, having to stay stooped over three-fourths of the time because the pine trees were closer together in this part of the bog and creepers laced the pine limbs together into an almost solid wall of vine and branch. Woodrow had crept through almost a hundred yards of this vegetation before he realized what it signified. He was getting close to a clearing. That's where the deer was headed.

The rain was coming down in sheets when Woodrow got to the clearing. Two hundred yards away, barely visible, was the deer. Woodrow could just make out that it was a buck—six, maybe eight points. He went back into the pines, barely avoiding a sinkhole at the lower edge of the clearing, and started circling. The rain was so loud he couldn't hear his own movement. He felt as if his skin had turned to some kind of shell. He didn't feel awkward, just stiff—except his bow arm. As he approached where he thought the deer would be, he moved faster and faster. What flashed through his mind as he slid between the soggy vines was a vision of himself, dry and calm, pushing down on Linda's elbow as she drew a simple recurve bow.

A few feet before he got to the clearing, Woodrow paused to catch his breath. Something was trying to flop over inside of him. It wasn't his stomach or any particular internal organ, it was just a general sense of rearrangement going on. He eased through the last veil of morning glory and instantly realized that he'd gotten even closer than he expected. Forty yards away, the deer was grazing in full three-fourths profile, slightly turned away from Woodrow. He counted eight points.

Going down on one knee, Woodrow decided to try to get a slight upward angle with his arrow. He wanted to hit just behind the left front leg. From this angle, he'd be sure to hit the heart. He made his draw, and with the button between his lips, Woodrow sighted over the four-bladed arrow, letting the bow know where that space between the ribs was. He felt the bow take hold. The button pulled from his lips, the string from his three fingers. The bow was pulling away from him into itself. It was a whirlpool drawing him and the buck together. The taste of iron was rising in his throat when he heard the deer bray and start to leap—only to collapse right where it stood. The rain had not let him hear the arrow strike the animal.

For a few minutes, Woodrow remained kneeling. He'd never heard such a bray before. It sounded like a child, but it also sounded like one of the black pines. The sound completely surrounded him, graceless, something whose life was borrowed and for that reason all the more attached to living.

As Woodrow walked to the deer, his stomach seemed to fill up with stagnant waves. He stopped about three feet from the animal and prodded it with his bow. He could see the ragged hole where the arrow had entered just behind the front leg. Part of a rib was visible. Woodrow prodded the deer again, harder.

He squatted down and touched the deer's flank. It was warm—damp from the rain. He ran his hand down the firm leg, all the way down to the small sharp hoof. He wondered if his arrow had gone all the way through. Surely it had. And the law of the hunt was that he had to find that arrow. He stood up and walked to the front of the deer. The arrow had split open its chest but hadn't been able to come completely out because the reverse barbs had severed the heart and snagged on the tough muscle, pushing it through the deer's chest and out the hole cut by the other two edges. The rain was washing the blood away.

Woodrow dropped down by the deer and watched the rain streaming down its face. Even with a perfect shot, the deer had felt enough to let out that bray and try to leap. Its life was too quick. Woodrow wished with the force of the sickness sweeping over him that he could have seen that leap, that silent leap.

He dragged the deer by its hind legs across the clearing down to the sinkhole. His heart was beating through him in the same vertical strokes as the rain. "This was not where he belonged," he said to himself as he pushed the deer down into the sagging mire, not sure who he was talking about. Even after the deer was completely submerged, Woodrow continued pushing it with his bow. Finally, the bow disappeared into the hungry mud.

Without the bow, he was able to move through the pine trees much easier. At this rate, he'd be home in plenty of time to drop by Erdahl's. There might even be time for them to go look at bows together—the kind that didn't require a man's measurements.

———————The Rat Becomes Light

In the finishing room, the chain, coated with layer after layer of stain and shellac, cannot make its usual clamor. It is easier to hear the other incidental sounds made in this part of the factory. The most noticeable sound is made by the spray guns. Their hisses are hypnotic. It is the sound of ocean water just after the wave has broken and the tide is rubbing back across the sand. Beneath the hissing is the hollow pulsing of the large air compressor that powers the spray guns. Its muted palpitations are felt more as a pressure against the skin than as a vibration in the ears.

When the stain has been applied to the furniture, the chain carries the moist dark pieces of wood out of the spray booth and into the rub room, where the excess stain is rubbed off before it streaks. In the rub room, the only sounds are the shuffling steps of men rubbing off the furniture. They move as if through a dream of punishment, stooped over, intent, and filthy. No one talks much in the finishing department because the vapors from the spray guns are thick and taste like a blend of tar and chloroform or of creosote and iodine. The sprayers are required to wear filter masks, but the rubbers are free from such rules.

The longer a man stays in the rub room, the quieter and the darker he becomes. Unless a man is made for rub-room work, he won't last long as a rubber. The fumes, the silence, the grime, and the monotonous pace of the job require a special attitude, a peculiar discipline, a distinctive need. Such a man was Rawley Pendergraft. He had worked as a rubber longer than anyone could remember. However, it was impossible to guess his age because his skin was so darkened by the stain. If the stain covered up his wrinkles, it also covered up any other distinguishing features. All that one remembered about Rawley Pendergraft were his shadow complexion, his muzzle-shaped face, and his pointed shoes—which were the same color as his skin and his clothes.

Rawley was short with narrow shoulders, but he wore clothes that bagged, particularly the seat of his pants. Since it was difficult to tell where Rawley's clothes ended and he began, people assumed that it was Rawley himself who bagged as well as his pants. Because Rawley had worked for years and years at the dirtiest job in the factory, everyone assumed that Rawley was dirty. These were the traits that led to the other factory workers calling Rawley Pendergraft the Rat. In fact, only three or four people knew Rawley's real name.

One of these people was Bullis Mullinax, who ran the cutoff saw in the rough end. As Rawley was scurrying between the freshly stained dressers, wiping off the excess with his wad of cotton waste—a gob of thick strings, which, from a distance, resembled Spanish moss hanging from Rawley's hands—he saw Bullis easing his way down the narrow corridor between the conveyor belt and the wall. Bullis was a very large man and had to walk sideways to avoid brushing up against the sprayed dressers. Rawley had a pretty good idea of what Bullis wanted.

"Shit, I don't see how you stand it in here," Bullis shouted in greeting. It was quiet enough to be heard without shouting, but the men who worked in the machine room and the rough end were so used to talking over their machinery that most of them had forgotten how to speak normally.

"It's quiet," Rawley replied and kept on rubbing. He was the only one working in the rub room today.

Bullis turned his head as if just noticing the absence of roars, rattles, buzzes, and shrieks. "Quiet enough, I suppose," he concluded, clicking his tongue against the roof of his mouth, already beginning to taste the vapors. His jowls tightened in distaste. "How in the hell do you keep from getting sick?"

"It's just brown air, Bull," Rawley answered.

Bullis started to lean against the wall but thought better of it and, instead, put both his hands inside the front of his overalls. He started to prop his right foot on the rail of the conveyor belt, but he noticed at the last minute the thick sludge built up on the metal. Rawley could also tell that Bullis had started breathing more shallowly than normal. Most people who weren't used to the thick air of the rub room didn't know how to breathe in it. Bullis had begun to hold his head down when he breathed in, as if the air around his chest were somehow cleaner than the air higher up.

"It's all the same in here," Rawley said, gliding to the next dresser.

Bullis glanced up as the small man rubbed the damp piece of furniture with two clumps of cotton waste. Bullis could feel his eyes turning red along the outer edges. For a moment, before he blinked away the buildup of fumes that was beginning to blur his sight, he had thought Rawley looked like some sort of saggy plant, something that might grow in two or three feet of swamp water. "We're having a game tonight at Gruber's," Bullis shouted. "Want us to save you a place?"

"Will Gruber have the grill going?" Rawley asked, not slacking his pace.

"If you bring the meat, he'll cook it for you," Bullis answered. "And he's going to have onion rings, too."

"I'll be there," Rawley said. He really didn't care for the poker games at Gruber's place, but he liked having a place to go. Usually at the Friday night poker game, he could find out where Saturday and Sunday night games were being played. Sometimes, Gruber's games would run solid from Friday until Sunday, but a lot of money had to be involved.

Although Gruber hadn't officially gone out of business, he didn't have regular hours for serving the public. Most of the time, he'd send one of his daughters in to unlock the doors, and she might sell potato chips or soft drinks, but Gruber saved his grill for his gambling customers. In addition to hot food, Gruber also offered—or his daughters offered—companionship and back rubs for men who needed to relax. Rawley had thought about going with one of the girls into the small room where there were a couple of cots, but he knew none of them liked him. But then, he didn't like the girls that much either. All of them looked too much like Gruber—round heads with no chin and squashed noses that only opened halfway. They were all built like butchers, too. Everyone in the family had a sour smell, a mixture of stale sweat and fried onions. The smell carried over into the hamburgers that Gruber cooked, but it wasn't so bad there.

What Rawley really liked about the poker games was the way the small dining room—it had only four tables—felt so filled up with people. The air would be gray with cigarette smoke, the yeasty smell of beer would be drifting around under the smoke, and beneath that, like marshy ground beneath a mist, would be the smells of the poker players. Years ago, Rawley had lost the ability to smell with his nose, but smells had slowly started coming back to him—as if through his skin. That was the only way he could explain it. And he could smell more with his skin than he ever could through his nose. He could even smell time. However, to smell something like that, he had to tilt his head back so his long neck would be exposed to the air where time was passing by, leaving behind it an odor of pineapple—that was how three-thirty smelled. Noon smelled like bread or machine-dried towels.

He could also tell what cards each man was holding—if he wanted to. Kings were peppermint. Queens were spearmint. Aces were wintergreen. Hearts were cinnamon. Clubs were pepper. Spades were blueberry. Diamonds were cherry. When he first learned to tell the cards and the numbers, Rawley had been able to win every hand, but almost as soon as he learned the flavors, he lost interest in winning. Money didn't please him, didn't satisfy him. Besides, he felt a little like he was cheating when he smelled or tasted the other men's cards.

At six-thirty, Rawley left his cinder-block apartment. It was number seven in a row of ten apartments at the end of a muddy street. By cutting across the cow pasture behind the apartments, Rawley could cut off fifteen minutes of his walk to Gruber's Grill. He had a car, but it was very mild for September, and the orange smell of six-thirty made him want to walk. He liked the emptiness of the cow pasture. Behind the apartments, the pasture sloped down to a small creek. Even the school kids avoided coming this way because on either side of the creek was marsh. However, Rawley knew exactly which clumps of grass would hold him up, and without slowing his pace he guided his pointed shoes through the marsh, over the creek, and up to the drier, higher ground on the far side.

Rawley stopped in the middle of the pasture. To his right, about three-fourths of a mile away, he could see the elementary school. To his left, he could see the identical white houses of the mill village. They were just far enough away so Rawley could doubt their existence. The cow pasture was like a moment of lost breath, a minute of not knowing what to say, a lapse of memory. For Rawley, as he walked through the rough dry grass, the pasture felt as if it had been scooped free of passing time. As far as he could tell, it had always smelled of cows, grass, and oak trees. In the middle of the pasture was a large grove of oaks. They were gigantic. Limbs were constantly dropping out of the high trees. Rawley suspected that more was going on in the oak summits than most people realized, but he felt too empty to know for sure.

When he reached the oaks, Rawley had to stop and rest. From the creek to the grove was a steady climb, and Rawley had come to mistrust air that he couldn't see. It didn't seem as predictable as the air in the finishing room, or as warm as the air he would be breathing at Gruber's Grill. He stood facing west, back toward his apartment. The sky was deep red. Rawley had to lean against a tree. Sunsets always made him feel turned out. During the week, when he had no place to go, he tried very hard to be indoors during sunset. But he could always feel it, like a bill collector about to knock on his door.

Having caught his breath, Rawley turned away from the red sky and walked east through the grove, noticing how the tree trunks looked like grooved monuments to deafness. The red light splashed against them like eye wash. It came to Rawley like the odor of a very strong shampoo—the kind that burned his eyes. Once out of the oak grove, he crossed the flat part of the pasture where the mill boys played football. This section of the pasture was more a part of the mill town, and Rawley felt he didn't really belong in it. It was for other people. So as he crossed it, he allowed himself to think about Gruber's. He shifted his hamburger meat from his right hand to his left.

For a long time, Rawley suspected that whoever had built his apartment building had also built the building in which Gruber's Grill was located. It was a cinder-block rectangle divided into four separate businesses: a beauty shop, a barber shop, Gruber's Grill, and a small motor rewinding shop.

Behind these four businesses, the town ended and the forest began. In the summer, Rawley liked to stand in the back door of the grill and look at the pine trees. The mumble of the poker games would drift around his back and make him feel safe. Sometimes, television could make him feel the same way, but he never had enough extra money to get one. Besides, there were times when Rawley felt he needed something more. Days would pass when all he could think about was getting with people to play poker. And the best place to play poker was at Gruber's because it had everything—hamburgers, onion rings, smoke, and Gruber's daughters walking around putting their hands on your shoulders. If the cards were coming up slow, Gruber would plug in the jukebox, which hadn't seen a new record in fifteen years, and they'd listen to music until the game picked up. Rawley's favorite song was "The Brown Mountain Light."

Drinking went on too. Drunk men were sad and beautiful to him. When he saw men pouring out glass after glass of whiskey, he knew they felt as empty as he did. During their drunkenness, they seemed to recognize something in Rawley that was invisible to them during the week. Whatever it was they saw, they were softened by it. That was another reason Gruber liked to have Rawley around. He could handle the drunks. The men who stayed sober were the ones who gave Rawley the most trouble because he stayed the Rat to them.

Rawley knocked on the grubby door of Gruber's Grill. The window in the door had been painted pale pink—paint left over from when the beauty parlor had been redecorated.

"Whatcha want?" Gruber yelled from inside. Rawley could smell him standing at the halfway point between the grill and the door.

"It's the Rat," Rawley answered. This was the hardest part of the evening for him, declaring who he was. This was the worst kind of judgment for him.

The heavy lock inside the door snapped open, but Gruber always expected his customers to open the door themselves. Doors made Gruber nervous. By the time Rawley was halfway through, Gruber was already back at the grill, turning over the hamburgers. "Lock it!" he shouted at Rawley.

Rawley did as he was told, then stood with his back to the door in order to study the eight men already playing cards. He knew them: Bullis Mullinax, Mayhew Blevins, Lanny Haigler, Horace Dula, Skeeter McCoy, Dayton Harley, Woodrow Redwine, and Dancy Evans. All of them worked at the furniture factory except Horace Dula, who sold insurance, and Dayton Harley, who had a hardware store. The men were sitting at two tables and must have just started playing because they were talking too much to be deeply involved in the game. Rawley sat at a third table, in front of the jukebox, waiting for more people to come. Only three of the eight men were smoking, and the air was still too transparent to comfort him. He was surprised to see Woodrow playing poker. He wasn't much of one for social events. Most of the time, he was at the archery range. Rawley watched Woodrow's face closely. He had never learned to read the Indian even though he had been working in the spray booth for five years now. Woodrow seemed to be trying to work something out. Rawley admired that because he felt he was trying to do the same thing. A man played poker just to fill up the time while he nursed his preoccupation.

Opening a pack of cards, Rawley nodded to himself. A preoccupation, that's what it was: growing inside him, filling him up, and at the same time making him feel empty. "Give me a burger," he called to Gruber, tossing the meat on the counter.

"Starting kind of early, ain't you?" Gruber called back, unwrapping the meat.

"I don't feel right," Rawley replied. "Maybe I need something in my stomach." He could smell the fried onions—or it might have been Gruber; both smells gave him a little comfort.

"Don't get sick on us, Rat," Mayhew Blevins said. "I want to get some of your money tonight."

"You always do," Rawley said.

"Your trouble, Rat," Mayhew continued, "is that you don't concentrate."

"It's them fumes he's always breathing," Lanny Haigler suggested.

"They don't seem to hurt Wood's card game," Bullis pointed out.

"I wear a mask," Woodrow replied.

"Leave the Rat alone," Dancy Evans advised. "He had a run of luck a while back."

"That's what it was—all that it was," Mayhew said. "And a man who plays poker as regular as the Rat can't depend just on luck."

"Who gives a shit?" Skeeter McCoy asked.

"Look," Mayhew replied, "I'm trying to help the Rat. He needs to learn the game better—"

"Then leave him alone," Skeeter said. "In a few more years, he'll learn."

Woodrow looked up from his cards. "He knows more than most of us already."

Bullis looked at Woodrow, then at Rawley, then back at Woodrow. He probably knew Woodrow better than anyone, but he'd never heard him speak up in defense of anybody. "How's that?"

"He's become a brother to that factory," Woodrow replied. "He's opened himself up to it, and the two of them have . . . they're brothers."

"Fume brothers." Skeeter snickered.

Woodrow simply stared at Skeeter for a moment. "Nobody else could take what he takes. I've tried it myself without the mask, and I can't do it." Woodrow looked at his cards and said,

"A card game." He let his hand fall on the table, then got up, unlocked the door, and walked out.

"Come on over here and take his place, Rat," Mayhew said.

Rawley went to the table, but he was thinking about how Woodrow had stood up for him. A man who'd not spoken ten sentences to him in five years, and there he was saying he was a brother to the factory. It was important he prove to these other men that what Woodrow said was right. In fact, he wanted these men to see that Woodrow was more than right. So when the cards were dealt, he decided to let the smell come to him as he had once before. He unbuttoned his top three shirt buttons and rolled up his sleeves.

"Whew! Looks like Rat is getting ready for business!" Horace Dula exclaimed.

"You're not going to win all our money, are you?" Skeeter asked, fanning his cards out under his nose.

Rawley was silent for a minute, sniffing with all his skin. "Not this hand," he answered. "But neither are you, with a pair of fives, a deuce, a queen—"

"Misdeal!" Skeeter yelled.

"It'll probably be Mayhew," Rawley continued, "with his three kings."

Everyone threw his cards down when Mayhew and Skeeter dropped their cards face up on the table. Then a silence settled over the eight men. The only person moving normally was Gruber, who walked from the grill and set the hamburger at Rawley's elbow. He saw that the men were taking a break from their game so he plugged in the jukebox and punched a few random numbers.

"How'd you do that?" Bullis asked.

"He probably saw a reflection somewhere," Skeeter replied, looking over his shoulder and up at the ceiling.

"A man could get rich with that trick," Lanny Haigler observed.

"He could get shot a lot sooner," Horace Dula pointed out. "Or maybe worse."

"The deck is marked somewhere," Mayhew said, rubbing his finger along the edges of his cards. Then he flipped them face down so he could study the backs.

Rawley began eating his sandwich. Nancy Sinatra began singing "These Boots Are Made for Walking." He realized this feeling of being a puzzle to other people was even more fulfilling than playing poker, than sitting in the smoky room cramped in a shabby chrome-and-vinyl chair. The music rested on his skin like butterflies, then sunk in. He could smell Nancy Sinatra and her music—it was chocolate and filled his throat the way a milkshake would sometimes back up in it.

"It was a new deck," Lanny Haigler shouted. "I opened it myself. If it was marked, it was done before the Rat got here."

"Him and Wood could have worked it out," Skeeter said.

"What about that, Rat?" Dancy Evans asked.

"I'm the cards' brother," Rawley answered as clearly as he could with his mouth full of hamburger and his ears full of Nancy Sinatra.

"If he's not going to tell us how he did that trick," Horace Dula said, "he can't play."

"Ever," Mayhew added. "Not until we know what you did."

"I don't want to play," Rawley announced; the news came as unexpectedly to him as to the other men.

Having punished him as severely as they knew how, the players calmed down, wanting to get back in the mood to play cards. But they didn't know exactly how to get the room back to normal. They could have laughed off a fist fight or a drawn-out drunken quarrel, but this interruption had the quality of a miracle followed by a trial.

"Way over yonder . . ." Tommy Faile began to sing on the jukebox.

"That's an old one," Bullis said, shuffling a deck.

"That's 'The Brown Mountain Light,' ain't it?" Horace asked.

"It shines like the crown of an angel," Lanny sang along with the record, "and fades as the mist comes and goes."

"I'd sure like to know what that light really is," Gruber said as he brought in a plate piled with onion rings.

"It says in the song that scientists have gone up there and tried to figure out what it was," Dancy said.

"That's true," Mayhew added. "I was up there once when a bunch was there. They were from N.C. State, that group was. And they had Geiger counters and radar and infrared cameras—"

> Many years ago a Southern planter
> Came hunting in this wild land alone
> And there so they say
> The hunter lost his way
> Never to return to his home.
> A faithful old slave took a lantern
> And searched day and night but in vain
> Now the old slave is gone
> But his spirit wanders on
> Just searching—

"Searching, searching for his master who's long long gone," Lanny sang again.

"That'd be one way for a man to make a name for himself," Dancy observed.

As the men were talking, Rawley leaned over to the jukebox and pushed the reset button. He had never heard the song the way he was hearing it tonight. The words were clearer to him now than they had ever been, even back when the song was new. He hadn't been to see the Brown Mountain light since he was seventeen or eighteen years old. He'd driven up to Brown Mountain the night before he started to work in the factory. He could feel his skin soaking in that light, pulling toward it all the way across the gorge, across the years that had passed since he'd last looked at it. He played the song four more times before the other men got sick of it. But before they started threatening to smash the record if Rat played it once more, he had made up his mind.

Rawley walked out into the September night, his mind as full of flimmerings as the night sky. He had never felt such large spaces in his head before. All he could compare it to was that time when he was a kid and he'd had a headache all day long. By the end of school, he was fit to be tied, knew he had a brain tumor or something like that, a blood clot maybe. But just before supper, he heard a click right behind his eyes. Then all of a sudden, his sinuses drained, a gush of liquid, so much that he was scared at first. But when he realized his headache had also drained away and he was no longer clogged up, he felt glad. His head felt ten times lighter than it ever had before. Inside his skull, he figured it must have looked and smelled like the street always did in the evening just after a light rain, fresh and shining. But tonight, his whole body felt fresh and shining.

When he got back to his cinder-block apartment, he packed what he thought he'd need—a loaf of bread, five cans of Vienna sausage, five cans of beer, a package of Oreos, two blankets, a roll of toilet paper, and a pair of socks—in his cardboard suitcase. Going out to his car, Rawley saw ten feet of cotton rope lying in the road. He decided to bring that along too. He might have to do some climbing.

From Boehm to Linville was about sixty miles, but because thirty of those miles were up steep roads, Rawley didn't get to Linville until nearly twelve o'clock. He parked on the overlook that faced Brown Mountain. Five other cars were parked on the overlook. Mostly, boys brought girls up here. In the summer, there would be so many cars that latecomers would have to park at the next overlook and walk a mile back if they wanted to see the Brown Mountain light.

After a brief struggle, Rawley got a blanket pulled around him. Then he took out three slices of bread. He halved each slice and rolled up a sausage in each half. Since seven sausages came in each can, Rawley had to eat one without the bread. Without the added flavor of the bread, the sausage usually tasted depressingly like liver to Rawley, but tonight everything tasted good to him. All the time he ate, he didn't take his eyes off the light.

The light looked like a misplaced star except it was about five times larger than a star. And the Brown Mountain light constantly moved, slowly and without design. But as Rawley watched it, he got the clear impression that tonight the light was moving in a very slow circle, and even though he was all the way across the gorge, he was in the center of that circle. He had to open a beer to help him think about this, because as far as he could remember, he'd never been the center of anything. The circular motion stopped.

The light dropped abruptly down to the very base of the mountain. Very slowly, it began winding up toward its original position. When it got there, it made its circle several times, then dropped back down and started its same winding ascent. After the fifth winding ascent by the light, Rawley was convinced that the light was showing him the way up the mountain. It was giving him a map of the trail to follow. For the rest of the night, Rawley ate Oreos and watched the light sending its message to him. By dawn, he could close his eyes and see the path as if it were burned on the inside of his eyelids.

All the other cars had long since left, but even if they hadn't, Rawley would have still climbed out of his car—after putting on his extra pair of socks—with his suitcase dangling from his right shoulder by his rope and climbed over the rock wall to drop into the rhododendron bushes at the bottom. The footing here was very unsteady because of so much litter and because the bushes were so thick. Still, Rawley liked the feeling of being swallowed up by the mountains.

Soon, the descent into the gorge became even more difficult because the slope of the mountainside was very steep, and Rawley had trouble threading his way through the rhododendron. His suitcase kept getting caught in the sprawling branches. After two hours of crawling, he stopped to eat a can of Vienna sausages. He had to cling to the limbs of the rhododendron with his arms around one tree and his feet in another, lower tree as if he were standing on a ladder. When he finished eating, he rearranged the suitcase on his back, wrapping the rope around himself and the suitcase several times.

Climbing through the trees was easier, but still not easy. From the time he had climbed over the wall, he could hear the faint roar of the river at the bottom of the gorge. As he squeezed himself through the dark limbs, sinking up to his ankles in the dark, loose soil when his feet would slip off the branches, he began to worry about how he would get across the river. However, by lunch, his worry was slowly being replaced by frustration. After hours of stumbling and slipping, the river didn't sound any closer than it did when he first started out. As he ate another can of Vienna sausages and drank two cans of beer, he could still see the path of light on the inside of his eyelids and figured the water couldn't be too far away no matter how it sounded.

He was having to stop to catch his breath more and more frequently, but finally, the river did start to sound nearer. When this happened, Rawley began to worry again about how difficult crossing it would be. Although it wasn't extremely wide, it was extremely rough. Rawley admitted to himself that if anything happened to that Southern planter, he was probably drowned trying to cross the river at the bottom of the gorge. It sounded more like an animal than a flow of water. It sounded like bad weather coming up behind you. Soon the water was so loud Rawley couldn't even hear his own progress through the bushes.

That evening, Rawley sat on a branch that extended a few feet over the cliff. He had arrived at a section of the gorge wall about twenty feet above the river and climbed out on the limb to see if there were any places above or below him that might be closer to the water. There weren't. It was five o'clock, and the light in the gorge was already getting dim. Rawley ate his last two cans of Vienna sausage and drank his last two beers because he didn't want any more extra weight in his suitcase than was necessary. He had a plan.

He tied one end of his rope to the tree limb where he was sitting. The other end, he dropped toward the water. It still seemed an awful long way down from the end of the rope to the river, but it was still closer than if he just dropped from the tree. Then he took his belt off, looped it through the handle of his suitcase, buckled it, and hung the suitcase from his shoulder. His hands were shaking, partly from fear and partly from fatigue. He hoped the suitcase would float long enough for him to find a place on the other side where he could climb up out of the gorge. Then he would be on the Brown Mountain side, where the light had traced out a path for him.

Closing his eyes once more to see the path on his eyelids, Rawley grabbed hold of the rope and slipped off the limb. The years he had clutched those gobs of cotton waste and rubbed furniture had given him very strong hands. He had no problem getting to the bottom of the rope. He did have a problem letting go. Just before he dropped, he tried to get clear in his mind which way he wanted to drift.

The river wasn't anything like what Rawley had expected. Dropping from ten feet, he struck bottom so hard that his knees collapsed completely, enough to strike him in the chin. Rawley had not realized how almost solid water can feel when it's moving in a swift current. He was pulled and carried, pushed into rocks, dragged over logs, sometimes on top of his suitcase, sometimes under it. When he thought, all he could think of was how cold that water was. It was as if he had lost a layer of skin.

As he clutched at rocks with hands he couldn't feel and tried to stumble to his feet on numb legs, behind his eyelids, the light's path got brighter and brighter. The gorge was dark. The higher mountaintops were illuminated in the last raw light of the evening, but despite his gasping and the burning in his lungs—or maybe because of the burning in his lungs and the blazing of his freezing skin, Rawley's sight was breaking down into bright points of vision. The river fell away from him, giving him up, and he found himself in a heap on a small rocky beach at the base of Brown Mountain.

He couldn't get his legs to work. His knees were made out of dough. But the light of the path was throbbing through his head. All around, he could smell the snow waiting for winter, the blossoms waiting for spring, the river waiting for stillness. A pale illumination bloomed over the lip of the gorge wall directly above Rawley. The light had come to meet him.